RACK AND RUIN

Book III of the Out of Orbit series

Chele Cooke

Copyright © Chele Cooke 2015.

All rights reserved. No part of this publication may be reproduced, distributed or transmitted in any form or by any means, including photocopying, recording, or other electronic or mechanical methods, without the prior written permission of the publisher, except in the case of brief quotations embodied in critical reviews and certain other noncommercial uses permitted by copyright law.

Publisher's Note: This is a work of fiction. Names, characters, places, and incidents are a product of the author's imagination. Locales and public names are sometimes used for atmospheric purposes. Any resemblance to actual people, living or dead, or to businesses, companies, events, institutions, or locales is completely coincidental.

Cover Design © Design for Writers 2015
Book Layout © BookDesignTemplates.com 2013

Rack and Ruin / Chele Cooke. -- 1st ed.
ISBN: 978-1-5170042-3-1

For Julia, Kathryn, and Elizabeth

*Fifteen years and six thousand miles
hasn't changed our friendship.*

*Here's to another few decades,
and maybe one day,
a few less miles.*

Damage Report

"It's been scrubbed, Volsonne. They didn't have time to mount a defence. The Cahlven troops wiped out everything."

"Survivors?"

The Agrah commander shifted his weight from foot to foot. The man beside him had been a soldier for near on a quarter of a century, a commander for almost ten. Maarqyn knew that he knew how to stand and report. Meetings with the Volsonnar weren't uncommon but they were at least usually invited to sit. Not today. Today, their Volsonnar was far too angry to invite them to relax in his expensive chairs and submit their reports over a drink.

"Some," he admitted carefully. "About a hundred managed to escape. They sent the distress signal."

"And it's the same with each of our bases?"

"Yes, Volsonne. The reports came in within hours of each other. The Cahlven synchronised their attacks.

We have survivors from each but the bases are wastelands. We will need new locations."

The Volsonnar leaned back in his chair and ran his fingers through his greying hair. His eyes were as shrewd and sharp as they had been a dozen years past, as calculating as the first time he had announced they would return to Os-Veruh. More wrinkles had appeared and he didn't move as well as he once did but his stature and presence were enough to command armies. Not that he'd actually stood a physical command for some time now.

He rounded on the commander, and those sharp eyes surveyed him, taking in each breath as if looking for something to give him away. He grasped his hands in his lap and raised a thin, dark eyebrow.

"And you, Maarqyn?" the Volsonnar asked, a sharp edge to his tongue. "Would you not like to gloat?"

A flicker of cracking resolve flashed across Maarqyn's face. He longed to gloat. This had been a long time coming and he had said as such. He lifted his chin.

"No, Volsonne. Gloating is for victories and we have won none here."

"I'm well aware of that, Commander," the Volsonnar snapped.

He sat forwards and swiped a long, agile finger across his tsentyl. The device lit up. It was still recording, no doubt for him to go over later. Perhaps he would spot something in the things they had told him; a pattern nobody else had been intelligent enough to see. Maarqyn knew he would find no such pattern. There was only a clear goal and they all saw it: annihilation.

The tsentyl flashed through the screens; numbers and figures winked at them from across the desk.

"I want numbers, Tzanlomne. Figures of our losses by the end of the week."

"Yes, Volsonne."

Maarqyn squeezed his own fingers behind his back. The Volsonnar had been furious before they'd even stepped into the office and yet he had still not mentioned the one topic they knew he craved to raise. It was only natural, after all. The Adveni diminished the ties of blood as often as possible, but there was nothing to completely disregard the bond of parentage.

"And the encampment in the north. Where are we on that?"

Maarqyn gritted his teeth and held back a growl.

"My teams have a layout of the encampment but it is well protected. Nyrahby ships are performing frequent passes. So far nothing has gotten through their shield."

"Agrah troops from the city have been dispatched, Volsonne," Tzanlomne said. "With their numbers they will—"

"They will do nothing," Maarqyn cut in. "It is a blessing that the Cahlven have not yet made an attack on the city. Troops from outlying areas are still being brought in. The disarray of the Agrah on this planet has held us back from formulating an offensive with enough strength to drive the Cahlven back. That is one of their Densaii ships stationed up there. The Agrah we had in the city will not be anywhere near enough to take it, even with the Nyrahby giving support."

"Because your Tsevstakre would have done a better job, Guinnyr?"

The Volsonnar laughed. They both turned back to him as the cruel sound rang in their ears. Maarqyn kept his face impassive, holding back a grimace.

"You claim this delay in a single attack is a blessing, Maarqyn? When we have lost a few hundred thousand troops? Oh, by all means, call it a blessing that the Veniche have not been harmed."

"Volsonne, you know that is not—"

"Be quiet, Maarqyn, I know it is not what you meant."

Silence settled over them. Maarqyn wrung his hands behind his back, gritting his teeth and staring over the Volsonnar's head. Even Tzanlomne seemed smart enough to keep his silence for the time it took their leader to swipe through the screens of reports they had sent him. The Cahlven numbers were limited to a single ship but that would change now that they had succeeded in destroying Adveni reserves. Once news of it got out, no doubt the number of Veniche fighting for the Cahlven would escalate as well. The Veniche were pathetic excuses for rats, running to whoever gave them the best protection. One thing was for certain: they could not count on the Veniche for anything more beneficial than refusing to take up arms against them. They could not be relied upon to join a fight against a new invader.

"I assume Ehnisque is scouting the encampment?" the Volsonnar asked, finally.

"Returned this morning with Uyan," Maarqyn confirmed. "They were one of the first units sent up there."

The Volsonnar gave them a distracted nod as he stared at the wall. The muscles in his jaw tightened and his dark eyes narrowed.

"And E'Troke?" he asked. "Tell me what has happened with my son."

Maarqyn could see the beginning of a smirk from

Tzanlomne. Of course the little idiot would find this amusing. The young Grystch had been under his command—his control—and he had defected. The Volsonnar's own son had changed sides under his watch.

"There have been no sightings of E'Troke since the destruction of Lyndbury Compound, Volsonne. However, we have the footage from the salvaged cameras and reports from the guards on duty. He was a part of the attack alongside the Veniche."

"There is no doubt?"

"You know that I questioned E'Troke's allegiances for some time, but even I never truly believed he would do something like this."

"That did not answer the question."

Tzanlomne stood silent and smug and Maarqyn wanted to tear him into pieces for his amusement.

"There is no doubt. One of the Veniche who went in with him was his own drysta."

"A drysta you wanted for yourself, Maarqyn. If my information is correct."

"It is correct," he said, straightening his back and holding his head high. "The girl had information on the escape of my own dreta. I wanted to question her, nothing more."

"And now my son uses her to liberate a prison and, I assume, help organise the other damages to the city."

"We can only make assumptions on his connection to the Belsa, Volsonne, but yes."

The Volsonnar shoved back his chair and rose to his feet. He turned to look out of the window, his knuckles white as he grabbed the frame. His reflection was tight and focussed and his jaw moved with the grinding of his teeth.

"I take on the mantle to continue our progression, to bring our people back to their homeland, and my own blood turns against me. He will not be the first if his betrayal is not met with retribution."

"Volsonne?"

He turned around. The son had certainly inherited his father's vicious glare. Maarqyn remembered the fierce and talented young man who had first joined his ranks, so desperate to prove himself against the name of his father.

"Your fear of lost loyalties led us to this problem. Had you reported your suspicions this could have been dealt with before it brought this storm down upon us."

"I can only apologise, Volsonne."

"You'll need to do a lot more than that if you are to keep that title you command. You will rectify this quickly."

The Volsonnar took his seat again and clasped his hands in his lap. He lifted his chin and took a steadying breath as he looked up at Maarqyn, though there was a knife's edge hidden behind his teeth.

"I want his Nsiloq mounted on my wall," he said. "Before his treachery—and your stupidity—cause me any more problems."

1 THE FIRST COLVOHAN

It was the second time the Cahlven emissary, Olless, had walked out of the room without warning. She had already spoken twice to Edtroka about his anger and the language that accompanied it. When he continued to curse, calling her some vulgar Adtvenis name, she had walked out again, leaving them all waiting for her to return, and for Edtroka to calm down.

He was still swearing rapidly under his breath. Beck sat and watched, sighing, tapping his foot in an unsteady rhythm. His gaze roamed the walls and furniture as he crossed and uncrossed his arms. Keiran paced, running his fingers against the backs of the chairs. Georgianna watched him, leaning forwards onto her knees. If he felt her gaze, he didn't show it.

It had been three weeks since Edtroka had led them in an attack against the Adveni, liberating prisoners from Lyndbury Compound and destroying some of the Adveni technology that was used against the Veniche. They had known they would need more people to fight to have any hope of driving the Adveni back, but it had taken a lot to convince Edtroka that removing the threats the Adveni held over them would give them what they needed. It had taken even longer for Beck and the other Belsa to agree to work with Edtroka.

The Cahlven had arrived not long after they moved north, away from the city. They had sworn their allegiance to the Veniche and promised to fight for Os-Veruh against the Adveni. Olless, their emissary, had been sent with troops, promising that one of the Colvohans would be dispatched once they had succeeded in wiping out Adveni reserve bases. Until the Colvohan arrived there was nothing to do but wait in the camp they had created and strategise attacks.

They had camped at Nyquonat Lake in the far north. It was pretty but becoming less habitable by the day as the cold rains preceding the Freeze set in, heralding the end of the Heat. Many had already complained that this location would not be suitable for much longer, and the ex-inmate, Dhiren, whom they had liberated from the Compound during their attack, was the only person whose spirits weren't dampened by the weather in the small protected camp.

The Cahlven had given them less than Edtroka had anticipated, and Georgianna wasn't surprised that he was letting out his frustration. They had taken a long time in making a decision over whether to attack the Adveni, and Edtroka's ranting in their frequent meetings made clear that he'd expected things to move faster now that they had arrived. Well, some of them. The leader of the Cahlven had still not appeared on Os-Veruh despite frequent promises that things were moving forwards.

Edtroka slumped into a chair, finally silent, and it seemed only moments before Olless returned. She strode into the room like nothing had been amiss, as if she'd simply left to collect some information or to give an order. Her lavender eyes swept over them with interest and she laid a small orb on the table already laden with maps, lists, and diagrams.

She lifted her hand away from the orb and the colours that had been shifting through it settled and faded to the dark purple of the pre-dawn sky. Georgianna recognised the sphere immediately. She had been on the receiving end of Edtroka's anger when he'd discovered her holding the one he owned; a device he'd been unwilling to explain at the time.

"Do you really think your shields will hold?" Edtroka asked, his frustration barely restrained. "They might be protecting us from the Nyrahby bombs but they won't stop the Agrah from flooding the camp with troops."

"The shields can be made solid enough that no being can pass through," Olless replied, keeping her cool much better than Edtroka.

"Great," Keiran said. "So the Adveni can surround us, watch us make the shields solid, and wait us out while we starve."

Edtroka stood, pointing at Keiran and nodding. He glared at Olless but held his tongue.

"We have been given notice of the progression on the strongholds," said Olless. "We cannot launch a full attack against the Adveni with the numbers we have."

"And you want us to sit and wait while the Agrah move on our position?"

Beck leaned back in the chair, crossed his arms, and watched as Edtroka and Olless sniped at each other. Keiran returned to his pacing. Sitting in a chair beside Beck, Georgianna picked at her thumbnail and listened.

She didn't know why she had been called into this meeting. She wasn't one of the leaders who had been chosen to speak for the Veniche; those places belonged to Keiran and Beck. She wasn't some person of great insight into the methods of war. She was a medic. Was she only here because she had been Edtroka's drysta? Even that was a pointless reason as far as she was concerned. Edtroka ignored her whenever they stepped inside the command room, focussing his attention on those with more useful opinions. Even Keiran and Beck ignored her most of the time. Beck only paid her attention when he was frustrated with the conversation and needed a break. He would come and sit by her and talk of his adopted daughter Lacie, who was training harder than ever to become a medic like Georgianna. Keiran had either forgotten she existed or was hoping he would forget soon. They had not spoken a word to each other since he'd been named leader. Their silence had become a battle of wills, one she had almost lost near on a hundred times.

"I am the emissary. I implement the orders I am given," Olless said. "We should bring in the Colvohan if you wish to change that."

She waved her hand towards the orb on the table and Edtroka shot it such a fierce glare that Georgianna imagined it might crack under the weight.

"Why did they even send you if you can't do anything?"

Olless gave him a thin-lipped smile.

"Because they thought I could keep you in your right mind, Adveni."

Edtroka swore under his breath but then, at the look Olless gave him, growled and waved his hand dismissively. He sank back into his chair.

"Fine. Get them."

Olless picked up the orb. Georgianna watched, edging forwards on her chair. As soon as the orb connected with skin it began to lighten. Swirls of cloudy colour stretched and slid across the surface. Maroon shifted to burning embers. Onyx waves crashed into a violet spray. It was so beautiful that Georgianna forgot what it was for. She glanced at Beck and Keiran, wondering if they found this as captivating as she did, but they both watched with impatience.

"Naltahn, First Colvohan," Olless said, holding the orb up before her.

The orb shifted further at the sound of her voice. Thick white veins spread across its surface like branches from the trunk of a tree. They wove together and split away again, forming a canopy. The top of the orb glowed pure white before the entire design faded away. Olless set it down on the centre of the table and waited.

Georgianna tapped her feet, her gaze flickering from the orb to the others in the room. Beck and Keiran showed no discomfort in the waiting, while Edtroka maintained his frustration. Only Olless remained alert and presentable.

The bells were quiet at first, melting into the silence, then got steadily louder until a short jingle sounded. Beck got to his feet, Keiran rounded the chairs, and Edtroka moved to the edge of his seat. Olless grasped her hands before her and straightened up, her long red braid falling between her shoulders.

Georgianna was the only one who squeaked in surprise when a man appeared before them. She covered her mouth with both hands but Beck had heard her. He glanced over his shoulder and grinned. She could imagine he'd had the same reaction the first time he saw it happen.

The man before them was dressed in the same neck-to-ankle suit that Olless wore, but he had covered his in a heavy overcoat. His ash-grey hair was slicked back where it curled behind his ears and at the nape of his neck. He glanced at each of them in turn, his gaze lingering on Georgianna before striding a few steps towards her. The squeak slipped past her lips before she could stop it, a shudder running down her spine as the man walked straight through the table. The only person who didn't blanch at the sight was Olless, though she smiled at their discomfort.

"Sir, if you wouldn't mind taking three more steps. You are currently standing in the middle of the table and the Veniche find it disconcerting."

He gave a curt smile as he walked out of the table and his legs connected to his body again.

"You needed me, Olless?"

"Yes, Sir. There is some disagreement over the course of action here on Os-Veruh."

"Has something happened to change your current situation?"

"No."

"Yes!" Edtroka said, leaning forwards.

The Colvohan turned to look at Edtroka and clasped his hands before him in the same manner as Olless. His eyes were the palest grey Georgianna had ever seen.

"Mr. Grystch, what do you believe has changed?"

"The Adveni have been amassing their troops. They're sending Agrah here, if they're not beyond the borders already. Before long we will be surrounded."

"And the shields hold?"

"Yes, Sir," Olless said before Edtroka or Keiran could argue.

"Then I do not see an issue that requires contacting me."

Edtroka got to his feet. He was at least a head taller than the Colvohan, and Georgianna saw the bristle of annoyance that passed over the projection's face before it faded back to a serene stare.

"If we give the Adveni time to surround us while you attack the bases then you will be looking at a slaughter the moment the shields are down. They will send every strength to wipe us out. You will have won the bases but lost Os-Veruh for good."

Edtroka kept his temper better than he had done with Olless but there was an edge to his voice that could not be ignored. Georgianna had never met Edtroka's father, the Volsonnar, but she wondered if that sharp and undeniable authority in his voice was something they shared. It wouldn't surprise her if the leader of the Adveni sounded like he could cut you where you stood with just words.

The Colvohan gave Edtroka's comment a moment to settle in.

"We are not giving the Adveni time to surround you. Aomel, Second Colvohan, is on his way to Os-Veruh with more troops and a fleet of Dalsaia as we speak. We expect him to arrive within the week. Once there, he will take command of the movements on Os-Veruh and we will begin the assault on the Adveni strongholds."

"When was this decision made?" Edtroka demanded. "We've heard nothing of this."

"Aomel's attack on Sollnadt was the closest to Os-Veruh. The moment the assault was complete he began the journey with the troops and ships he had under his command. It was the most convenient option."

The orb rocked as Edtroka slammed his hands down onto the table. The projection flickered and trembled.

"We were not told! We brought *you* to this fight, not the other way around."

"You lacked both the provisions and the strength to bring a fight of this scale to the Adveni." The Colvohan's restraint was cracking, just like Olless' had done. From what Georgianna had seen of the Cahlven, they were models of calm and organisation. Against the fire of an Adveni and the disorganisation of the Veniche, their serenity grated and splintered.

"I don't see why you are surprised, Edtroka," Beck said, stepping forwards. "The Adveni didn't care for our opinions when they invaded. I don't see why the Cahlven should be any different now that it's their turn to conquer."

Beck didn't wait for a response. He gave Georgianna a grim frown as he strode past her, and then opened the door with a thwack of his hand to a plate on the wall. He disappeared around the corner and his footsteps faded along the corridor.

Georgianna turned back to the others to find that Olless had flushed pink, her eyes cast to the ground. The Colvohan stared at the doorway.

"Olless, I trust you will make the necessary arrangements for their arrival."

"Of course, Sir," Olless said without looking up.

"I'll have everything ready and will report any changes."

"Ensure you do so."

The projection flickered as the Colvohan reached for something they could not see and in an instant, vanished without another word. Georgianna stared at the space he had occupied. Olless turned to Edtroka.

"How dare you speak to the Colvohan like that?" she hissed. "You came to us because you wanted help, help we have given you. Get in line and make sure Casey does the same. I will not be shown up like this again. Do not make me regret vouching for you, Grystch."

Edtroka rounded the table, glaring down at her, his lips pulled back in a snarl that showed his teeth. Even Georgianna leaned back in her chair away from him.

"The whole point in you coming was so that this line would be a joint decision. You named us leaders here and yet we are not informed. So perhaps you should bring the Cahlven in line, Olless, before we decide we do not want your Colvohan's opinion on our fight."

Olless spluttered as Edtroka swept past her. He didn't look at any of them as he followed Beck through the door and stalked away. The air he left behind was tight and suffocating, dripping with accusation.

Standing by the table, Olless hissed and murmured, staring at the maps and diagrams they had been poring over. Keiran slunk into one of the chairs and cradled his head in his hands, staring at the floor. Georgianna thought he looked lost. He'd been given the command, and to look at him now she wasn't sure he wanted it. She didn't even know how it had happened. Perhaps it was because he was one of the people Olless and the Cahlven had known before their arrival. Beck held the Belsa; he was the obvious choice. So why Keiran?

Georgianna shifted and rose to her feet. She stepped towards Keiran, but as soon as she came close to him he turned further away without looking up. Gritting her teeth, Georgianna gulped. He'd walked away from her. He'd claimed she had betrayed him, even after she'd stopped Alec and the other Belsa from killing him. He thought she held his actions against him, despite everything she'd done to prove otherwise. It wasn't up to her to fight for his attention. He needed to get over it.

Georgianna threw one last look at Olless and hurried out of the room, hoping she would at least be able to catch up with Edtroka.

2 Fighting Talk

Georgianna grasped the doorway of the small transport ship before descending the steps. Though she'd visited the big ship a couple of times over the past weeks she still couldn't get used to the sensation of her feet being stuck to the floor, as if walking through thick mud. Edtroka had said that the huge Densaii ship was used for travelling between planets. He had told her that once out of the atmosphere, gravity no longer had any control. His explanation didn't make the sensation any nicer.

The steps receded behind her and the door slid closed, disappearing into the shell of the ship. She turned away, trying to spot Edtroka. He shouldn't have been difficult to see, standing at least a head taller than any Veniche. She set off towards the tents they'd set up on the lake shore, bending her head against the cold wind.

The sky had been slate grey for a week. Clouds swirled overhead, darker with each passing day. While most expressed their relief at the end of the Heat—the long months where Os-Veruh travelled so close to the sun that prolonged exposure could drive a man to insanity—Edtroka had spent the last few days despairing at the impeded visibility. Sure enough, while Georgianna was sure that the Cahlven had technology to locate incoming ships and transports, the low-hanging clouds had given the Adveni an advantage over those on the ground.

Ripples rolled across the surface of the lake as low waves washed the rocky shore and a tremble ran through air and earth. Georgianna sprinted across the open ground between the tents and clutched the trunk of a tree, holding herself against it. The tremors shuddered beneath her feet, vibrating through the bark. She lifted her head and gazed up through the canopy of reddening leaves as a thousand bolts of lightning flashed across the sky, looking for a space to pierce through the shield. They spread, flickering and cracking like flames licking at a log. Georgianna squeezed her eyes shut and lowered her head, hands over her ears.

As the bomb exploded against the shield, her eyelids burned white and her ears screamed with the vibrations. The wet earth beneath her feet slid and shifted. Blinking away the red spots in her vision, Georgianna glanced up, watching for more of the artificial lightning. None came. The clouds retained their innocence.

Water washed high onto the lake shore and a group of Veniche shakily gathered their belongings as the momentary tide threatened to carry them into the lake. Georgianna steadied herself against the tree trunk, waiting for the vibrations to fade.

Despite knowing that their bombs would not pierce the Cahlven shield, the Adveni kept up a steady pace of daily attacks. Sometimes the Nyrahby sent three or four launches in the space of an hour. Whether they were hoping that a repeated onslaught would let something through, or they simply planned to keep those within the shields scared, Georgianna didn't dare guess. It wouldn't be the first time the Adveni had hurt people just to prove that they could.

Straightening up, Georgianna headed over to the tents, only to pause as she spotted someone further into the trees. She frowned and moved closer, and was almost at the shield border before she realised who it was.

"Alec, what are you doing out here?"

Alec jumped and turned around. He grinned, waved her forwards, then glanced through the trees again.

"What are you doing?" repeated Georgianna.

"Shh, they'll hear you."

She stepped forwards and Alec grabbed her hand, leading her through the trees. He stood so close that Georgianna could feel his warmth against her back and smell the rain in his hair. She gritted her teeth. A thick patch of trees separated them from a pair of voices and Alec had to point through the branches for her to pick out the speakers.

"I don't know why you expected anything different. Conquering armies care little for the opinions of the conquered."

Dhiren sat on a thick fallen branch turning a knife in his hands while Edtroka paced back and forth. A copaq hung from Edtroka's fingers so casually that it might have been an extension of his hand. When he gestured, he swung it without care. While Georgianna grimaced, Dhiren didn't seem the least bit perturbed by having the weapon so close.

"The Cahlven were not supposed to be a conquering army," Edtroka said, his voice deflated.

"What did you expect them to be, E'Troke? Saviours? They came with the intention of staying. Otherwise, why would they care?"

"I expected to be involved in the decisions that would affect us."

"Well, I wouldn't know anything about that, would I?" Dhiren said. "I was never involved in any decisions that affected me."

Georgianna turned away from their discussion, shoving both her hands against Alec's chest.

"You shouldn't be listening to this," she whispered, glancing over her shoulder.

"I didn't want to. There was no other choice."

"Yes, and I can see how horrible it was for you."

Dhiren smirked up at Edtroka in bitter sarcasm and Georgianna felt another stab of guilt for listening in on them. She shoved Alec again and, glaring at his grin, made her way around a trunk.

Edtroka crouched, his hand on Dhiren's knee. The space between the two men shrank as Georgianna looked for an opening into the clearing.

"Dhiren, come on. You know it was for the best."

"And maybe this is for the best, too," he said. "Perhaps you will see that later."

Alec grasped Georgianna's arm, trying to pull her back.

"Stop!" she hissed, yanking her arm free of his grasp and tripping through the gap in the trees, bursting into the clearing. Edtroka snatched his hand back from Dhiren's leg and stared at the eavesdroppers, his eyes wide and his mouth open. He pushed up out of his crouch and took a few steps backwards, busying himself with straightening out his shirt. Dhiren glanced at Georgianna, then Edtroka, and laughed.

"Look at that," he said, pointing the knife between them. "A Veniche makes the big strong Tsevstakre squirm. Who would have guessed?"

Edtroka scowled and turned away from them, fitting his copaq back into his belt. A flush of blood rose up his neck, threatening to capture his cheeks. Georgianna glanced at Alec, who looked suspiciously between the two of them. Dhiren seemed to be the only one who found the comment amusing. Hurrying away from Alec, Georgianna sat down next to Dhiren on the fallen branch.

"What will happen, Edtroka? The Colvohan is already on his way. Will they send him away if we don't agree?"

"Of course they won't," Dhiren said.

"What are you talking about?" Alec asked.

Dhiren glanced at Alec and pointed his knife at the ship hovering above them.

"One of the leaders of the Cahlven is on his way here. None of our exalted leaders were told until just now."

Alec didn't look happy about this news but, unlike Edtroka, he kept his thoughts to himself. He frowned and leaned against one of the tree trunks, folding his arms.

"As I was saying," Dhiren continued, turning back to Edtroka, "you don't have a decision in this. You can either accept it or you can fight against it. But if you fight they will keep you out of all further decisions."

"You're saying I should apologise?"

"It wouldn't hurt."

Georgianna grimaced and bit her lip. Edtroka snorted and sneered as his hand went back to the copaq strapped to his hip. He fingered the grip but didn't pull it from the straps.

"So we just let them come in and take over?" Georgianna asked. "I'm with Edtroka. That's no better than the Adveni."

Dhiren stabbed his knife into the ground between his feet and leaned onto his knees, hands clasped together.

"That depends."

"On what?" Alec asked.

"On how they treat us once they have control," he said. "If they simply take over the Adveni rule, then true, it's no better. But if they offer technology and a chance to rule alongside them?"

Alec rolled his eyes.

"And how do we know they'll do that? If what he's said is anything to go by," Alec said, jabbing a thumb in Edtroka's direction, "they have no intention of letting us have a say."

"Well, it'll certainly be more likely if they think they can work with us."

"So you're saying I should apologise," Edtroka said again, rolling his eyes.

Dhiren didn't answer. He looked at Edtroka unabashed until the Adveni growled and turned away.

"Fine!" he snarled, and stalked out of the clearing and into the trees. Georgianna lost sight of him within moments and Dhiren shook his head, chuckling.

"This is why I usually stay away from people."

"You seem to have a pretty good handle on him," Alec said, nodding in the direction Edtroka had just vanished.

Dhiren shrugged and turned instead to Georgianna. "Another lesson?"

"That'd be good. I was in that meeting on the ship all morning and did absolutely nothing."

"Lesson?" Alec asked. "What are you teaching him?"

Georgianna stood and grinned.

"I'm not. He's teaching me."

Dhiren grabbed the handle of his knife and wrenched it from the soft soil. Swiping the blade across his trouser leg, he tugged another knife from his belt. Alec jumped forwards, his hands curling into fists. Tossing the knife blade over handle, Dhiren caught the blade between his fingers and, with a smug grin at Alec, offered the knife handle-first to Georgianna.

"Teaching you what?" Alec hissed. "You know you're not supposed to be leaving the shield without an escort."

Georgianna glanced at him, took the knife, and swept her hair back over her shoulder.

"We're not leaving the shield," she said. "Dhiren's teaching me to fight."

Frowning, Alec crossed the clearing and took the seat Dhiren had vacated. He slid his hands under his thighs and watched warily as Georgianna and Dhiren circled each other.

"Why? You're a medic."

"Because being a medic has protected me well so far," she said sarcastically.

Georgianna turned the blade in her hand, gritting her teeth and watching Dhiren prowl around her. He tossed his knife from one hand to the other with a casual grace. His mocking grin was infuriating as she had barely managed to even nick him so far. She didn't want to hurt him, but it would have been nice to know she could actually land a blow. Lunging forwards, Georgianna groaned as he once again slid away from her jab, leaving her stumbling to regain her balance.

"You're too predictable," he chastised. "You put all your weight into the motion and give your opponent every clue to where you're going."

Georgianna turned the blade around in her hand. Dhiren stopped and shook his head.

"Don't hold it like that. You don't have as much flexi-bility on the angle of the blade from there."

Lowering her gaze, a warm blush rising into her cheeks, Georgianna adjusted her grip and returned to circling him.

"Why are you learning with knives, anyway?" Alec asked. "The Adveni aren't going to be coming at you with knives."

Dhiren didn't so much as blink before he attacked. He spun his knife and jerked forwards. She jumped away from him, but with better balance than before. Dhiren pushed forwards, driving her up against a tree until his knife was at her throat. Grasping Georgianna by the front of the shirt and holding her still, he looked over his shoulder at Alec.

"Because you need to get close. If you're going to learn to kill, you have to get close, to know you can do it."

He patted Georgianna's cheek and stepped back, scuffing his boots across the littered earth.

"Plus, guns are afternoon training."

Leaning forwards, Alec frowned.

"How long have you been doing this?"

"About a week," Georgianna said. "Not exactly a lot else to do while we're waiting for the Cahlven."

"But the Cahlven soldiers are giving the others training. Why didn't you just join in with that?"

Dhiren snorted and pointed the knife at Alec.

"I know how to stand still and take orders, thanks," he scoffed. "So does George. After your time with the commander I'd have thought you'd have had enough of that, too."

Alec gave him a wry grin and got to his feet. Dhiren

watched him pass by, moving to stand behind Georgianna. He slid his hands down to grasp her wrists, pulling her arms up into a better position.

"You want to protect your core," he said in her ear. "Getting stabbed in the arm is better than getting stabbed in the stomach."

Georgianna nodded, allowing him to move her around. He turned her to the side, keeping her arms close to her body. Each touch was gentle, his voice warm and familiar. She leaned back into him, remembering a time when Alec would have been the one to offer to teach her to fight, when he would have thought it was essential she knew how to protect herself from the Adveni. That felt so long ago now. Her breath caught in her throat. Standing close to Alec only reminded her that Keiran was keeping his distance. She wished Keiran was the one standing close, teaching her. The sight of him turning away from her on the ship flashed in front of her.

"You want to keep your weight balanced," Alec said as he took hold of her hips. "If you overstretch it'll be easy to knock you down. Get closer to them instead of extending your arm all the way."

"That makes it easier for them to get me!"

"True, but it's easier to run when you're already on your feet."

Alec stepped away from her, returning to the branch and taking a seat. Dhiren glanced at him and raised an eyebrow.

"Are we ready to go?"

Alec waved him on as Georgianna nodded in agreement. She took smaller steps now, keeping her side to Dhiren instead of facing him, the knives always in the space between them.

"Come at me!"

Georgianna faltered. She didn't want to attack him when he was ready for it and give him a better opportunity to throw her off. She pushed forwards, keeping the weapon close to her body. At the last moment, she flicked the knife to the side and Dhiren let out a hiss. Georgianna jerked in surprise, her mouth dropping open. He didn't pause. He grabbed her arm and yanked her back. Twisting around, the handle of his knife came in against her stomach, his lips at her ear.

"Never drop your focus. One cut doesn't make a win. You don't stop until they're dead."

"Are you hurt?"

He laughed and lifted the knife away from her, releasing her arm. She looked down at his arm and saw a trickle of blood running down to his wrist.

"Dhiren!" she squealed. "I told you we should be using dull knives!"

Dhiren chuckled and wiped his hand along his arm, smearing the blood over his skin. The slash she had given him was superficial, but it didn't make her feel any better about it.

"I should put a dressing on it," she said.

"I'm fine, George."

The ground was covered in leaves but Dhiren jumped to snatch one from a low-hanging branch. He placed it over the cut and held it there, rolling his eyes. Georgianna took a seat next to Alec and used a handful of leaves from the ground to clean off the edge of the knife.

"What happened in the meeting?" Alec asked.

"The Cahlven are sending one of their leaders. They told Olless to stay here until they arrive, which Edtroka doesn't agree with. He thinks we should fight now, as the Adveni will be sending Agrah. He says once they arrive it will be too late."

Alec stared at her. When she didn't say anything, he waved for her to continue. She sighed and shrugged.

"Edtroka and Beck are angry that they weren't told the plan. Three named leaders and they were given no input."

"E'Troke and Beck were angry," Dhiren repeated. "What about Keiran?"

Georgianna turned the knife around in her hand and held it out to Dhiren, handle-first. He slotted it into his belt. Since they began their training, he had claimed many times that he didn't mind a few cuts, but the sight of his blood made her unwilling to try to spill more of it. Alec was right; she was still a medic, after all.

"He didn't say much. He just listened."

"I doubt he cares," Alec sneered. "He's been hiding behind Edtroka for years, right? Now there's someone bigger and scarier to do the job. He certainly knows how to choose the side he thinks can protect him best."

Jumping to her feet, she spun to face Alec.

"Keiran helped free me! He helped gather information against the Adveni and he helped Edtroka in contacting the Cahlven. We weren't getting anywhere against the Adveni, and Keiran helped change that."

Alec flushed and bared his teeth, ready to snap back at her. Georgianna stepped further away.

"If you can take down the Adveni without help, Alec, go do it and show us all. Otherwise, stop acting like you know better."

She turned away before either man could speak. Twigs and leaves crunched under her boots as she stalked back through the trees. Whether she was angry at Keiran or not, whether he ignored her and she him, Georgianna wasn't going to let Alec or anyone else diminish what he had done.

Behind her, Dhiren chuckled.

"You know, Cartwright, for someone who spent years being beaten for doing something stupid like using the wrong Adtvenis term of respect, you still have a big mouth."

3 The Metal Map

Georgianna slowed once she was clear of the trees. Certain that Alec wasn't following her, she made her way along the edge of the lake. She wasn't in the mood to get into a war of words with him, especially not about Keiran. Fighting wouldn't help. It wouldn't bring Keiran back to her.

Shelters had been erected along the shores of Lake Nyquonat in a way that made Georgianna's heart ache. A lifetime of living on the trail with the changing seasons had left the Veniche skilled at building their shelters from day to day and it seemed that this had not been forgotten under the Adveni reign. They had returned to their old trades without question, like putting on their most comfortable clothes. Those who were skilled with building helped others in creating temporary homes and were paid with meat, clothing, or whatever was to spare.

A troop of Cahlven soldiers accompanied all hunters past the shields, though the Veniche regularly complained about their loud voices and unskilled tracking. The Cahlven didn't seem to mind the mockery. In fact, some of the soldiers had become regulars around cook fires in the evenings, sharing stories and listening with interest.

Georgianna returned to the tents they'd set up on their arrival. The supplies Edtroka had hidden in Lurinah Forest just north of Adlai were still scattered inside, including clothes, food, weapons, and a medicine pack that he had given to her. Most of the clothes were far too big for her, but in exchange for healing injuries and illnesses amongst the other Veniche, she had managed to get some of them taken in and shortened to fit her more comfortably.

Beck sat in the mouth of a tent, cleaning a rifle with a rag. There were three other weapons on the ground next to him and it was clear he'd been here since leaving the meeting, taking out his frustration on the metal. Lacie sat on his other side, her sunset hair tied back in a neat braid. She stirred a pot of broth and chuckled at something Jacob had said to her. The dark-haired ex-drysta, Jacob Stone, had a collection of plants around him, torn up from their roots. He separated them with nimble and scarred fingers. Georgianna dropped down on the other side of the small fire, reaching out to warm her hands.

"You don't look happy," Lacie said.

Georgianna pouted at her.

"Boys are ridiculous."

Lacie smiled and looked down at her knees. Beside her, Jacob quickly took a deep interest in one of the plants next to him. He spread the leaves apart and plucked off the small buds inside, one by one. Beck chuckled.

"Which one is it, this time?" he asked.

Georgianna grimaced.

"All of them. They either don't talk or they talk too much."

He nodded absently and flicked back a switch on the rifle, detaching the clip and setting it on his knee.

"Yes, that meeting was filled with too much talking if you ask me. Too much talking and not enough information."

Lacie dropped something else into the pot and stirred it before turning to the piles of plants next to Jacob. He handed one to her and she repeated his motions in removing the buds as he watched with an encouraging smile. When Georgianna looked back to Beck he was observing their quiet company with an amused smile.

"Will that change now the Colvohan is coming?" she asked. "There's no reason to keep plans secret now, is there?"

His laugh was hollow and bitter. He picked up the clip from his knee and gestured with it, waving to the shelters around them.

"When they arrive, I expect the farce of our involvement in this war will finally end. We will be shoved off to the side for our own protection, no doubt."

"Would that be so bad?" Lacie asked.

Beck placed the clip down at his side and leaned forwards. There was such affection in his face that Georgianna wondered why he had never had a family of his own before taking Lacie in. He'd never joined, nor had any children. He had always been just Beck before the Adveni arrived.

"If we take no part in this fight, then we will owe the loss or victory entirely to the Cahlven."

"So?" said Lacie.

"So that will put them in a position of absolute power

over us. Which is no better than the situation with the Adveni, now."

"But what if they're nice?"

"Physical violence isn't the only threat of power," Jacob murmured. "Their manipulation could be quieter and cordial, but it would still make us slaves."

Georgianna's eyes widened. Jacob had come out of his shell since beginning to heal, but he was still quiet and private. She rarely heard him speak, especially not in front of people like Beck, who, he had once told her, scared him. Beck gave Jacob an approving nod.

"The boy has it," he said, ignoring the rising blush on Jacob's cheeks. "It could start out small but the power would be there. That imbalance would travel generations. They would pass their rules and force their authority by holding this win over us. *'You'd be slaves to the Adveni if it weren't for us, so you should let us change this rule to suit us.'* You see?"

"I guess," Lacie said. "But will that change if we take part? We have such small numbers."

"The numbers are not as important as you might think."

"They're not?"

"No," Georgianna agreed. She dipped her finger in the broth. Before Lacie could smack her hand away she popped the finger into her mouth and sucked off the juice, grinning at the younger girl. "We have a much better knowledge of the land, of the cities. Our knowledge will help their troops. Their force is in numbers, ours in history."

Light shot across the sky and the ground trembled beneath them. Beck dropped his rifle and grasped the handle of the pot, holding it steady. The shudders ran in ripples through the ground and lightning forked and flashed over the shield. The giant Cahlven ship looked monstrous with lightning reflected across its smooth, sharp shell. As Georgianna squeezed her eyes shut and covered her ears, the explosion rocked through her. She lifted her head and glanced at Lacie and Jacob as another flash flooded her eyes with white-hot light.

Screeching, Georgianna gave up protecting her ears and dug the heels of her hands into her eyes, shielding them with the cool black shade of her palms. Red and white spots bloomed and faded with the rippling vibrations. A deep groan grew to a rumble and she brought her hands away to see blurry rocks tumble down the mountain slope into the northern edge of the lake. The water swelled and rocked, waves crashing high on the shores.

"They're increasing frequency," Beck boomed over the ringing in their ears.

Jacob's plants lay around him in disarray, forgotten in the blast. He clutched Lacie's hand, and both trembled far harder than the earth beneath them. The young redhead looked at Georgianna as Jacob murmured into her ear. She pulled away her hand, a blush brighter than her hair colouring her cheeks. Jacob looked briefly upset by the lack of connection until he caught Georgianna watching them. His ears were pink beneath his dark curls and he looked away. Georgianna turned to Beck to find him watching them as well.

"Why are they wasting firepower?" she asked.

"No idea. They have to know they won't get through the shields."

"They don't want to get through the shields," Jacob said, his voice quiet under the lingering buzz. "They don't care whether the bombs get through the shields as long as *we* also don't go through the shields. They're keeping us penned."

Beck watched Jacob with interest. There was a respect in his smile as he nodded and drummed his fingers against his knee.

"Stop us from making a move. That's a good theory, Jacob."

The tint at the edge of Jacob's ears spread down his neck and underneath the collar of his shirt. He didn't look at Beck as he smiled and reached for one of the discarded plants.

Lacie grabbed the spoon and stirred the broth again. She used its handle to poke the fire underneath, raising the flames higher against the pot. Bubbles popped across the surface and the warm, tempting scent coiled into the air around them. Beck fitted the rifle together as Georgianna rested her elbows on her knees and watched the bubbling broth.

"Smells good!"

They all looked up as Dhiren approached. He had a scrap of linen wrapped around the part of his arm where she had nicked him with the knife, and a small spot of blood had seeped through. It didn't seem to be bothering him in the slightest. He scuffed his foot against the loose dirt but made no move to sit beside them.

"Thank you," Lacie squeaked, avoiding Dhiren's eye.

"Olless wants us," Dhiren said.

Beck collected up the other weapons and stashed them in the back of the tent. He zipped the front flaps closed and rose to his feet with a tired groan. He placed a kiss on top of Lacie's head and patted her shoulder.

"Keep some warm for me, okay?"

Lacie nodded and Dhiren scuffed his foot again.

"She wants all of us."

"All?" said Georgianna.

Dhiren waved his hand to each of them.

"All."

Jacob and Lacie shared a worried glance. Releasing a deep sigh, expecting another hour or two of sitting and saying nothing, Georgianna grasped the handle of the pot, lifted it from the fire, and set it next to the opening of the tent. Lacie got to her feet, shook off the small sheet she'd been sitting on, and laid it, clean side down, over the pot. Jacob collected his plants and dropped them into a canvas bag before throwing them into the next tent along.

Georgianna grinned. That was Wrench's tent. Eli Talassi—known as Wrench to most of his friends—was skilled with technology and had been the one to remove Jacob's collar after he escaped from his owner. A few months ago, Jacob had helped them heal Wrench's wound when he was hit by the chemical gel of a copaq bullet. She wondered whether saving each other had bonded them in some way, or if Jacob simply wanted to remain close to Lacie.

Once they were all ready to go, Dhiren led them over to the waiting transport to take them up to the ship.

* * *

The room was bigger than the one Georgianna had been taken to for the meetings with leaders. A huge low table stood in the centre of the oval room, and chairs were fitted into the walls with tables that folded down between them. Jacob and Lacie, who had never been up into the ship, stared, in awe of everything they passed. Alec and Keiran stood facing opposite directions, silent and stubborn, while Taye shifted his weight from foot to foot.

Georgianna had been friends with Taye since childhood; they had grown up in the Kahle tribe together. However, despite Georgianna's helping him rescue his girlfriend, Nyah, from her Adveni owner, Taye had become cold and suspicious after she'd agreed to work alongside Edtroka.

"Where's Nyah?" Georgianna asked him.

"She wasn't invited."

He didn't look at her, and she remembered the way Taye had been quick to question the Cahlven's involvement in their fight. While they had been friends a long time, Taye seemed to have forgotten the affection they'd once had for each other, and avoided her whenever possible.

Dhiren led Georgianna over to the low table. She winced as Keiran came to stand beside her. There was only a slim gap between them but the space felt as impenetrable as the shield above. She looked down to avoid his eye, staring instead at the table. A thick powder covered its surface. Slate grey, it shimmered under the lights. Keiran reached out, picked up a handful, and let it trickle through his fingers.

A small cough brought them to attention and, under Olless' glare, Keiran dropped the rest of the powder and brushed his hands together.

"Miss Wolfe will not be needed for this," Olless said calmly, turning away from Keiran. "We have Mr. Cartwright. That will be enough."

"Nyah knows more Adtvenis than Alec," Taye said, crossing his arms over his chest.

Alec's gaze lingered on Georgianna. He shoved his hands in his pockets and glanced at Lacie and Jacob.

"It's better she isn't here," he said.

"Well, there is no reason for Lacie to be involved in whatever this is!" Beck said. "If you need something you can get from us, I will not—"

"No, I'm staying!" Lacie squawked. "I want to help!"

Beck took her elbow but Lacie pierced him with a glare and extracted herself from his grasp, turning back to the table. Raising an eyebrow in amusement at the silenced marshall, Dhiren barely concealed his grin. He turned away from Beck and waved his hand around the table.

"Beck, Keiran, and Edtroka are nominated as leaders and everyone else bar myself and *him*," Dhiren nodded to Taye, "used to be dreta."

Georgianna glanced around the table. He was right. When she looked at Edtroka, he had a smug grin as he looked down on the ex-inmate.

With no more arguments, Olless pulled out a flat white device. Every gaze was on her as she tapped in a series of commands. With a gentle whoosh, the powder flew up from the table. A few, including Georgianna, recoiled. Edtroka seemed impressed, Dhiren and Taye curious.

The powder vibrated. Sparks of light reflected off the shards and bounced in every direction. Olless typed in a few more commands and the powder shifted again. Some of it fell into deep valleys while other parts rose into tall mountains. When it finally settled, a circular spread of land lay before them in tiny metal shavings.

"It's a map," Alec announced.

"Correct. Mr. Flynn stands closest to our current position." Olless reached over the map and circled the valley at the bottom of the northern mountain range in front of Dhiren's hips. "And Mr. Stone by Adlai."

Adlai was easily identified by the various spires and buildings, even though they were too small to make out individually.

Dhiren moved in a flash. His fist pierced through the range of mountains, knocking off their tops and sending a spray of metal powder over the landscape. He chuckled and beamed as he extracted his hand. The powder recreated the mountains instantly but the look of annoyance remained on Olless' face.

"If you're quite done."

"I am!" Dhiren said, unabashed.

Olless shook her head and rolled her eyes as sniggers rippled around the table.

"You have all been asked here due to your individual expertise. Mr. Rann, as I am informed, has an extensive understanding of the tunnels beneath Adlai, due to his Carae dealings. Mr. Cartwright, Mr. Stone, Miss Cormack, and Miss Lennox have knowledge of different areas of the dwelling quarter and the places their owners used to take them."

"I've got a pretty good mental map of the compound," Dhiren said, holding up a hand. "Oh, wait."

"You know the northern lands better than anyone here, Dhiren," Edtroka said, though his amusement was clear. "Your knowledge could be invaluable."

"The Adveni have increased the frequency of their attacks," Olless continued, ignoring Dhiren's jibes. "And our scouts inform me that there are troops of Agrah on their way to this location."

"What a surprise," Beck grumbled.

"Our shields can protect us from the projectiles of the Adveni ships but will not be effective against troops unless we solidify."

"Solidify?"

Georgianna didn't need to look up to see who had spoken. She was sure they were all thinking the same thing. They had no idea what Olless was talking about.

"Our shields have the ability to become solid. They will not allow anything to pass. We have held off from this measure so far to allow for Veniche to come and go collecting food. If we were to solidify, this would no longer be possible."

"How long would the shields be solid for?" Dhiren asked.

"Once they are solid, they cannot be changed back without removing them completely. Unfortunately, we suspect that the Adveni commanders are aware of this."

"So, they block us in, force us to solidify the shields, and then only have to wait until we have to remove them before destroying us completely," Edtroka said, nodding. "It's what I'd do."

Alec raised an eyebrow. He didn't say anything but Georgianna could imagine what he was thinking: of course Edtroka would do something that cruel.

"I have brought you here in the hopes of getting an idea of prime targets," Olless said. "As you all may have heard by now, the Second Colvohan is on his way to Os-Veruh. We hope to begin our response the moment he arrives with reinforcements."

Dhiren leaned across the map, mountaintops brushing his chest. His shirt sent a tiny landslide of powder cascading down the mountainside to collect at the bottom.

"There are four lakes near Adlai, not including Nyquonat," he said, pointing to the valleys dipped into the land. One extended off the side of the table nearest to Lacie. "Those are the main sources of water to the city."

Alec shook his head and grasped the edge of the table, leaning forwards.

"That won't matter once the Freeze sets in. If we were still in the Heat, perhaps, but water will be readily available through the rain run-off and then easily collected from the snow."

"That will save the Veniche," Beck argued. "But would the Adveni think of it?"

Everyone turned to Edtroka. His eyes widened. "Most Adveni will have received at least a minimum of survivalist training," he told them. "Cutting off the water would cause discomfort but would not cripple them."

"Electricity might," Taye said. "Cutting the power? Veniche can survive easily without that. We've done it for generations."

A nod went around the table, though Edtroka and Olless looked sceptical. Georgianna wondered whether they had ever lived a life without electricity and their technological devices. Had they ever warmed themselves in a Freeze with nothing more than open fires and layers of clothes? Had they ever cooked on an open flame and relied on torches to light their way?

"Can you make Adlai bigger?" Taye asked.

Olless drew the device from her pocket and after a few clicks the powder vibrated and fell to a flat layer a few inches off the table. A couple more taps and the city of Adlai spread across the table, a perfect view from above. They took a few minutes to acquaint themselves.

Georgianna reached behind Dhiren's shoulders and tapped Edtroka's arm before pointing to a tall square powder building.

"There's your apartment," she said with a grin. Edtroka smirked back at her.

"From what I've seen," said Taye, "electricity lines are built into the walls along the main lines. I couldn't tell you where each one leads but I've seen people down there fixing things."

"What about buildings?" Lacie asked. "They have all their systems and records."

Beck laid his hand on Lacie's shoulder and beamed at her as she pointed out a large building off Javeknell Square.

"None of this matters," Keiran cut in. "We can disable whatever we like and it'll make no difference. As soon as the Adveni feel they're losing, they'll evacuate and blow the Mykahnol. We'll lose everything and all of these targets we've spent our time on will be useless."

Georgianna looked up at him. He was staring at the map but there was a blank, hollow look in his eyes. He chewed on the inside of his cheek and plunged his hands into his pockets, rocking back on his heels. His voice was raw and quiet, and now Georgianna looked closer, she realised he seemed thinner, skin pale and eyes dull. Had he not been eating since they arrived here? She glanced around the table. Was there anyone here who would have made sure he was okay after everything that had happened?

"He's right," Edtroka agreed. Keiran didn't look up or acknowledge the words.

"That's good then," Olless said with a smug grin. "That means the device should be our first priority."

4 Terms of Truce

The last thing Georgianna remembered was her legs cramping, and sitting down. They'd been stood around the map table for hours debating the best way forwards. For every suggestion someone made there were two people who disagreed, and for every dissention there was another idea. Nobody at the table had concrete knowledge of where the Mykahnol was set up or how to disable it. Even Edtroka was clueless. The Mykahnol had never been under the control of the Tsevstakre.

In the late evening, Olless had brought in a technician called Tohma. He listened to their explanations of the Mykahnol but in the end told them that he wouldn't know how to disable a weapon he'd never seen. They had heard rumours of what the Mykahnol looked like, and they certainly knew how it worked; but without a good look or at least some plans, nobody could know for sure.

Georgianna woke with her shoulder and neck muscles hot and aching. While she'd been sleeping, someone had laid a blanket over her. It was made of such soft material that she spent a couple of minutes stroking it; the blanket was as warm as the soft black behind her eyelids. Finally opening her eyes, she found that she was not the only one who had succumbed to exhaustion. Jacob and Lacie were asleep in adjoining chairs, Lacie's head resting on Jacob's shoulder. The corner of his lips touched the top of her head, and her hair fluttered with each of his gentle breaths. They too had been draped in a blanket but showed no signs of waking.

Georgianna shifted her shoulder and winced. Most of the room was empty. Only Dhiren and Edtroka remained, bent over the table. Edtroka straightened and shook his head, laying his hand against Dhiren's shoulder. Dhiren looked back, but quickly returned his attention to the map, his jaw tight. Even from her chair, Georgianna could see that the table had been reset to the bigger map of the land instead of the detailed Adlai map Olless had created from the powder. Edtroka brushed his finger idly over the top of a hill, his dark eyes fascinated by the metal that came rolling down.

"This is far enough north that no one would think to look," Dhiren said, waving his hand over an area Georgianna could not see. "There is water close, forest."

Edtroka turned his attention from the hill and followed Dhiren's hand. Resting his fist against the edge of the table, he leaned over and pointed at something.

"It's also completely open," he argued. "There is no protection here, Dhiren. An attack could come from any direction."

Dhiren stood up straight and folded his arms. His foot beat a steady rhythm against the cold floor. He turned away from the table.

"Will you ever find anything safe, E'Troke?" he demanded. "Except a compound with guards and no escape?"

Edtroka gulped. He straightened and didn't look at Dhiren as he turned away from the table and perched himself on its edge. Even leaning like this, he was as tall as the other man. He reached out to touch Dhiren's elbow but was denied contact as Dhiren took a step away.

"Dhiren," he murmured. "Come on. How many times will I have to explain myself?"

"It's not your explanations I want."

"Then what is it? I'm making these plans, aren't I?"

There was a desperation in his voice that Georgianna placed in an instant. She'd heard him sound that way before, back in the compound when he had been begging Dhiren not to kill him. He had said he'd *promised*, but she had no idea what the promise had been. Before that moment, she'd not even known that Dhiren and Edtroka knew each other.

She looked at Dhiren and, as he turned away from Edtroka, searching for anything to look at besides the Adveni, his gaze landed on her. There was no smile, no familiarity in his expression. He gritted his teeth and his fingers clenched into his sleeves.

"And how many does this plan include?" he asked, looking at Edtroka again.

"Ah, good, you're still here."

Both men jumped and Edtroka leapt a foot from Dhiren as he pushed himself from the table and turned to Olless. She strode into the room towards them. Her hair was free from its usual braid and the top button of her suit was undone. There were no windows in the room, but Georgianna guessed that it was the middle of the night. She shifted in her seat, pushing herself a little higher. Dhiren glanced at her and looked away again.

"What is it?" Edtroka asked.

"If you don't mind, Dhiren, I need to speak to Grystch alone."

Dhiren's nostrils flared as he set off. Edtroka grabbed him by the elbow.

"Whatever it is, Olless, I trust Dhiren implicitly."

Olless frowned but didn't say a word against this. Dhiren yanked his arm from Edtroka's grasp and, once he had his attention, nodded in Georgianna's direction. Georgianna's eyes widened as Edtroka glanced at her, but he gave a small shake of his head and turned his attention onto Olless.

"Well?"

Olless shifted her weight from foot to foot and wrung her hands before her. She gazed down at the table and, when Edtroka urged her to continue, didn't meet his gaze. Georgianna frowned. She'd never seen Olless be anything less than blunt. Even though she knew Edtroka and Beck were angry that she'd not been sharing all information, she'd never truly hidden it before.

"The First Colvohan ordered that I contact him immediately."

"And?" said Edtroka.

"And when I did, he told me that a truce has been offered by the Volsonnar."

"A truce?" Dhiren hissed a laugh. "You're kidding?"

Olless shook her head. Her long hair fluttered down her back, catching the light. She looked pale behind its curtain.

"They want a meeting once the Second Colvohan arrives."

Edtroka stepped closer and scratched his neck. He chuckled.

"Congratulations to them," he said with a sneer. "Why would the Cahlven even consider a meeting? You said it already: your troops have knocked out the majority of their bases. You've already taken out their defences."

"A truce could end this without more losses," she said.

Olless turned away from them, her gaze sweeping over the room. She watched Jacob and Lacie for a moment, and Georgianna was sure to close her eyes just enough to feign sleep. She didn't dare move or even breathe until she saw the swish of hair through her eyelashes as Olless turned to stare at the table.

"Are they considering it?" Dhiren asked.

"The Adveni will come to the table and Os-Veruh will be decided over without violence. Once a decision is made, all Mykahnols will be disabled and removed. But the meeting depends on one thing."

"You really think my father will sit down and discuss terms? Land ownership?" Edtroka gave a bitter laugh and shook his head. "The Veniche will never agree to this."

Olless nodded absently and gave a heavy sigh. Edtroka made a full circuit of the table.

"Which is why you came to tell me about it and not them, right?"

"No!" Olless screeched. "That has nothing to do with it."

Edtroka chuckled and rolled his eyes. He perched himself on the edge of the table again, accidentally sitting on the side of a mountain. He didn't even notice.

"What's the catch?" Dhiren asked.

When Olless looked at him in surprise, Dhiren raised an eyebrow.

"You said that the meeting depended on something. What is it?"

Edtroka froze and stared at Olless. She looked away from both and ran her fingers through the metal powder. She took a moment to compose herself, her chest heaving in steadying breaths, before lifting her head. Edtroka pushed himself upright again.

"The Adveni will come to the table to discuss a truce if the Cahlven comply with their demands within five days."

Dhiren's eyes narrowed as he stepped forwards. Edtroka reached to stop him but seemed to think better of it, dropping his hand. Shuffling a little higher in her seat, Georgianna held her breath.

"What are they demanding?"

Olless gulped but she didn't look at Dhiren. She stared at Edtroka as her jaw trembled. But when she found her voice, it was with the same cool authority that she'd displayed upon the Cahlven's arrival to Os-Veruh.

"They demand that you be handed over to stand trial for treason."

5 The Absent Vote

The sun was rising as Georgianna jumped down from the transport steps, more surefooted than before. Bolts of peach light pierced the clouds and struck the sides of the mountains, brightening the dull rocks to copper and gold. The beams sliced into the lake, leaving swirls of indigo and teal in their wake. She jogged along the rocky shore, chewing on her bottom lip and brushing the wrinkles from her clothes. He'd not spoken to her in days and it had been over a week since she'd last seen him crawl into a tent. It would take hours to search the camp beneath the Cahlven shield and she didn't have hours to spare.

Wrench groaned and rolled over when she shook his shoulders. He was sprawled across the tent, one foot sticking out of the opening. He grumbled into his pillow and tried to shake her off, but Georgianna slotted her hand in underneath his face, covered his mouth and nose, and held on until he spluttered and sat up.

"It's not even light, George."

"Where's Keiran?"

"Hell if I know."

Wrench flopped back down onto his pillow, groping for his blanket. Georgianna reached over his shoulder, searching for his nose again.

"Alright, alright! Gerroff! He's been sleeping on the ship. Comes down to eat and walk. If he's not up there, he's probably on the shoreline."

"Thank you, Wrench," Georgianna said sweetly, bending over and kissing his cheek. He was still grumbling curses even after she'd left the tent.

Georgianna ran back along the shoreline. The vast Densaii ship cast a wide shadow over half of the black and bottomless lake. Two men sat on rocks next to the water's edge, gutting fish, while six more waded up to their waists, each carrying a large net. One of them waved and Georgianna gave a nod in return, slowing to a walk.

He was sitting on a tall rock at the base of a slope where the land began to climb towards the mountains. In the shadow of the ship he seemed to have been carved from the same stone he sat on. As Georgianna came closer, she could see his fingers working through a rope, twisting and turning it with small, delicate movements. She stopped at the foot of the rock and watched him.

"And who wants a meeting now?" he said, not looking up. "First they send Cartwright, now you? Anyone would think Olless didn't actually want me to attend."

"I was looking for you."

The rock was slippery. There were no crevices to get a decent footing and it was too tall for her to haul her-self up by her arms. Keiran sat, eyes fixed on his rope.

She circled, and found a lower rock on the other side. Climbing precariously across the gap, she fell with a thump next to him. Keiran huffed.

"So, you finally decided I was worthy of your time?"

"Worthy of my time?"

He drew his knee up to his chest and dug his heel into a crack in the rock. A half-finished net hung down towards the water, the rest of the rope coiled beside his hip.

"How long has it been since you said two words to me?"

"You could easily have spoken to me, Keiran! I'm not the one who went off to sleep on the Cahlven ship to avoid everyone."

"Because you needed time!"

"Time?" Her voice was becoming shrill and squeaky as she turned to look closer at him. "What time did I need?"

"To figure things out. I told you I couldn't forgive Cartwright for that mark and you... you blamed me. I know you did. What happened to him was my fault."

"I..."

Georgianna stopped. She wanted to tell him that she didn't blame him. She wanted to say that it didn't matter whether he forgave Alec. There were a thousand things she wanted to tell him, but his silence—the way he'd avoided her—all crept up until she couldn't find the words. Instead, she sighed.

"The Adveni have offered a truce if the Cahlven hand over Edtroka."

"Truce?" he asked. "Is that possible?"

"They say the Volsonnar will meet with the Colvohan to discuss terms without violence and..." She shook her head. "That isn't the point, Keiran. They want Edtroka to be given to them so they can put him on trial for treason."

"Technically, he is a traitor."

"He'll be killed before anyone hears a single thing he says."

Keiran stared at the rope. He wound it around his fingers into knots, fitting them into the net with perfect precision. Georgianna snarled and took hold of the rope, pulling it sharply and undoing his most recent knot with a yank. He hissed and rubbed his fingers where the rope had pulled on his skin.

"What?"

"I just told you that the Adveni will kill Edtroka if he's handed over and you don't say anything?"

"What am I supposed to say? I don't know why you're even telling me."

He extracted the rope from her grasp and began fitting it back into place.

"I thought you might—"

"You've not spoken to me in weeks, Georgianna. And now you come and tell me this. Why? I would have found out from Olless or Beck. Why are you coming to me?"

Georgianna picked up the coil of rope and laid it in her lap. He watched her warily but she didn't try to tug the net from his grasp again. Instead, she fixed the rope into small neat coils that would be easy to draw from.

"I don't trust the others."

"Olless?"

"Any of them. I don't trust them not to hand him over just to bring the Adveni to the table."

"And what? You trust me because I've betrayed my people before so I'll probably do it again?"

"If you're a traitor, Keiran, then I'm just as guilty as you are," Georgianna said, shoving the coil off her lap and into a mess on the rock between them. "I helped Edtroka ensure your safety even before I knew what you were doing. You knew you were helping bring the Cahlven here. I didn't. I only wanted to save you."

Keiran stared at his knot. Drawing in a slow breath, he finally met her eye. He looked tired and drawn, his stubble growing into a full beard, his hair messy. But none of it could hide the sunken hollows of his cheeks and the dead grey in his eyes.

"It doesn't matter what we did, Keiran," she said, reaching across the gap and taking his hand in both of hers. "We're here. We're in this. Edtroka is a good man. You know it as well as I do. We can't let them hand him over like some bargaining chip."

When he shook his head, Georgianna feared she had lost him entirely. She pulled back, burying her face in her hands. Her breath came as a desperate sob she couldn't hold in any longer.

"I just... I don't know what you want me to do about it."

She peeked at him through her fingers. His eyes were beautiful, even dulled as they were in the shadow of the ship. They watched her from beneath his furrowed brow. Georgianna searched for the flecks of blue in the mass of grey, each one a reason to trust him with the fears that had been clawing at her.

"You were named one of the leaders of the Veniche," she whispered.

He gave a bitter laugh and rolled his eyes, turning those reasons away from her. Dropping her hands into her lap, she leaned forwards, trying to catch his gaze again.

"You have a vote, Keiran. Call for a vote on how to proceed. Even if Beck and Olless vote yes, you and Edtroka will stalemate them. If the Cahlven want to keep up this story of collaboration, they'll have no choice but to back down."

Keiran nodded slowly and looked down at his rope. He didn't move to make another knot; he simply stared at it.

Georgianna leaned closer to him. It felt like so long since they had talked to each other, since they had been close. The gap between them felt bigger than ever. Her pride had stopped her from closing it before, but clinging to pride was no longer an issue for either of them. She laid her hand on his knee.

"You are going to vote 'no', aren't you?"

He didn't answer and yet she still stared at him, waiting for him to tell her that he was friends with Edtroka, that he had worked with him for two years. Of course he would vote no. The silence stretched on, only broken by the water lapping at the base of the rock.

"Keiran?"

"George! Keiran!"

Keiran turned away first and she stared in disbelief at his cheek, at the curve of his ear and the slope of his nose. Tears gathered in her eyes and she brushed them away with the side of her hand.

"Dhiren, up here!" Keiran called down.

Dhiren jogged towards the rock. Stopping at the rock base, he put a hand to his waist, pressing hard against the own flesh. His jaw looked so tight that Georgianna thought he might shatter his teeth with the pressure. She moved backwards on the rock to get a better look at him. He was pale and sweating, eyes wide. He looked as scared as she had ever seen him.

"What is it?"

She slid across the top of the rock towards him. As he glanced around, she realised he was shaking.

"Dhiren, are you alright?"

"It's E'Troke," he said. His voice wasn't as solid as usual. There was no humour, no mockery. His words cracked as he looked across the lake towards the mountains. "He's gone."

6 Edtroka's Choice

Keiran shoved the chair away.

"We didn't get your help so you could bow down the moment the Adveni ask."

"No one is saying—"

"The fact you're even considering this truce says everything."

Olless rolled her eyes and slid into one of the seats. She crossed her legs, her foot jiggling. She'd not been impressed that news of the offer had spread so quickly, which had only made Keiran and Beck angry that they'd not been informed in the first place.

"The offer came in and I told Grystch of its contents," Olless said again. "As it directly affects him, I thought it best."

At the doorway, Dhiren snorted.

Beck stepped forwards.

"It directly affects all of us, Olless," he said. "Any offer of peace with the race who forced ours into servitude... affects us."

"You know that wasn't what I meant."

"Then what did you mean?" he asked, folding his arms. "Please, enlighten us."

Olless took a deep breath and ran her fingers through her hair. She still didn't look her immaculate self. Georgianna threaded her fingers through her own hair, self-consciously. If Olless didn't look good then she could only imagine she was an absolute mess.

"The message offers truce in exchange for Grystch's life. I meant that since he is named, he should be the first to know, whatever is decided."

"So you admit that it's his life?" Keiran asked. "We'd be handing him over to slaughter."

"From the Adveni track record when it comes to traitors—"

"This is ridiculous! We're not handing him over," Dhiren said.

Georgianna wrapped her arms around her legs and rested her chin on her knees. This wasn't helping, and Edtroka was getting further away. She wondered if he'd truly believed they would hand him over; if he thought that he meant so little to them that his only option was to run. He probably hated all of them for this. He would hate her, too. It was only through her insistence that he'd revealed himself as a traitor to the Adveni before the Cahlven arrived. If she'd not lied to Beck and told him they were planning to destroy the compound, he'd probably still be in his home and at his job, fighting the quiet fight. He'd still be safe, instead of on the run with both sides hunting him.

"I cannot say where I would stand on Edtroka," Beck said as he took a seat. "One life to save thousands."

Dhiren pushed himself off the doorframe, eyes bulging.

"But the Adveni have done too much wrong here," he continued before Dhiren could argue. "We cannot stand aside while you hold discussions about which lands they claim."

Olless shook her head.

"It does not mean that. It means that their Volsonnar and our Colvohan will meet to discuss terms. Whether these are terms either side will accept is still in question."

Georgianna hadn't been able to truly see why Edtroka was so angry before. He and Beck were always talking about how frustrating it was to not get the proper information. What did it matter if they were told that the Colvohan was on his way to Os-Veruh before he left or while he was making the journey? To her, there was little difference, not much to get so worked up over.

Now she could see it. She could hear it in the words Olless used, the way she placated each worry without proving their concerns unfounded. They weren't discussing land, they were discussing terms. It was all just a word game that made little sense.

Dhiren punched the doorframe.

"Forget the fucking meeting!" he shouted. "What is being done to find E'Troke?"

Olless got to her feet and peered curiously at him.

"Why does that matter?"

Georgianna knew Dhiren's history. She knew the brothers of the Compound had used him to intimidate prisoners into doing what they wanted. They'd done it to her, though in her case they had sent another prisoner to hurt her and, when Dhiren came to help her, his protection had been withheld in order to sway her to their side. She could see it in him, the way he stalked forwards. She could see the fury in the way his gaze fixed unwavering on Olless. She could see the name they'd given him: Coyote.

"Why does it matter?" His words were little more than a snarl, and Olless took a step away, rounding the chair to put it between them. The obstacle didn't hinder Dhiren in the slightest. He crept towards her, pushing the chair away with a brush of his hand.

"He made his choice," Olless said, taking another step away. "Whether he's gone to Adlai or has run to hide, he made that choice. There is nothing to be done but wait and see."

Georgianna uncoiled herself from the ball she'd curled into. She set her feet on the ground and immediately felt the sensation of once again being stuck to the floor. Olless was retreating from Dhiren, weaving her way around chairs to keep him at bay. Even though she wanted to avoid Dhiren's anger, Georgianna grabbed him by the arm.

"Dhiren, leave her alone. She got the message—she didn't write it."

Dhiren turned to her. He looked truly feral, teeth bared. She'd never seen him so angry, so hateful. He brushed her off, his hands balled into fists.

"He saved you. He made sure Maarqyn Guinnyr didn't get to you and use you the way he uses all his pretty little things," Dhiren sneered. "And what have you done for him? You should be arguing against this with all your breath!"

For the first time, Georgianna relished the feeling of being rooted in place. A shudder ran down her spine and into the tips of her fingers. She wanted to run but the floor held her steady. He came closer, waiting, watching for her mistake. Straightening up, she gulped.

"Olless is right," she said. "She told Edtroka about the message and he made his choice. We shouldn't take that choice from him."

Dhiren's face twisted in a spasm of loathing. Georgianna had never had a problem with him before. He'd always been cheerful and kind with her. Even when she had seen his skill in fighting, she had never been afraid of him. Until now. As he glared, she was sure that he hated her more than he hated any of the others. More than Olless and her infuriating rules, more than Vajra and Ta-Dao and their petty cruelty. More than the Adveni who had handed him over to that life.

She was the one who was supposed to fight for Edtroka. She was supposed to make sure they found him and brought him back. She'd been his. He'd protected her as Dhiren had said. Edtroka had gone against his family because he didn't agree with the Adveni, but he'd been caught because of her.

He raised his hand. Buckling against the pressure, Georgianna shielded her face. A twitch ran down his arm and he bared his teeth before turning away. He brought down his hand in a heavy blow, knocking over a chair as he stalked away. He didn't stop for anyone. Keiran moved to the door but Dhiren shoved him aside. He had disappeared down the corridor before anyone thought to try calling him back.

Georgianna squeaked as her breath returned. She covered her mouth, holding onto the sound, onto the fear it revealed. They were all staring at her with varying degrees of suspicion. Keiran's glare was the worst. Was it anger, like Dhiren's, or simply disappointment? She had begged him to save Edtroka, and now she'd simply let him go? No wonder he couldn't understand.

"You need a new leader," Georgianna said, when none of the others spoke. "You elected three and one is gone. You should elect another."

Olless opened her mouth, but Georgianna didn't wait to hear what the Cahlven emissary had to say. If she spoke, Georgianna didn't hear, as she pulled herself from the sticky sensation and followed Dhiren.

7 Contingency

He stood as still as the trees around him, staring through the shield border. He made no motion to show he had noticed her approach, but he knew she was there, and she'd made no effort to be quiet. Twigs and dead leaves rustled beneath her boots, and her clothes had snagged on branches more than once as she followed him through the trees.

Truthfully, she was glad for her lack of skill in silent tracking. She didn't want to surprise him. Back on the ship, he'd looked ready to punch her, and she was concerned that he might take the opportunity to do it now and blame it on being surprised.

"Go away, Med."

Georgianna brushed a branch aside and moved to join him, stopping just short of the barrier. Only a shimmer showed its existence, like hot air rising from burning ground. It rippled and distorted the forest beyond its border. Wide patches of ground were burned on the other side, trees scarred and fallen. The Adveni had bombed around them as they searched for the limits of the shield. That was what they did. They destroyed whatever they could touch until they found the problem. She couldn't see how the Cahlven could even consider calling a truce with people who would burn everything down, given the chance.

Dhiren didn't move away as she stood next to him and stared out at the desolation beyond their little protective bubble. He ground his teeth, then flexed his hands, balling them into fists. She didn't recoil.

"Do you think he's gone back?" she asked.

He didn't speak. He didn't look at her. Even with only a breath of air between them, he looked completely alone, lost in whatever he thought was outside the barrier.

"You were planning a back-up before the message came in, right? A place to hide and wait out the war. Would he go there?"

Dhiren's resolve broke with a heave of his chest. He shook his head.

"The back-up was my idea," he said. "I had to beg him to even consider it."

"He seemed to be on board."

"He was humouring me."

Georgianna frowned.

"Why, though?"

"E'Troke knew he wouldn't be allowed to live. He knew it in that prison cell," said Dhiren. He flexed his fingers in and out of fists. "He knew that if I didn't kill him, the Adveni would. Better to save someone who doesn't have a clock ticking over his head."

Georgianna turned to him, her arm brushing the barrier. A shock ran through her body which made the hairs on her arms stand on end. She sidestepped away from the shield and rubbed her hands vigorously over her skin.

"So you think—"

"That he's gone back to hand himself in? Yes."

As little as Georgianna wanted to believe that Edtroka would walk willingly to his death, she knew Dhiren was right. One person didn't win a war. Edtroka had told her it was bigger than them all. Even Alec had known that Edtroka would sacrifice people if it meant giving them a chance to win the war against the Adveni. She'd just never thought he'd martyr himself, not like this.

"Who would he go to?"

"His father."

She drew her bottom lip between her teeth and chewed on it as she gazed past Dhiren at the trees. He turned to her, his arm grazing across the barrier edge. He shook it off with a grimace and glared.

"Why do you care?"

"What?"

"You said that we should let him go, that he made his choice," he said. "So, why do you care?"

Meeting his gaze, Georgianna forced a half-smile.

"I said that to Olless," she said, propping her hands on her hips. "Do you think they would have turned down the chance to finish this war quickly without more bloodshed? At the loss of just one life, they end the bloodshed by talking round a table."

"But you just supported it."

"I said what she wanted to hear so she'd look the other way." Glancing over her shoulder, she peered through the trees before turning back to Dhiren. "If we're going to stop Edtroka, we need to do it ourselves."

Dhiren straightened up, eyes narrowing as he looked down at her. For a few seconds he simply stared. And then he grinned.

"He won't be easy to track," he said. "E'Troke has training. He knows the land."

"He'll also have the tsentyl he used on the way here."

"How do you know?"

"He's wanted as a traitor. He'll need to make sure he isn't killed before the commanders know the Cahlven are agreeing to the deal, right? You said he'd go to his father. Nobody would let him anywhere near the Volsonnar unless he organised it in advance."

Dhiren opened and closed his mouth. He scratched the side of his neck and jaw, and huffed.

"But how would we even track that? We don't have the technology to send him a message, let alone figure out where he is."

Georgianna clapped Dhiren on the shoulder, giving him a broad smile.

"No, but he used that tsentyl to contact the Cahlven once they were in range," she said. "Keiran can get the information for us."

"Keiran, who you've been avoiding since we got here?" he asked. "How are you going to convince him?"

Georgianna felt like he'd let all the air out of her. She'd been winding herself up, convincing herself that they could do this, that they could help Edtroka and make sure the struggle wasn't for nothing. But with a single question, Dhiren had unravelled everything. She'd not even considered that Keiran may not agree to her plan. In fact, for a few glorious minutes she'd managed to forget that Keiran was upset with her.

What if Dhiren was right and Keiran couldn't be convinced? He'd been given an important position by the Cahlven, not that he seemed to be taking to leadership. If anything, he'd been much happier when no one knew what he was doing.

"I'll figure something out," she said, brushing aside Dhiren's words, and her own worries. There was no room for fear within the shield. "After all, we traitors have to stick together, right?"

Dhiren's laugh was bitter, and he turned back to the barrier, reaching out to slide his finger through the ripples.

"Right."

* * *

Keiran paced. Wet leaves clung to his boots, mulch gathering in the treads with every step. He glanced down at her but didn't stop moving, back and forth, back and forth. It hadn't been easy to get him out here, and the silence as they walked had been excruciating. Georgianna wasn't sure how to begin. She'd sat on a log and patted the space next to her, but he didn't sit. He just paced, and she had lost what she'd been planning to say.

She thought that maybe he would be more inclined to listen to her if she apologised. Helping Edtroka was more important than her pride. But the words still wouldn't come.

"Did you bring me here just to stare, George?"

She shook her head and stabbed the mud between her feet with a stick.

"I need your help," she said. "*We* need your help."

"We?"

"Dhiren and me."

Keiran nodded and clasped his hands behind his back. He stopped pacing and looked down at her, waiting. Georgianna was reminded of sitting in front of her father as he berated her over one wrongdoing or another. It was the way he looked at her, as if he knew exactly what she was about to say.

"You're going to leave."

It wasn't a question, and Keiran's expression was blank and emotionless. His gaze swept over her face, and she wished that he'd look at her the way he used to. She longed for those nights in his shack down in the tunnels where he would memorise her face, taking in each detail as if he'd never see it again, and he needed the moment to remember. Now there was nothing.

"We need to find Edtroka."

"You said we should let him go."

"I lied."

He smiled, without humour.

"Yes, I think quite a few people are beginning to realise you're better at that than they'd expected."

Heat burned in her cheeks. She looked away and scraped the muck from the bottom of her boot. It gave way easily, sloughing from the stick onto the ground. She sniffed and rubbed her thumb under her nose. Not all marks were as easy to remove as the dead leaves and dirt. Keiran knew that as well as she did. The Grutt mark on his shoulder that branded him as a traitor would never truly heal.

"I lied because I don't trust the Cahlven to help Edtroka."

"You'd be right," he said. "Olless has no intention of finding out where he has gone."

"We can find out. If you want no part in it after this, I'll understand. You have a position here and you can try to change things, but please do this for me, Keiran."

She met his gaze and he folded his arms, frowning. Taking a deep breath, he broke eye contact and stared over her head. He rolled his shoulders and stretched out his neck.

"What is it you're asking me to do?"

"Edtroka will have the tsentyl with him. He used it to contact the Cahlven on our way here. We need to track it in order to find him. The Cahlven must have that technology."

He swept his tongue across his bottom lip.

"And if I say no? How will you track him then?"

"We can't."

Keiran let out a low hum as he turned and resumed pacing, watching the ground passing beneath his feet. Georgianna waited, but the silence stretched on and he didn't seem keen on sharing his thoughts.

"You owe me this, Keiran. You owe *him*. I saved your life with his help."

Keiran stopped but didn't look at her. He stared at the trees in front of him and she could see as he drew his drawn cheek between his teeth. His nostrils flared and he flexed his fingers against his sleeves.

"Is that how it's going to be, then?" he asked, his voice as hollow as the look in his eyes. "Trading scores on what we owe each other?"

Georgianna flung the stick down into the leaves and forest debris.

"You tell me! Since you seem so keen on trading on what I do and who for. I talk to Alec and you think it's a slight against you. I help you and he sees it as a personal attack. So, why don't you tell me who is keeping score, Keiran?"

Keiran frowned at the tree. He shifted his weight and unfolded his arms, burying his hands in his pockets.

Georgianna got to her feet and moved in closer. Standing behind him, she touched his elbow, sliding her hand up his arm. His skin was warm and welcoming through his shirt, but he flinched at the touch. She pulled her fingers back.

"Will you help us? Will you add another mark to my score?"

The sun began to sink behind the horizon and he still didn't answer.

8 Olless' Order

Georgianna traipsed up the stairs, her footfalls heavy against the metal rungs. She'd never been this high into the ship before. Usually her trips were confined to the rooms on the lower levels where Olless held meetings. This time there had been no summons, no official gathering to sit through. This time, Olless would listen and Georgianna would talk.

Although the ship looked massive from the ground, it was nothing to the interior. Corridors stretched and snaked, interconnected and twisting. A great clear box rocketed up and down, through a zig-zagging staircase, carrying people and supplies through the centre. Curious gazes shot past as she continued up the stairs, only to pause at each floor to see if it was the one she wanted. With her high station, Olless had been granted a place above the barracks of the general Cahlven soldiers. Georgianna had already peered through three windows onto long rows of beds; some empty, some not. Her heart beat harder with every floor and her palms were slippery on the metal handrail. The next one. It would be the next one.

Keiran had told her how to find Olless, and she didn't want to think about the way her heart had burned at the knowledge that he knew where the emissary slept. She focussed on his instructions: up the stairs until she'd passed the barracks and then along the corridor to the right. The door would be marked, she would recognise it.

When she finally came upon a corridor without a row of beds on the other side of the door, Georgianna pushed through and hurried along, checking each door.

The shout was nothing she had ever heard before and Georgianna spun on her heel, jumping towards the wall. The man in the black suit marched over, speaking in a tongue she didn't understand.

"I'm sorry?"

Heavy lines came between the soldier's brows and his lips puffed out as he glared at her.

"What you doing here?"

Georgianna glanced down the corridor and grasped her hands behind her back the way she'd seen Olless do when in front of the projection of the Colvohan.

"I'm looking for Olless," she said.

"You not here."

Georgianna blinked.

"I am here."

"You not be here!"

"Do you mean I'm not meant to be here?"

He nodded vigorously.

"Olless?" she asked hopefully.

The soldier considered her for a few moments. His lower lip was thicker than could be considered natural as he pushed it far out and looked both ways down the corridor. Finally, he huffed.

"Next!" he said, pointing along the corridor. "Then, you not here."

"Absolutely! I promise."

Georgianna beamed at him and crossed a finger over her heart. He stared at her chest and mimicked the motion back to her like a salute.

With no time to explain the meaning behind the gesture, Georgianna hurried away down the corridor. When she looked back, the soldier was gone.

The door was marked with a small copper plaque. Olless' name and title had been engraved in the centre in both Veuric and the Cahlven tongue. The metal gleamed in the artificial light and Georgianna guessed that it hadn't been there long. She wondered whether Olless had commissioned it especially for the trip. It didn't make a lot of sense that the label was written in Veuric as well, but it didn't matter now.

Her knock echoed in the long corridor, rebounding back from all sides. She stepped close, craning to hear something on the other side of the door. Nothing. Not even muffled movements. Apart from the sound of her own fading knocks, all was silent.

Georgianna jumped a foot into the air when the door slid unexpectedly open with a soft whoosh. Straightening herself up, she attempted to smile. It fell flat and she settled for tucking her hair behind her ear.

Olless wore a long dress in a thin material that flowed out from her hips and swayed silently, swirling like water. Her hair was free of its usual braid and cascaded to her waist. Georgianna stared. Olless was beautiful in a way she never looked in her uniform. Unrestrained and relaxed.

"Miss Lennox," Olless said, her lavender eyes surveying her as Georgianna continued to stare. "What can I do for you?"

Georgianna coughed and looked up.

"I want to talk to you about Edtroka."

"I was under the impression that particular conversation was finished."

Olless leaned against the doorframe, her bare shoulder malleable against the hard metal. Dark tendrils of ink spread across her pale skin like vines all the way down to the wrist. She smiled at Georgianna's wandering gaze.

"A different mark than the Adveni," she said, reaching up and tracing a long slim finger along one of the lines. "This one, for example, was not required as some rite of passage."

"Why did you do it?"

"Because I liked it."

Georgianna nodded absently and glanced both ways down the corridor. She took a step away from Olless, grasping her hands behind her back. She couldn't let the Cahlven emissary see that her fingers were shaking.

"You wanted to speak to me about Grystch?"

"You always call him that."

Olless gave her a smile that, for once, didn't look polite or forced. She blinked twice, those wide eyes ever brighter under the unnatural white lights.

"Would my calling him E'Troke—or Edtroka as you Veniche pronounce it—make it easier for you?"

"No. But Grystch—"

"Is his father's name, I know."

"He's not his father."

"No," Olless said. "But we all suffer the sins of our fathers. Having him remember that—"

"Is unfair! He's nothing like his father."

Georgianna strode a few steps down the corridor away from Olless. She ran her fingers through her hair, pulling it back from her face. Olless pushed herself from the doorway and followed.

"Have you ever met the Volsonnar, Miss Lennox?"

"No."

"Then, how are you so sure that Edtroka shares none of his traits with the man?"

Georgianna turned. Olless was so angular, as if her body had been made for a singular purpose, with nothing to spare. Even the flowing dress didn't hide that. If anything, it made her shape more impressive.

"The Volsonnar invaded Os-Veruh and ordered the enslavement of the Veniche. Edtroka fights against that very thing."

Olless smiled broadly.

"Both very bold actions, wouldn't you say? Perhaps even a little thoughtless?" she asked. "Both men acted without a full understanding of the ripples their actions would cause. The two are more similar than you may think. Their motives may be as different as the sky and ocean, but their actions are rock and stone."

Georgianna turned away from her again, letting out a heavy huff. She heard the footsteps behind, following her further down the hall. She turned back.

"Are you trying to find him?"

At the other end of the corridor, Keiran's footsteps were silent and Georgianna had to fight to keep her gaze on

Olless' face. She wondered if he was even wearing boots, for surely no one could tread so quietly. She didn't dare look and risk Olless following her gaze.

"I must admit, I am surprised you care so much," Olless said.

He crept forwards and Georgianna crossed her arms over her chest, glaring up at this woman who was nothing but professional as he slid along the wall like a shadow. He disappeared through the doorway Olless had left open behind her.

"Why shouldn't I?"

"You care deeply for the man who purchased you like a prize. While he may not have made you wear one of those horrendous collars, he put the mark of slave on you just the same."

"He did that to protect me. The Tsevstakre commander wanted to buy me. He—"

"Is that what he told you?"

Olless' smile was too broad, her tone too sweet. Her eyes crinkled in amusement. She raised her brow and her face looked stretched and tight. Too tight, in fact, like it had been made for another person.

"A week before your purchase, Edtroka contacted me for instructions on how to proceed. He seemed wary of two slaves who had escaped from the commander's service."

The cold metal around her began to leech warmth from Georgianna's skin, down through her toes and out through her fingers. Her stomach began filling with ice water, a drop for every word coming from Olless' thin lips.

"He was worried that Mr. Cartwright and Miss Wolfe may have taken information with them. Information that, if used, might make the commander more suspicious than he already was. Edtroka had been working against his race for some time and despite his father's position, he knew he was not untouchable."

The cold spread down her legs, solidifying into hard ice. Even without the odd artificial gravity, Georgianna wasn't sure she'd have been able to lift her feet to walk away now.

"He told me that there may be a way in, a method to contact these two..." Olless paused and gave her words—and the ice—time to settle before she continued. "You, Miss Lennox. He told me you might be able to make contact with them if you were freed from the compound."

"No..."

Keiran peeked around the doorframe. He held up the device as he slipped away along the corridor.

"Your brave, honourable Edtroka Grystch purchased you on my orders. No more."

"You're lying."

"You were a means to an end, Miss Lennox," Olless said, the false kindness slipping from her voice to reveal the venom underneath. "You were useful, I grant you. You saved Keiran for us and I have allowed you into the meetings to keep their attention."

Georgianna took a step away but Olless made no move to follow her this time.

"You are welcome in the camp and once we move on the Adveni, of course. We can always use more medics, even if they are of limited skill compared to our own. However, should you meddle in affairs above your station, I will have no trouble ensuring your presence is no longer necessary. Are we clear?"

Georgianna's throat tightened as she tried to force a gulp.

"Perfectly."

Olless' pure, polite smile was back in place.

"Then good evening, Miss Lennox. I will leave it to Beck or Keiran to keep you apprised of our progress."

Georgianna turned and ran along the corridor without returning the courtesy of a goodnight or goodbye. Her hands shook harder than ever and her breath came in shallow pants. She could only pray that Keiran would be able to get the information they needed from the device, because there was no way she was marching into war behind the Cahlven now. Dhiren was right; they'd learned how to stand still and take orders for far too long.

9 Beyond the Shield

The sun was barely above the horizon as they approached the Cahlven shield and the barrier to the camp. Ever since the Cahlven up in the ship had detected Nyrahby craft beyond the borders, trips outside the shield had been limited to those gathering food, and all Veniche had to be accompanied by Cahlven soldiers.

Dhiren had wanted to leave in the middle of the night, cloaking their departure in darkness. It had been Keiran who shut him down. If the Cahlven had a way of monitoring people going through the shield, he said, then passing through at night would only alert them all the quicker. At dawn, it could at least be conceivable that a party were going out to hunt. Dhiren wasn't happy with the delay, but at least he'd agreed.

The shield shimmered before them. Rays from the rising sun bent and spread across the forest floor, dappling the leaves into fractals of colour—from a burning red sunset to the deepest indigo. Georgianna hitched her bag higher onto her shoulder and patted the knife in her belt.

"Point of no return," Dhiren said.

Keiran reached out and touched the shield with the tip of his finger. The hairs on his arms stood up and he let the shudder run through his body, visible to all.

"Theft, disobeying orders, I think we're already past that."

Georgianna had to agree with Keiran. After stealing the device from Olless, packing up supplies and weapons, and disobeying the orders given to them by the Cahlven, she highly doubted that crossing through the barrier would make any difference.

She wondered if it would only be the Cahlven who were angry with them. Beck and the others might believe they were setting back the war by stopping Edtroka from handing himself over. They might think them traitors, running to save their own skin. Dhiren had never done anything questionable against the other Veniche in the camp, but his incarceration had been enough to sow the seeds of distrust amongst the others within the shield. He had told Georgianna the reason for his detention—murder, three Adveni, that they'd caught him for—but after hearing conversations between him and Edtroka, she wondered if there was something else to his past that they hadn't told her. Dhiren had been a little too angry at Edtroka's disappearance, but even she didn't trust his temper enough to ask him about it and hope for an honest answer.

"Come on, we're wasting time," Georgianna said.

She balled her hands into fists, squeezed her eyes closed, and stepped forwards. The electricity in the shield buzzed through her. It wasn't unlike the cinystalq, but where that had caused searing pain, this was like pushing through thick grass as it tangled around her limbs, holding her back. With another step, the sensation was gone, little more than the tingling of the current finding its escape.

Dhiren snorted loudly and she opened her eyes.

"What?"

He waved his hand in her direction.

"I'm sorry, but your hair is ridiculous."

Georgianna spun to look at him. Both Dhiren's and Keiran's hair stood on end, waving lazily in the breeze. She rolled her eyes and nodded to each of them.

"You look great, too. Both of you."

Reaching up, she realised that her own hair was just like theirs, only worse. Long strands floated aimlessly in the air and she had to rub her hands repeatedly over her head to make her hair behave. Dhiren licked his palm and slicked his back, which seemed to do the trick. Keiran merely grimaced and shook his head.

They trudged east through the remnants of forest. What hadn't been destroyed by the Nyrahby bombs was thick and hard to pass through, and wide sections had been reduced to little more than charred debris. Dhiren had told them of a ridge that ran south a few miles east of the shield. If they could get behind it, they would be able to travel a decent distance without being spotted by the Cahlven. How they would avoid the Agrah and the Nyrahby, on the other hand, they would just have to work out as they went along.

"This would have been a lot easier with Wrench here," Keiran grumbled.

Georgianna glanced over her shoulder. Keiran was

rolling a cigarette, barely watching where he was stepping. Dhiren forged on ahead of them.

"Why?" Georgianna asked.

"He could have helped with the technology. I don't know what you plan for me to do with this device. I can just about turn it on, but if it's in their language, we're screwed."

"The bigger the party, the bigger the chance we're spotted," Dhiren said, brushing a branch out of his way. "I don't particularly want to be followed and dragged back to the Cahlven's troops before we get half a mile."

"Yeah, well." Keiran brushed off the comment and licked the edge of his cigarette paper as Georgianna turned away.

She quickened her step, catching up to Dhiren, and considered overtaking him. He knew where they were going better than she did, but she figured if she just walked straight he'd tell her if they needed to change direction. She didn't want to think about the other reasons Keiran might want Wrench with them, like perhaps having someone to talk to so he could go back to ignoring her as often as possible. He was doing this for Edtroka, she knew, not because he wanted to do something for her. Personally, she wondered if it wouldn't have been better if he'd stayed behind. With Edtroka and Keiran now missing from the Cahlven camp, the responsibilities of the Veniche would fall entirely on Beck. He'd do his best and he was a good leader but she wasn't sure how well he'd be able to withstand the demands of Olless and the Colvohan with no one there to back him up.

Georgianna bristled at the thought of Olless and her revelations, but she couldn't disregard the words that now spun around her mind. Even if Edtroka had bought her on Olless' orders, he'd still done it, he'd protected her. So why did the idea of Olless ordering him to buy her sit so uneasily in her stomach?

The click of Keiran's lighter snapped her alert. She could smell the smoke as he blew it into the air.

"Alright, what's up with you?" he demanded.

"Who?" Dhiren asked.

"George. She's been... off."

"How would you know if I've been on or off anything?"

She pulled her bag tight against her back, grasping the straps to keep herself from fidgeting. She glared ahead, focussing on the sound of the leaves beneath her boots. With the echoes from the tree trunks, it sounded as though there were more of them walking. She checked behind but saw nothing.

"And there it is." Keiran chuckled. "The off-ness! You were all hopeful words and pleading for me to help yesterday and now you've barely said a word since I got the damn machine you wanted."

Georgianna shook her head and rolled her eyes. Dhiren appeared at her side and leaned forwards to get a good look at her face.

"Yeah, I see it. She's pissed."

"I'm not. Leave me alone."

"Oh, okay. I'll upgrade that to *really* pissed," Dhiren said with a grin. He walked backwards a few steps, looking at Keiran. "You do something, Zanetti?"

"Apart from help her? No. You?"

"I'm sure I've always done something. But in this case, I don't think it was me. So, who else do we have?"

"Well, there's Cartwright..."

Keiran appeared on her other side. Both of them

grinned at Georgianna and each other, waiting for her to crack. She scowled and concentrated on her feet. Let them be amused by their new game. Let her be the source of their entertainment. It seemed it was a running theme in her life, people using her for their own gains.

"Maybe she's pissed E'Troke left without saying goodbye," Dhiren said. "Poor abandoned little drysta."

"Leave it alone!" Georgianna snapped.

"And we have a winner!" Dhiren cheered, clapping his hand against this thigh. "So, E'Troke pissed you off. Was it because he left?"

"No," she said. "I mean, yes!"

Keiran raised an eyebrow, leaning towards Dhiren with a knowing smile.

"Lying."

Dhiren nodded his agreement.

"Did he leave you locked in a compound for two years?" he asked, smiling blandly at their stares. "No? Just me? Okay... Did he kill someone?"

"He lied to me, alright?"

Dhiren snorted.

"Join the queue, lovely."

"What did he lie about?" Keiran asked.

Georgianna scuffed her boot against the leaves and growled under her breath. She didn't want to talk about it but they had a long way to go with little else to discuss. Keiran certainly wouldn't want to talk about their relationship with Dhiren listening in, and truth be told she wasn't sure she wanted to discuss it, either. No doubt, if she didn't tell them, they'd just find other ways to torment her until she did.

"When I was talking to Olless last night she told me that

Edtroka bought me because she ordered him to. He wanted me to contact Alec and Nyah."

Keiran frowned and blew out a cloud of smoke.

"And my deal with him had nothing to do with it? I agreed to make his trip in return for getting you out, or have you forgotten that?"

Georgianna glared back at him. A crunch echoed between the trees and she glanced at their feet, brushing leaves aside in the hope of seeing twigs hidden beneath the leaves. Dhiren paused when he realised she'd stopped.

"Are you sure that's all it was?" she asked Keiran as she turned in a circle. "That he didn't have some other agenda?"

Keiran frowned at her. He shrugged.

"Of course he isn't sure."

The cigarette fell from Keiran's fingers. The three of them spun around. The cigarette hit the ground and Dhiren and Keiran had both drawn weapons before the last word was out of Alec's lips. He stepped out from behind a tree trunk a short way back, a smug grin on his lips. Holding up his hands to show them empty, he walked towards them.

"He didn't care as long as he got what he wanted. Never really cared about consequences, did you?"

While Dhiren snarled and replaced the knife at his hip, Keiran launched himself across the gap. He grabbed the front of Alec's shirt and slammed him back against the nearest tree.

"What are you doing here?"

Georgianna hovered between Keiran's fury and Alec's amusement. Dhiren approached and grasped Keiran by the shoulder. Shrugged off, Dhiren waved Georgianna forwards as Alec was slammed into the tree again.

"What are you doing here?" Keiran demanded again.

They pried Keiran from Alec, hauling him back. Alec brushed himself off and checked the back of his head for blood.

"I saw you packing bags and knew you were about to do something stupid, so I followed you."

"We're not going back," Georgianna said.

She adjusted her stance and folded her arms. Alec grinned at her and rolled his eyes.

"Run back and report to Beck, Cartwright. Send people after us, see if we care."

"You're going to find the Adveni, right?"

"What do you care?"

Alec grinned and stepped forwards.

"Because if you're going to Adlai," he said, plucking Keiran's battered cigarette from the leaves and holding it out to him, "then I'm coming with you."

10 Divisions

Georgianna hopped on the spot. She flailed her arm to keep balance and smacked the heel of her boot against the trunk of the nearest tree. Dhiren watched with amusement but didn't come closer or offer to help. Rocking uneasily on one foot, Georgianna upended her boot and three small stones tumbled out onto the mossy ground.

The pebbles had been bothering her for hours. As she trudged through the forest, each step shifted them under the arches of her feet and between her toes. She'd complained about the irritation twice but tried to ignore it, assuming they would find Edtroka quickly once they reached Lurinah Forest. After all, they had a map on the device Keiran had stolen for them.

Hours later and they were no closer to finding Edtroka than when they had first stepped between the tall trees. She'd finally given up, telling the others to stop. As she unlaced her boots, Keiran had taken the opportunity to prod at the Cahlven device again.

"Look closer on the map," Alec said. "Most of them can do that, you know. Make the map look bigger."

Keiran glanced at Alec with a raised eyebrow and shook his head, going back to the device. He slumped down on a large tree root and chewed his lip, staring at the screen. Alec approached and stood at Keiran's shoulder, leaning over him.

Georgianna tugged her boot back on, balancing against the tree trunk. The rains had drenched the ground even beneath the cover of the leaves. After so long walking with stones under her feet she didn't want to spend the rest of the afternoon with one wet sock.

"All the tsentyls have it," Alec said. "You just need to change the measurements."

Jumping to his feet, Keiran faced Alec and shoved the device at his chest.

"Here. You're such an expert? You work it!"

Alec took the device in his hand and looked down at it. Scowling, he turned it around and glanced over at Dhiren and Georgianna.

"I can't read the Cahlven stuff."

Keiran smiled, and he snatched back the device.

"Oh, can't you? Join the club."

"So, we're working from a map none of us can change," Alec said, "and we're searching an entire forest for one man? Fantastic!"

Lacing up her boot, Georgianna kept her head down and tried not to listen to the bickering. It had been four days of the same thing. Since they'd left the Cahlven, everything Keiran had done was wrong in Alec's eyes, and everything Alec said was to wind Keiran up. When they really went for each other—which happened at least once a day—it was Dhiren who had to pull them apart. She'd tried getting between them once when Dhiren was busy hunting and wasn't keen to try again. Her shoulder was still sore from being shoved so roughly aside that she'd toppled over. Alec and Keiran had both apologised, blaming the other, and she had decided that next time she would just let them fight it out.

Dhiren rubbed his hand over his face, glaring at the two and the growing argument. Georgianna thought that he would be used to people's bickering, having spent so long inside the compound. But the longer the snapping continued, the less patience Dhiren had for them.

Tucking his hands into his pockets, he shuffled his feet.

"You do both realise that the person we're looking for is a skilled hunter," he said. "If we had any chance of finding him, your incessant fighting would let him know we're coming and give him a chance to run."

He rolled his eyes and, after checking that Georgianna was ready to move again, set off through the trees. She noted with a smug smile that Keiran and Alec both looked embarrassed at Dhiren's words. Grinning at them, she followed Dhiren at a jog, catching up with his long strides.

"Dhiren, how did you meet Edtroka?" she asked.

The look he gave her was sceptical. He pulled his hands from his pockets and flexed them into fists.

"It's just that you two obviously know each other well. You said he was making a back-up plan for your benefit. You were close, right?"

"We met during the Wash, before I was caught and sent to the compound," he said, scuffing his boot against a clump of moss. "He told me he was against the Adveni. He knew no one would believe me if I told them. I started helping him after that."

"So you were in contact with the Cahlven?"

Dhiren shook his head and glanced at her.

"This was before. E'Troke needed a second person to contact them, protocol or something, and that was going to be me. I was arrested before we could do it. He started working with Keiran not long after."

The other two had caught up to them. They trudged along behind, Keiran following with his gaze still set on the device in his hands. He frowned and cursed under his breath, tapping at different parts of the screen.

"He didn't get you out?" Georgianna asked.

"Couldn't," he said, though there was bitterness in his voice. Dhiren had made comments about Edtroka's leaving him in the compound, but she'd not understood it before. She couldn't work out why Edtroka would have had anything to do with Dhiren's capture if they were friends.

"He couldn't have bought you or something?"

"He convinced someone that I could be kept in the compound, made me sound like a good catch for Ta-Dao and Vajra. They put a bid in with the guards pretty quickly, otherwise I would have been executed with the crimes they had me on. They wouldn't have let me be sold, he knew that."

"So he left you there?"

Dhiren raised an eyebrow.

"Hey, no one questions that more than I do, Med," he said. "Given him a lot of grief about it too, but he's a good man."

Behind them, Alec snorted and swiped at a branch above his head.

"Yeah? If he's so good—on our side and all that—why don't you just shout that it's you?" he suggested. "Face it, that's why you're scared he'll hear us coming. You're scared he doesn't want us to find him. You're scared he didn't run off for some noble cause."

Dhiren's bag hit the ground with a wet slap. He spun and jumped over it, mud flying up from his boots. He grabbed Alec by the throat before any of them had realised what was happening. A single swift kick around Alec's ankle was all it took for him to go down. Dhiren landed on top of him, still holding him tight at the neck. Driving his knee into Alec's stomach, he hovered over him, growling.

"I'm sick of your shit, Cartwright!"

Georgianna stepped forwards as Alec spluttered, but the larger man only tightened his grip on Alec's throat, holding him still.

"If you're so against E'Troke, why don't you just run off back to the Cahlven?" He gave a snarling laugh. "Or better yet, your owner? Tell him what awful, traitorous Ven we are."

Alec opened and closed his mouth. His legs jerked and he twisted in the mud. Gurgles squeezed past Dhiren's grip but nothing more.

Dhiren looked ready to spit blood.

"E'Troke didn't come back to Adlai because he's stupid. He didn't leave because he was running and he thought the south would make a nice camping spot." Alec grappled at Dhiren's wrist, his nails leaving gouges in the flesh. "He came to turn himself in, you idiot. That's why he'll run. Not because he's a bad guy but because he doesn't want us stopping him."

Alec's cheeks were pale, his lips purple. Georgianna groaned and grasped Dhiren by the shoulder. Without a second thought, he flung her backwards with his free hand. She saw a brief glimpse of his face, how flushed he was. His teeth were bared. He had that feral look about him again. She staggered backwards, scared to return to him.

"Let him go," she begged. "Please, Dhiren, he can't breathe!"

Even Keiran looked uncomfortable with the turn in Dhiren's mood. His hand hovered by the gun at his hip.

"I'll let you go if you promise not to open your mouth on the subject again," Dhiren said.

Alec nodded frantically. Slapping his hand against Dhiren's shoulder, he seized and jerked.

"One word from you and I'll snap your neck before anyone thinks about putting a collar around it again."

The gasp that rattled through Alec's throat as Dhiren released him was sweet and painful to hear. Dhiren rose to his feet and gave a flick of his hand. Blood from Alec's nail gouges splattered over the younger man's face. Alec's eyes were wet with tears but he didn't bother to wipe his face as he scrambled to his feet, staggering as far from Dhiren as he could.

The chuckle made all of them jump. Spinning around, they stared into the trees. They heard it again; closer but not where the first sound had come from. The laugh rumbled through the spaces, making Georgianna shiver. A crunch and a squelch under boots, a rustle of leaves. The noises circled them. Gulping, her hand went to the handle of the knife in her belt. How many people were around them?

Were they Veniche or Adveni? She drew the knife from her belt.

Keiran had pulled the gun from his hip. Dhiren balled his hands into fists.

"It's been a long time since anyone threatened to kill to defend my honour," Edtroka said as he finally stepped out of the bushes. Keiran groaned and replaced the gun in his holster as Edtroka straightened up, brushing leaves from his shoulders.

"It's been a long time since you had any honour to defend," Dhiren replied.

The flush of anger in Dhiren's cheeks receded to something warmer. He crossed the gap in two strides and the embrace between them was tight and desperate. Edtroka's hand reached to the back of Dhiren's head; his fingers threaded into his short hair. Georgianna turned away from them, staring at the ground with wide eyes.

'Close' was not the right word for their relationship.

Alec rubbed his neck and glared at them. True to his promise, he didn't say a word. Keiran put the device into a pocket on his bag and leaned against a tree.

"Could have made it a bit easier on us," he said. "How long have you known we were here?"

Edtroka pulled back from Dhiren. He shrugged.

"Few hours."

Dhiren growled under his breath.

"Thanks."

Edtroka's smile was short lived.

"Well, you've found me," he said. "And now it's time for you to leave."

11 THE COUNTDOWN

Edtroka led them through the forest to the place where he'd camped. He said he'd arrived the day before and had been gathering his courage to send a message to the Volsonnar when he heard people coming. Not wanting to be discovered before getting in contact with his father, he'd tracked the noises until he came upon Georgianna's group. Apparently, it had been funnier to watch them traipse around the forest than to reveal himself.

They came to a small clearing in the middle of a patch of large-trunked trees. Edtroka jumped to reach the lowest branch, where he'd hidden his things. The sack he'd brought with him was small compared to their own. Georgianna stared at the ground, shuffling her feet.

She knew what he planned on doing.

The moment they'd seen the dot on the map blinking, they'd all known Edtroka's plan. Even Alec, with his snide comments, couldn't have denied what it looked like. But as

Edtroka was only a dot on the screen of the Cahlven device, the idea of his turning himself in remained abstract and far away. Standing there, seeing his lack of supplies and knowing he hadn't intended on needing them—it was too real to think about. As the others spoke, she busied herself with taking off her own bag and searching through it for food.

"You're being stupid," Edtroka said, settling against a tree. "The Cahlven can protect all of you. You shouldn't have come."

Dhiren harrumphed and sat as far from Edtroka as he could in the small space between the trees. His joy at seeing the Adveni had faded with Edtroka's explanations and before long he was sullen and quiet.

Alec and Keiran also chose to sit on opposite sides of the clearing, shaping them all in a circle. Unsurprisingly, Alec sat as far from Dhiren as he could. That did, however, put him next to Edtroka, which surprised everyone as he sat down without comment. He threw a cautious look at Dhiren and quickly began searching through his bag for supplies, following Georgianna's example.

"You shouldn't have left," Dhiren said.

"Why? The Cahlven have taken control of this whole thing, you've seen it. My involvement was to bring them here. Now that's done, their use for me is gone. I can't help them by staying any more than any of you can. But if my handing myself over buys you time for a peaceful negotiation, why shouldn't I?"

Georgianna pushed her bag away. She leaned over her knees and glared at him.

"You're talking about it as if you're going to be slapped on the wrist and sent back to work. You'll be killed! That is, if they don't decide to torture you for information first."

"George…"

"No! Don't say it like I don't know what I'm talking about. Have you ever worn a cinystalq, Edtroka? Have you?"

He frowned and leaned back against the tree.

"No, I haven't."

"You were the one who said that Maarqyn would never just accept that I'd told him everything. Do you think your father will be any better? They'll keep digging until you'll tell them anything just to make it stop. You said it. You'll die revealing your deepest secrets."

Edtroka's gaze flickered from Georgianna to Dhiren and back again. He lowered his eyes and stared at his boots, rubbing his hands up and down his legs.

"And if I accept that?" he asked. "I can buy you time, George. Time you desperately need."

"We don't, not at this cost."

Keiran dug the point of his knife into the ground and began scratching at the wet soil.

"Don't you think your knowledge is useful?" he asked.

Edtroka looked at him warily but Keiran didn't lift his head. He was carving out channels in the dirt with his blade. When Edtroka opened his mouth to argue, Keiran continued.

"You know more about Adveni systems and methods than the rest of us put together. Who gives a sun's turn about Veniche travelling habits, or which tunnel gets you to the Oprust district the fastest? Without you, we're walking blind." He looked up, fixing Edtroka with a stare. "Even the Cahlven are in the dark here."

Edtroka wrapped his arms around his legs and clasped his hands, wringing his fingers.

"I don't know where the Mykahnol is, Keiran," he said. "I can't help them any more than you can."

"But you can tell them the standard responses to attacks. You can outline formations and technology." Keiran glanced at Alec and licked his lips. "You managed to get me out of that ambush by knowing their tactics and movements."

"What good is that if we can't stop them from blowing the city sky high?"

"They hate Maarqyn," Alec croaked. His voice was raw and he winced and coughed at the words. Rubbing the side of his neck tenderly, he avoided their eyes and leaned against a tree, watching the leaves. "People are scared of him but they hate him. I was with that man for two years and I saw enough of you."

Edtroka's eyes widened. Georgianna, on the other hand, was transfixed by Alec's quiet words.

"You were their friend, their equal. You weren't someone ordering them about and humiliating them when they failed. Maarqyn has few friends in the city. The only people who like him are Volsonnae, and even they are scared he'll destroy them if they don't lick his boots."

"That doesn't matter," Edtroka said. "It just means they'll do whatever he asks because they're scared of what happens if they don't."

"But they'll do what you ask because you ask it," Dhiren cut in.

Their gazes met across the space between them. Neither looked away. Dhiren's face was a model of determination, though Georgianna wasn't sure whether his intention was to win the war, or simply to convince Edtroka against going through with his plan.

"They won't."

"I saw their reactions to you. From within the compound and before. They respect you. Some of them were scared you would call in daddy, but they respected you because you did a good job."

"What's your point?"

"Do you think your father would have made your betrayal common knowledge, knowing how it would damage his reputation?" Dhiren asked, mirroring Edtroka as he drew his knees up and bound his arms around his legs.

"Perhaps, I don't know."

"Then we still have a chance to get to some of the people you knew. Maybe you can get information out of them."

Edtroka got to his feet, rubbing his hands vigorously around his face. When he realised there wasn't enough space for him to pace, he stood still, staring down in frustration.

"So instead of walking into Adlai to give myself up and buy you all time, you want me to walk into Adlai and ask for information that may not even help?" he sneered. "Like that won't get me caught, anyway? If I do that then I've not even bought you negotiation time."

"We don't want negotiations," Georgianna said. "Beck doesn't, either. The Adveni have done too much to be allowed to stay here. Olless keeps talking about it like it's just a conversation and it doesn't mean anything. She hasn't been here. She hasn't seen the extent of what they've done to us."

"We want them dead or gone," Alec agreed hoarsely. "Not sitting around a table. These negotiations are only a good idea if we can use them to keep their leaders busy while we destroy them."

Edtroka snorted and rolled his eyes.

"You're all talking like we can do this alone. We can't."

"How do you know that?" Georgianna asked. "How do you—"

A high beeping sound cut through her words. Georgianna looked around, heart thumping hard against her ribs. She knew that noise. Keiran pulled his knife from the ground and Dhiren jumped to his feet. He turned in a circle, threatening the trees before his gaze settled on Edtroka's bag. A blue light blinked through the canvas.

"It's my tsentyl," Edtroka said, extracting the small black cube. "I had it set to minimum communication but I'd turned it on fully just before I heard you all."

"If you had it off, how were we able to track it?" Alec asked.

"We had the signal from when he contacted the Cahlven," Keiran said, patting his pocket and thrusting his knife into the dirt. Dhiren sank back to a crouch. Edtroka grinned at Keiran.

"I was wondering how you'd found me," he said. "It makes sense. Tsentyls give off an individual signal so you can find a specific one if needed. This one isn't registered to me so they wouldn't have known to look for it. It would have been just another dot on a map, indistinguishable from the tsentyls of those in the Nyrahby who were busy bombing us."

"Why did you turn it on?" Georgianna asked.

"I was getting ready to contact my father."

He swiped the tsentyl from its cube form, letting it slot into a flat square screen in his palm. He clicked through it; the light from the screen bathed the small clearing in an eerie blue glow. Georgianna watched as he frowned and blinked. His lips parted and he let out a heavy breath that cut through the silence. Even the wind had stopped to hear the news.

"Well?" Keiran asked. "What is it?"

Edtroka was silent as he locked down the tsentyl and closed it into a cube again. He bent down and placed it into his bag, taking his seat against the tree trunk.

"E'Troke?" Dhiren pressed.

"It was a final warning for all Adveni stationed in Nyvalau to evacuate," he said. "The Mykahnol has gone into final countdown."

He lowered his gaze to his knees. A fist of fear grabbed hold of Georgianna's chest, squeezing so tight she could hardly breathe.

Edtroka buried his head in his hands.

"We're out of time."

12 FIVE-MAN FIGHT

The darkness had swallowed them inch by inch. Dry grass licked at their legs and the breeze tasted their hair, wafting the scent into the wind. They walked between two rows of stone teeth, disappearing from sight.

You make sure that man of yours looks after you, my girl.

He had brushed under her eyes as tears gathered along her lashes. Even though he hadn't wanted to leave without her, he had been stronger than she was. He had accepted her advice and given in to her pleas that they would be safer. He had hugged her so tightly—the way he always did—that she couldn't breathe against his barrelled chest.

Georgianna couldn't breathe.

"But what was the benefit?" Alec asked, stabbing a bent spoon at one of the stale packets of food. "The Cahlven are north. They haven't even shown an interest in Nyvalau."

They'd mostly waited out the countdown in silence. Edtroka claimed that it would be an hour before the southern Veniche city was destroyed. Dhiren joked that it would become an even bigger crater than it already was but when nobody laughed he gave in to the quiet. Keiran passed Georgianna a packet of food, but she didn't taste anything other than sand in her mouth.

There were maybe only minutes left. She'd tried counting but her thoughts kept going back to her nephew Braedon asleep on the back of the cart as they'd left her. He'd been so excited to travel for the first time. His grand-father had told him about travelling for most of his life. Braedon's giddy joy had made him so useless in packing that they'd sent him off to play.

"It was a show of power," Edtroka said, his voice tired and dull. "The Cahlven destroyed the Adveni bases. They were probably proving that both sides could play that game."

"But there was nothing of value. The Cahlven were destroying reserves, troops and weapons. What were the Adveni destroying?" Alec asked.

"Veniche." Dhiren stabbed at the ground with his knife. "The Cahlven have claimed to be siding with us against the Adveni, so the Adveni took their numbers away from them."

Georgianna set the food packet aside, propping it care-fully against her bag so that it wouldn't spill.

"You think?"

"Or they were taking away a place to run to. They know Adlai will be the main target, so get rid of the back-ups."

She'd told them to run. She'd begged them to. Every-thing had been getting so complicated that she couldn't worry about them as well. They'd wanted her to leave with them—they'd had the papers for it—but she'd said no. They would be safer outside of Adlai. Safer without her.

They would be safer. She'd promised that they would be safe, that she would be safe.

Georgianna got to her feet and turned away from them. The trees were thick in this part of the forest; large rough trunks she couldn't wrap her arms all the way around. The branches, heavy with leaves, blocked most of the light from the moon and stars. Knots of bushes scratched at her boots. The tangles tore at her legs and hips. She didn't push them away. She let them tear at her. Trudging through the undergrowth, she didn't watch where she was going, she just walked.

We're out of time.

They were out of time. Their time was gone. They were gone.

He touched her elbow first, bringing her to a stop. He circled her in the cramped space between the trunks, his fingers drifting up her arm to her shoulder. Breath wavered in and out of her mouth, unable to pass through the tightness in her throat. His blue-grey eyes looked like the closest stars, sad that the dawn was almost upon them. He didn't brush the tears away from under her eyes. He let them creep down her cheeks and splash from her jaw. Without a word, Keiran wrapped her in his arms, pulling her tight against his chest. Georgianna dissolved against him, along with the barrier of anger and pride that had been between them for weeks.

Breath became harder and harder to come by, each gasp like swallowing fire. Her lungs and throat and body burned and the tears came thicker, faster, hotter. Still he clung to her and let her cling to him.

Gasps became sobs that echoed in the dark.

He drew her down onto the ground, leaning against a tree trunk and cradling her against his chest. She gripped his shirt so tightly that her knuckles whitened and her fingers ached. It was a good pain; the pain of hanging on.

"You don't know," he whispered into her hair once the sobs had given in to the silent flood. "They might not have made it that far."

Georgianna squeezed her eyes shut and kept hanging on.

* * *

Cradled against Keiran's chest, Georgianna stared at the patch where her tears had soaked through his shirt. Black gave way to moss green in a fuzzy ring. The material clung to her cheek, sticky and hot, but she stared at the blurred line and didn't move, blinking against the soreness of her eyes.

At some point she had fallen asleep. The darkness had given way to the warm and unthinking black. He had held her, still held her, his fingers buried in her hair and his body as comforting as the quiet behind her eyes. She didn't know whether he'd also slept, but if he hadn't then he hadn't complained about it.

The morning sun fought to pass the canopy of leaves above them, light winking through the gaps, disappearing with the slightest wind. Georgianna heard the soft trudge of footsteps through the moss, approaching with caution. She watched Alec's approach out of the corner of her eyes. He stuffed his hands down into his pockets, shoulders hunched and head drooped, looking just like the boy who had once been told off alongside her brother, Halden. The scars of adulthood had taken their toll on the innocent face she had once known. The mark of the Adveni was as visible on Alec as it was invisible on her.

"You're awake," he murmured.

Keiran jerked beneath her and tilted his head to get a better look at her face. He gave her a tentative smile that she didn't return.

"Hey," he whispered. His fingers flexed in her hair, brushing the back of her neck.

Alec shuffled where he stood and scuffed his boots against the moss. He looked anywhere but at her. He swallowed and stared up at the canopy of leaves.

"We need to make a decision," he said. "On what we're going to do. Edtroka says he had the tsentyl on too long. If the Adveni haven't realised already, they may do soon. We should leave."

"Okay," Keiran said. His chin brushed the top of her head as he nodded.

Georgianna peeled herself away from him. His shirt clung to her cheek as far as it would reach before falling back against him. He tried for another smile as he stood and took her hands, helping her up. Her body protested every movement.

"Can I have a minute?" she asked.

"Course."

Stepping close, Keiran brushed his thumbs under her eyes and kissed each cheekbone before he strode back through the trees.

She rubbed her hands over her face, erasing the tears and the kisses. She pulled her fingers through her hair and hugged her body, trying to conjur that feeling of hanging on. There was nothing to cling to but her own flesh.

Tears began gathering again. She sniffed and tipped her head back, willing them to slide away behind her eyes so that she could hold on to them. She deserved them.

"Gianna?"

She gasped and lost the tears. Now there was just the sound of her name; the name only those who had known her as a child had used. It was a name that reminded her of her mother braiding her hair and of her father carving and telling her stories. She turned around. Alec was still standing there, still boy-like, his hair mussed and his gaze reproachful.

"Are you…" He cracked under her gaze and stared at the floor. "Are you okay?"

Georgianna took a deep breath that seared her throat. She straightened herself up. She would not look away, not now. Beneath the tears, beneath the fear and the pain, there was an anger that flared at his standing there looking so lost and forlorn. He had told her to send them away. He had tried to send her with them, getting the papers and convincing her it was best.

"No," she said.

She walked past him without another word, picking her way through the trees and bushes, back to the clearing, leaving him alone with her anger.

Dhiren and Edtroka sat hip to hip with a small fire before them. The smell of cooked meat hung in the air as smoke coiled and bloomed above the flames. They both looked up but, upon seeing her, remained silent until she'd taken a seat. She picked up the packet of food she had left the night before and prodded it with the spoon. Dhiren reached around the fire and passed her some chunks of rabbit that had been left to cool in one of the empty pouches.

She gave him her best attempt at a smile and moved her spoon to this new meal.

Alec returned a few minutes later and sat as far away from everyone as he could manage within the small space. In the flickering light, Georgianna could see thick lines of purple bruising around his neck. A flicker of guilt shot through her but as he glanced over and quickly averted his gaze to the fire, his lips pursed, and the guilt was licked away by new flames.

Dhiren drummed his fingers against his leg and frowned, before putting on a bright smile.

"Okay, so we have to leave here. We have two choices. We go back to Olless and receive a whipping for disobeying orders, or we go into Adlai and fight this thing."

"There are five of us," Keiran replied. "How are we supposed to fight?"

"We had small numbers to keep ourselves being spotted by the Cahlven. The same could work getting into Adlai."

"And once we're there?"

"We find some of Edtroka's friends, see if we can convince them to help us," Alec said.

Georgianna should have been surprised that Alec was open for help from Adveni, but she was focussing on chewing the meat. She thought through each bite, each movement of her jaw, anything to keep her thoughts from returning to her family. The meat was greasy and overcooked. It also tasted like sand.

"And if none of them decide to help, we have nothing and a city full of Adveni knowing we're there," Edtroka said.

"Why would they help us?" Keiran asked.

"You're an idiot," Dhiren said. "We're not going to walk

up and say, *'Hey, we want to destroy your entire race. Could you help?'* You were playing both sides for two years and you didn't learn how to convince people of something they didn't want to do?"

Edtroka shoved his elbow into Dhiren's ribs but it only made the hunter grin all the broader.

"We lie," Alec said. "Edtroka tells them he knows the Cahlven have information on the Mykahnol. He's worried they'll try to destroy it, so he needs the information to change the protocol to something the Cahlven won't be able to work."

Dhiren chortled and leaned over to slap Alec on the shoulder. Alec flinched away from him.

"See! Cartwright's got it. Milk the vtensu!"

"How did you learn to be so devious?" Edtroka asked.

Alec glanced at them and his worry melted into a smirk.

"I lived with Maarqyn."

All four of them laughed. When Keiran glanced at Georgianna, he stopped and placed his hand on her thigh. She scooped up another piece of rabbit, stared at it for a moment, and dumped it back into the packet.

"We're going to Adlai," she said. "We're bringing the vtensu down."

13 Tears in Rain

"She was registered, even before becoming your favourite little house pet," Dhiren muttered, not nearly quiet enough that they didn't hear him. Georgianna guessed he wanted them to hear so that they could talk her out of her plan to go to her family home.

"That's got nothing to do with it," Keiran said.

"It's got everything to do with it. They're after Edtroka, or had you forgotten?"

Keiran glanced over his shoulder and rolled his eyes.

"Going to the Med's house is almost as bad as us hiding out in his apartment." Dhiren jabbed his thumb in Edtroka's direction. "Do you think they won't look because it's too obvious? Like we wouldn't be stupid enough to try that? That's because they'd be right. It *is* stupid!"

Keiran stopped in his tracks long enough for Dhiren to catch up to him. He yanked him to one side and, though Georgianna was sure that Dhiren could have Keiran flat on his back within a matter of seconds, Dhiren allowed himself to be tugged away.

"She's lost her family, alright, give her a break," Keiran said. Like Dhiren, he tried to keep his voice low, but with no distraction bar the sound of their footsteps, he would have had to whisper in Dhiren's ear to stop the others from hearing completely.

"The camps will be the most inconspicuous," Alec said loudly. "They'll give us the most covered path into the city and we'll have time to plan so we know we have a place to regroup if needed."

Keiran released Dhiren and hung back to join Georgianna as she trudged behind them. He reached out to slide his hand into hers but she pulled back, giving him an apologetic smile. He nodded.

Out in front, Edtroka was stubbornly ignoring the lot of them. He stormed ahead, as if eager to get the whole thing done as fast as possible. By the end of the argument in the forest he had been the only one who favoured returning to the Cahlven. Or, at least, who favoured the others' return to the Cahlven. He had still planned on handing himself in to prevent further bloodshed. It didn't matter that the clock had run out on the offer the Volsonnar had made; he was sure that his appearance would convince his father to reconsider.

Georgianna watched him, wondering what he was now scheming. If Edtroka intended on throwing his life away, she feared there was nothing they could do to stop him. He might suddenly disappear or walk them headlong into an Adveni patrol to ensure his capture. No. While she wasn't sure that Edtroka was willing to save himself, she trusted that he would do everything in his power to keep them safe.

He already had. He was travelling with an escaped convict, a known Belsa, and a commander's drysta. All three would face death if they were caught and Georgianna didn't know what the Adveni would do with her. They knew about Edtroka's involvement in the destruction of Lyndbury Compound and so surely they knew about her, too. She would probably be killed with the rest of them. Edtroka wouldn't risk their lives even if he was willing to give up his own.

The rain came down in earnest as they neared the city, plastering their clothes to their skin and their hair to their faces. Dhiren shook his head every minute like a wet dog, sending water flying in every direction. They'd taken a wide route around the north of the city to reach the camps in the west, and through the sheets of grey the houses on the outer ridges came into view, dark under the slate sky.

"Now or never," Alec said.

Dhiren didn't look happy but he nodded just the same. Edtroka extended his already long strides, almost disappearing through the dark cloud of rain. This time Georgianna let Keiran take her hand as they set off at a run after him, bags bouncing on their backs.

Water poured from the rooftops, splattering mud. The houses spotted along the ridge became more frequent until two waterfalls of overflow splashed down on the alleyways. Edtroka ducked into a gap and let them pass. Georgianna took the lead with Keiran and Alec behind her. Edtroka and Dhiren—who were less familiar with the camps—brought up the rear, Edtroka hunching himself over to disguise his height, a trait of the Adveni.

Weaving around the backs of the houses, Georgianna ran the familiar path until she spotted the one she wanted.

Releasing Keiran's hand, she vaulted over the fence into the small patch of garden. Skidding on the wet grass, she caught herself just before she tumbled face first into the mud. It caked the bottom of her boots and the hems of her trousers, making her feel like she were wearing the large sled shoes they used for trekking across snow. Her clothes were soaked and hung heavy, splattered with dirt.

The back door of the house stood open; a large pool of rainwater spread across the kitchen floor. Alec settled his hand on Georgianna's shoulder, urging her back. He drew his knife. Keiran and Edtroka raised their weapons and followed him inside. Dhiren nodded to Georgianna and held out his arm for her to go first. He closed the door behind him.

The large cooking pot lay on its side in the middle of the kitchen. The chairs were gone and the table-top lay in two pieces on the floor, its legs broken off. Georgianna braced and walked further inside.

The rain drummed against the walls of the small house, echoing her heartbeat and with the anger at what she was seeing. Any belongings her family had left behind were strewn through the rooms. All valuable and useful items had been stolen.

She stood in the doorway of what had once been her room. Her trunk, built by her father while her mother had still been pregnant with her, was gone. Her mattress had been split open and the grass and straw pulled out. Her clothes were ripped and trampled. The frame of her bed had been taken; there was nothing left but the splinters where they had broken it apart.

"I'm sorry, George," Dhiren murmured from behind her.

"People here knew my father. They knew Halden.

They'd probably seen Braedon every day of his life and they still—"

"I know," was all he said. He squeezed her shoulder, sending a stream of cold rainwater from her shirt cascading down her back.

He left her alone in the doorway and followed the others through to the front room. Georgianna searched around for anything salvageable before moving on to the room her brother shared with Braedon. The sight was much the same. Furniture had been stripped and broken apart. What clothes remained were torn and useless. A rag toy of Braedon's had been left behind untouched and she gathered it up and clutched it against her chest.

This time, there were no tears. She wandered through the house, observing the destruction of her family's lives but not truly seeing it. Her father's room had been turned upside down and if he had left anything of value behind, it was gone now. Georgianna clung tight to the rag doll as she thought about the bag of belongings she had taken with her to Edtroka's apartment, now lost to her as well. The Adveni had killed her family but it had been the Veniche who wiped out almost all trace of them. She brought the doll to her nose, inhaling deeply through the worn material. She wanted nothing more than to recognise a scent, for it to bring happy memories, but there was nothing but dust and cold rain air.

The front room was the last and the worst. The furniture her father had so painstakingly made was broken or missing. The stool he'd always sat on to whittle lay in pieces in the corner. That didn't make any sense. If they'd needed firewood in the middle of the Freeze then perhaps she could understand it; sometimes people were driven to desperation. But here they had broken things apart for no other reason than destruction. The tears that now sprung to her eyes were not drawn from sadness or loss; they were from anger.

She didn't see the object until she sent it spinning across the floor from an absent kick of her boot. She watched it rock and lie still, the tiny eye peering up. Zello, the toy wolf her father had carved for her as a child—her favourite—lay on its side. She crouched and picked it up, turning the smooth wood over in her fingers. One of his back legs had snapped off and she figured that someone had trodden on it while moving through the room.

Her father had clutched that wolf so tightly when he had thought she wouldn't return from the compound. Convincing him that it really was her, and not some cruel spirit sent to haunt him, had been heart-rending. Now, holding the wolf was ripping her in two.

"We should move on," Georgianna murmured. "It's obviously not safe here."

To his credit, Dhiren didn't laugh or brag about being right. Keiran moved to her, but Edtroka held him back. He shook his head and Keiran's jaw tightened as he glanced between the two of them.

"Can... Can I stay a minute before we leave?"

"We'll be in the kitchen."

Edtroka ushered the others out of the front room. Back in Edtroka's apartment, Georgianna had often wondered about the lack of personal items. Everything Edtroka owned had been functional. There was nothing that gave any hint to his family or his life before arriving on Os-Veruh. Now, standing in the rubble of her family, she understood why.

Remembering them was too painful. Edtroka's family were still alive, most of them at least, but they were no longer a family to him. Georgianna knew she would give everything to have her family alive, even if she never saw them. But for them to think of her as a traitor? To want her dead? She wasn't sure she would handle that any better.

She turned over items strewn across the floor, looking for anything she could salvage, things that would remind her of them. Even though her family were already gone, she couldn't cut them from her life the way Edtroka had done. Tears of fury and desolation blurred her vision. She wanted to take everything, from the broken stool to the ripped clothes. For anyone else to have them would be wrong. For them to rot in this house, a waste. Even though she knew there was no use for them, she had still gathered an armful of items by the time she slung her bag from her shoulder and opened it to put them inside. Dhiren or Edtroka would probably call her mad but she didn't care.

Standing, Georgianna walked back to the doorway. There was nothing left for her here. There was nothing left for any of them. The bag hung low, slapping against her calf with every step. In the corridor, she glanced through the open front door and out to the street. She froze.

Ehnisque's dark hair was knotted tightly at the base of her skull. She looked perfect, despite the storm. Her pale skin shone through the dark rain, in stark contrast to the black of her uniform. She wasn't as tall as her brother but she was statuesque, standing there in the rain, a small smile already on her lips.

Georgianna placed the bag down just inside the living room door. She didn't dare look behind to check for the others in case Ehnisque saw. She couldn't even hear their voices over the pounding of the rain. She stood still, listening and waiting, but there was only the steady beat of the rain.

Ehnisque stared at her, hands clasped calmly. She wouldn't have come alone. Georgianna already knew that there would be little chance of escape. If she tried to run the Adveni would close in and capture her. They would catch them all.

There was only one option. She would set off the trap herself. If she walked directly into the net then they wouldn't be able to throw it so easily over the others. They would have time if she could warn them.

It was only fair that the Adveni got the whole Lennox line, wasn't it? She'd see her father again. He would be furious, she knew, but he would hug her and tell her it was alright.

She wanted to turn and run. She wanted to scream. She wanted to draw out the knife Dhiren had given her and prove he'd been able to teach her something.

Instead Georgianna stepped out to meet Ehnisque Grytsch in the rain.

14 Bet and Bluff

Ehnisque didn't move as Georgianna walked forwards. Raindrops pounded her skin like pellets and ran down her face into her soaked clothes. She looked up at the woman. It was almost laughable. Ehnisque was dramatically taller than her. Every inch of her body screamed power and speed; it was a body made for the duty it had been given. The rain rolled off her Tsevstakre uniform as easily as it slipped down her cheeks.

"You won me a bet, Ven," she said, her grin broadening.

"You're welcome."

Georgianna didn't know where the determination was coming from, but she couldn't let Ehnisque see her squirm. She would face her like a woman, like a warrior. Her family had been taken from her but she would protect Edtroka from his.

"You see, my men here thought that you wouldn't be stupid enough to come here, but I knew," Ehnisque jeered, waving her hand to two more Tsevstakre. They moved through the rain like shadows. "The silly little medic, so sentimental."

"I hope you got something good for your win."

"Oh, I did, Ven. I got you."

"Well, I'm sorry I'm not more presentable for you."

Ehnisque's laugh sounded so much like Edtroka's that it threw Georgianna off. She didn't want to compare this woman to Edtroka. Although they resembled each other physically, their characters were completely different. Edtroka wanted to help people, where Ehnisque was best at destroying them, at least from what she'd seen.

"Did you do this to the house?" she asked. "A taunt to draw me out?"

Ehnisque looked past her and through the open doorway.

"While I would love to have claimed that carnage, I cannot." She leaned closer, her dark eyes sparkling through the rain. "Though, I cannot claim to have stopped it, either. We took bets on whether you'd cry, too."

Georgianna gulped and steeled herself against the cold and the anger that would have her body tremble. Ehnisque straightened and looked over her head at the doorway.

"Who else is in there?"

"No one."

"You always have someone, Ven. Some pathetic man willing to hurt himself for your pretty face. Is it my brother this time or have you abandoned him?"

"You said it, Ehnisque. I'm silly and sentimental. I wanted to see my home. I came alone."

Ehnisque motioned for the two Tsevstakre soldiers to move forwards.

"Check the house," she said. "If there is anything more

than a bug in there I want it dead or in front of me. If it's E'Troke, I want him alive."

Georgianna turned away from Ehnisque and watched as they advanced. They slipped towards the house, their weapons raised, moving soft and slow, silent. She gritted her teeth. If they went too far then they would find the others. They would trap them and submitting to Ehnisque would be for nothing.

"Do you really think your brother would be stupid enough to come here?" she demanded, returning Ehnisque's cruel smirk. "After all, he was smart enough to outwit Maarqyn for years. He outwitted you, too, didn't he? Even your father, the vtensu Volsonnar wasn't smart enough to see his betrayal. So, if you think he's stupid enough to come here it makes me wonder how your family ever took power."

Ehnisque's fist flashed forwards and there was a second where Georgianna didn't even register the motion. Then, like thunder, the pain cracked through her. Georgianna covered her face and howled as loud as she could, doubling over in pain. She howled and swore, stamping her foot.

"You dare talk about my family like that?"

Had it been enough?

Straightening up, she dabbed her thumb under her nose and scrunched her face to test the pain. It hurt. She faced Ehnisque again. The Adveni was sneering down at her.

"Yes," Georgianna said. "You mentioned mine."

"Your pathetic excuse for kin are where they belong."

Tonguing her teeth to make sure none of them were wobbling, Georgianna swiped across her lip with the back of her hand. She couldn't taste blood, just rain and fury. She was digging her own grave. It would never be planted with grass or given a marker, but the least she could do was deny the Adveni the satisfaction of forcing her to it, kicking and screaming. She would go willingly, and take many of them into it with her.

"And soon your psychotic friends will be where they belong," Georgianna said. "Say, how is the commander?"

"You stupid little—" Ehnisque grabbed her by the collar, pulling her forwards.

"Stupid little what, Ehnisque?" She grabbed Ehnisque's wrist, driving her nails down into the flesh. "A stupid little Ven that he obsessed over more than he did you? And you call me pathetic."

The Adveni drew her fist back but, before she could strike again, she glanced over Georgianna's head and her snarl of rage turned into a grin of triumph.

"Stupid little Ven," she said. She glanced down at her. "Did my brother not tell you that you should know your hand before you bluff?"

Georgianna jerked back, trying to look over her shoulder. Ehnisque tugged her closer.

What if they hadn't heard her? What if those Tsevstakre were dragging them out? No, she would have been able to hear them fighting. Dhiren and Edtroka had taken on guards by themselves. They would have been able to fight the two soldiers. They would have at least tried. She knew they would. Ehnisque would have been more worried; she would have grabbed her and used her to make them stop.

She would have heard it.

"You're too sentimental," Ehnisque said. "That's why you'll never win."

She feared it was Edtroka. He'd wanted to hand himself in to give the Cahlven time. He'd even offered to sacrifice himself within the compound. What if this was how he finally got his way? He'd had the tsentyl powered up for too long, he'd said it himself. Perhaps it had been his plan all along to ensure his capture.

Ehnisque released her. She spun around.

It wasn't Edtroka. Two soldiers were coming out of the house and between them, not fighting or shouting but walking calmly, to meet his fate, was Keiran.

Georgianna's heart fell further the closer he came. He stared past her at Ehnisque. She could see the same determination in his face that she had tried to use to mask her own fear. She wondered if he was scared.

"Well, well, well. What do we have here?"

"If you're stupid enough to need—"

"Quiet!" Ehnisque snapped. "You will hold your tongue or I will cut it in two."

She pointed at the door.

"Were there others?" she demanded. "Did you see anything?"

"There were multiple treads inside," one of the soldiers said. "We called in for Vosqra and Dtron to move around back to try to cut them off, but nothing so far."

"Who was there?" Ehnisque said to Keiran, her voice as sharp and cold as broken ice. "Who were you with?"

Her gaze snapped between them. Keiran's jaw tightened and he stared right back. Georgianna held her tongue and kept it in one piece.

Ehnisque shoved Georgianna, sending her splashing down onto the soaking ground. Pain shot up her back.

"I said, who was there?"

"No one," Keiran said. "It must have been the looters' footprints."

"That house has been empty for a week." Ehnisque said. "My men have seen to that."

Georgianna got to her feet and stood next to Keiran. The backs of his fingers brushed hers. He twitched.

"They saw you approaching the house. There were more of you. They told me there were five."

"Maybe your men count as well as you do your job," Georgianna said.

Ehnisque smacked her with the back of her hand. Georgianna staggered back as Ehnisque beckoned the soldiers closer.

"They do not move. They so much as sniff and you put a bullet in their knees. I need to report this to the commander."

She turned away as the soldiers flanked them, both clamping a hand down on their arms. Ehnisque pulled a tsentyl from her pocket and swiped it open. She stabbed it forcefully with her finger, as if it had been the one to insult her, and within moments, a monotonous tone buzzed through the air.

Georgianna looked at Keiran. He pressed the back of his hand against hers and returned her gaze out of the corner of his eye. He gave a tiny almost indiscernible nod. She didn't need to ask. He knew what she was afraid of and he knew what she wanted. He'd always known what she wanted.

Edtroka, Dhiren, and Alec were gone.

15 Left to Lose

The cell was dark, with only slivers of light squeezing through the tiny window at the top of the back wall. The bars across the entrance were thick and so close together that there was no chance of getting an arm through the gap, let alone being able to twist and unlock the door. Ehnisque had hooded both of them the moment they left the camps and Georgianna hadn't been able to keep up with the turns they'd taken. After entering a building, they had been shoved down a flight of stairs and they were now deep underground. Even Edtroka wouldn't be able to blow out a wall and help them escape.

Keiran had finally stopped pacing. He sat against the wall, hands clasped in his lap. He closed his eyes and rested his head back against the wall, but he was too stiff to be asleep. Georgianna kept mobile, hopeful that her pacing might relieve some of the tension and help her to forget her fear. She ran her hand back and forth along the bars as she walked, listening for footsteps amid the random melody of fingers against metal.

"It was stupid!"

She returned to her tirade with the same fervour as the first time she'd let the words tumble from her. Keiran sighed and cracked one eye open.

"I shouted so that you would know to run," she said. "You should have run."

"So you're angry with me for sacrificing myself after you... sacrificed yourself," he said. "Don't you think that's a little hypocritical?"

"I wanted you to run. What benefit is there in both of us being here?"

"Alright." He pushed himself further up. "Let's discuss the benefit of you sacrificing yourself to a man who has already expressed interest in buying you and torturing you for information."

"It would have given you the chance to get away."

"And when you offered to stay with the brothers in the compound? Whose benefit was that for?"

Georgianna spun on her heel so fast that she smacked her elbow into the bars. Hissing, she cradled her elbow in her hand and glared down at him.

"That's got nothing to do with this."

"I think it has everything to do with it," he said.

"It doesn't matter."

"Let's say it does."

Georgianna rolled her eyes and went back to pacing.

"This isn't getting us anywhere."

Keiran's laugh was brash and bitter. He flung his arms out and beamed a belittling grin.

"Look around, George! *Nothing* is getting us anywhere."

And since you seem so intent on proving how stupid I was for giving myself up, I think I deserve the right to do the same."

"If you think I am so stupid, why did you follow, then?" she hissed, pleased for a moment that she had the upper hand.

"Do you really need to ask that?"

She stopped, staring through the gap in the bars and not daring to look back at him. The corridor was as dark as their cell. She couldn't even see the doors from here, just the black of the stone walls. The empty gloom looked almost comfortable, quieter than the questions and desolations running through her head.

Georgianna couldn't ask him again why he had followed her, because she didn't know she could bear to hear the answer. After spending weeks wondering and worrying about the gap opening up between them, she knew what he was going to say, but didn't want to hear him say it. She didn't deserve it; not after everything that had happened. Her family were gone because of her. She didn't deserve the comfort of knowing Keiran had walked into this hell to protect her. If anything, that made it worse. She had lost her family and she was letting Keiran follow her to a grave.

"You're meant to be one of the leaders, Keiran," she whispered. "You were meant to be… you were meant to help us win and rebuild. I've lost everything, already."

Keiran frowned as she turned to look at him. She could see his eyes through the darkness, bright and sad. He rubbed his hands against his thighs.

"You really think you have nothing to lose?" he asked. "What about the people losing you?"

"That's not what I meant."

They'd been so distant, so angry. Despite the good they'd done, she wanted to rewind it all so she could have him back again; go back to when things had been simpler. Or, at least, when it had been easier to lie. She couldn't lie any more.

"The point is, any of the others would have received an instant death sentence. They don't know about me."

She looked away from him. He'd followed her because he thought she was safe. Her lungs filled with stones.

"They know."

"What?"

"They know about you. They'll have searched Edtroka's apartment by now. They know you helped Alec and Nyah escape. They know that you convinced Edtroka to free me from the compound."

She remembered how she'd felt when she saw his name on a list alongside a map that detailed their escape route whilst freeing Alec and Nyah from Maarqyn's ownership. She'd been confused and upset. She had wanted to trust him but too many things didn't make sense. Of course, that had been before she'd realised that Edtroka wasn't on the Adveni's side and that the list was to help them.

Returning to his side, Georgianna slid down onto the floor next to him. Beside her, Keiran rubbed his face and stared at his knees, heaving a sigh.

"Why didn't you run with the others?" she asked.

Keiran licked his bottom lip as his gaze searched her face.

"Because if I'd let them take you, I'd have been right where you are."

He reached up and brushed the hair back from her face, his eyes so close that they blurred in her vision. His breath was warm and damp against her skin. It was the most intimate they'd been since he comforted her over her family, and closer than they'd been for weeks before that.

"Nothing left to lose."

Georgianna slid her hand into his and squeezed. She kissed the back of his fingers. She splayed their hands and kissed his palms. She lay her head on his shoulder and shared her fears with him as he pressed his lips against the top of her head.

"It's too late now, anyway," he murmured into her hair.

"Too late," she agreed.

* * *

The door at the end of the corridor hit the wall with a crash. Georgianna jumped, scrambling to her feet. Backing away from the bars at the front of their cell, she pressed against the wall, running her fingers along the brick. Footsteps echoed down the corridor and into the small cell, boots heavy on the stones. Keiran climbed to his feet beside her. He slipped his hand into hers and squeezed tightly, but it brought no reassurance.

Night had fallen. The small window at the top of the wall no longer let in any light. A bright blaze shone briefly through the open door and down the corridor but, just as quickly, it was gone as the door slammed closed behind whoever was approaching. The outlines of the bars glinted through the gloom and Keiran stood silhouetted next to her as her eyes adjusted.

She knew who was coming before he appeared. Ehnisque had mentioned contacting the commander and Georgianna only knew one Adveni commander who would care that she had returned to her family home. She gulped and gripped Keiran's hand tighter.

Maarqyn Guinnyr strolled in front of the cell and looked inside. His dark hair was perfectly styled, his uniform without flaw. His eyes glittered and he took a long moment to look them both over, his gaze lingering on their linked hands.

"How adorable," he drawled with a smirk.

He waved someone forwards. A soldier unlocked the cell and pushed the door inwards. It smacked against the bars, the clang of metal on metal deafening within the confines of the cell. Georgianna pressed her back harder against the stones. She'd been certain of her choice. She knew it was for the best. But that didn't make it any easier, to stand in front of a Tsevstakre commander.

Stepping forwards, he rubbed his hands together and surveyed the two of them.

"Imagine my joy when Ehnisque called in her little capture," he said. "She was hoping for her brother too, of course. Nothing like a little sibling rivalry to get the blood flowing."

Maarqyn gazed at her, his smirk broadening.

"But, of course, Miss Lennox, you know all about that, don't you? The report came in after your foray into the compound and subsequent disappearance: three others with the last name Lennox had passed through a checkpoint going south. They had the proper paperwork but we had to check. I'm sure you understand."

Her insides became as heavy and solid as the stones at her back. The weight of her stomach almost buckled her knees and at the same time, she was completely hollow.

She clung to Keiran's hand so hard it hurt, the question already burning on her tongue. Had the Adveni stopped her family from going south? Maarqyn was surely vindictive enough to punish innocent people to compensate for those who got away from him. Maybe he had brought her family back to Adlai in the hopes of luring her out.

Georgianna wanted to burn off her tongue for even thinking something so self-obsessed.

She didn't want to ask him. She didn't want to ask anything of Maarqyn, least of all news he knew she would care about. But the words were bubbling in her throat, and they fell from her lips before she could stop them.

"Are they alive?"

Maarqyn clasped his hands in front of him and adjusted his stance.

"Does it matter?" he asked. "After all, you'll never see them again. Well, maybe we can arrange something if you are under my ownership."

Georgianna gritted her teeth as Keiran tightened his grip into fists, so tight she thought he might break her fingers.

"Perhaps we can come to an arrangement, you and I," he said. "I might even spare this one from being collared if he agrees to behave. With Alec and Nyah gone, I could use more help."

The growl that bubbled in Keiran's throat never made it to his lips. He rolled his shoulders back and straightened up, glaring daggers back at the Adveni commander. Maarqyn grinned broadly.

"I must say, Medic, I was unsurprised when Ehnisque told me a man had given himself up during your capture." He kept his gaze on Keiran. "It seems to be a talent of yours, doesn't it? Getting men involved in your little problems.

We did hear an awfully interesting story from one of the inmates within the compound. He screamed for your death quite vehemently. Seemed quite eager to tell us everything he knew, once I suggested that we might return you to him to do as he wished."

Georgianna paled and stared at him.

"You want to give me to Ta-Dao?"

Maarqyn's laugh was so cold that it ran straight through her.

"Give our little bird to a murderer? I think not. That would be a waste, wouldn't it? Over far too quickly." His eyes narrowed as he looked her over. "I have better plans for you, for both of you. I'm sure you'll sing quite nicely if given the right incentive. Plus, the inmate was quite mad by the time we spoke to him. I think it was best for all involved that he didn't speak any more, don't you agree?"

Maarqyn let the question hang in the air as he turned back to the soldier outside the door and waved him forwards. The man stepped into the cell, waiting. Maarqyn turned back to Georgianna and Keiran, and surveyed them both for a few seconds before nodding.

"Take him first," he said and even then, the glee was evident in his voice. "Let us see how much he will endure before he cooperates."

The soldier stepped up and grasped Keiran tightly by the arm. He tugged him forwards and Keiran didn't fight. He gripped Georgianna's hand, stretching their arms between them as he was pulled away. His fingers slipped from hers and he didn't look back as he was dragged from the cell. The soldier led Keiran out of sight and yet Maarqyn still watched her.

"Enjoy the show, little bird," he whispered.

He swept from the cell, closing and locking the bars behind him.

Georgianna slumped against the wall, sliding down it. She wrapped her arms around her legs and rested her forehead on her knees. A tremor of fear wracked through nher body with each ragged breath.

Further down the corridor, a door opened and there was a shuffling as Keiran was pushed inside. They didn't close the door behind them.

She didn't hear the questions they asked him. She couldn't make out the threats or orders. She couldn't even hear if he answered anything Maarqyn asked, if he told them what they wanted to know. For the rest of the night, alone in the darkness, Georgianna could only hear Keiran's screams.

16 THE NSIQO

The long chair was sticky. The thick, leathery material was an odd texture she'd not felt before, like it had been varnished and hadn't dried. Wriggling against it, trying to get comfortable, she tugged at the blue cords which secured her wrists to the armrests. The end of one cord hung from the knot in a coil on the floor. So far, at least, it hadn't been connected to anything.

Maarqyn stood in the corner of the new room, watching her; arms folded, drumming his fingers against his elbow. Georgianna shivered and leaned back in the chair. It propped her feet up, stretching her out. She felt exposed and no matter how she twisted and turned, no position could ease the feeling that she'd been displayed for his amusement.

Maarqyn hadn't touched her yet. He had stood in the corner of the room, watching, as she was strapped down. He stayed perfectly still as the soldier made sure each knot was secure before leaving. He'd not even asked her any questions. Perhaps he was expecting that Keiran's treatment had broken her, that all he had to do was wait for the cracks to start opening.

They hadn't let her see Keiran. He'd been taken to another cell further down the corridor. A soldier stood outside each door, ready to shoot them with copaq gel if they tried to speak. The sun had risen and set, and all she had seen of Keiran was the trail of blood where they had dragged him down the corridor. She didn't want to think about what they'd done to him. She couldn't think about what they might do to her if she refused to cooperate.

"Where is E'Troke Grystch?"

His voice was quiet and soft but too cold to be friendly. He didn't move from the corner of the room and he didn't look away from her face. Georgianna shook her head, her hair sticking to her cheeks and neck.

"I don't know."

Maarqyn waved a hand towards the coil of blue cord on the floor.

"Technology really is ingenious, isn't it?" he said. "With the use of such things I don't even need to touch you to make you answer my questions."

His boot clunked against the stone. She looked away as he came closer, and it was only then that she realised he had closed the door. When they had taken Keiran, they hadn't seemed to care if the torture was heard outside the room. Through those hours of being unable to do anything but listen to his screaming, she thought perhaps that Maarqyn wanted her to hear. Strapped to the chair, the closure of the door now scared her more than the idea of pain. She shuddered and tried to push herself further up in the chair.

"I don't know where he is," she said again.

"It rarely leaves marks. No unsightly injuries to have to look at every day. Just a nice, complacent drysta who knows her place."

"I don't!"

Her voice dropped to a squeak and Maarqyn smiled. Placing a hand on top of her arm, he brushed his thumb back and forth against her skin and leaned over her.

"But it's boring," he whispered. "So impersonal."

She squirmed under his touch.

"You see, it's not just the memory of pain that keeps a drysta docile. It's the memory that I gave it to them, that I alone control what happens to them. Cinystalqs are useful to a degree but there comes a time when you have to truly leave your mark on a person. Am I right?"

"I don't know."

He stood up straight, his grin bemused.

"You don't know where E'Troke is? You've already said that. Or is it that you don't know if I'm right? Well, that'd be no surprise, I suppose. You don't seem like the type to mark another person, to claim them."

"You haven't claimed them. You can't claim a person," Georgianna murmured.

Clicking his tongue against his teeth, Maarqyn moved closer and took a seat on the edge of the chair, close to her knees. His slim fingers brushed the top of her thigh, up towards her waist. She jerked her leg away but had nowhere to go.

"How much you have to learn, little bird. Every time a drysta looks at a scar, they will connect it to the one who gave it to them." He walked his fingers across her stomach and her muscles tensed. "They will think about the giver of a mark every day for the rest of their lives. Is that not claim enough?"

He lifted his hand away from her stomach and placed it on her knee again, giving it a gentle squeeze. His eyes shimmered when he smiled, wrinkles appearing at their corners. He was in his forties, probably nearing fifty, and yet there wasn't a single grey hair on his head. She searched closer; anything to stop herself from looking at those amused eyes, or the vicious smile playing on his lips.

"While we were talking to your friend, we discovered something quite interesting," he said, tapping his fingers against the inside of her leg. "He has a mark on his shoulder, one that the Veniche use for a traitor. What is it you call that?"

Georgianna gritted her teeth. When she didn't answer, Maarqyn rolled his eyes and drummed his fingers harder.

"Now, now, Medic, this is hardly going to bring the downfall of your race, is it?"

"Grutt," she said. "We call it a Grutt."

"*Grutt*. Such a vulgar term. Coarse."

She was sure he'd known the word all along. Where was this leading? Shaking his head, Maarqyn leaned in closer.

"Do you think he'll remember the person who gave it to him?"

Her stomach churned. Alec had given Keiran the mark, thinking him a traitor for working with Edtroka. Keiran had already said that he would never forgive Alec for marking him. She wondered if Keiran had told him that, already.

"When we searched E'Troke's apartment for clues to his whereabouts and his plans, we found an interesting list of names," Maarqyn continued when she didn't answer. "Was Keiran Zanetti working with E'Troke before your capture?"

She felt sick. Her stomach rolled and clenched. Her fingers trembled and she felt heat spreading across her skin. Her gaze flickered to the cord around her wrists. It wasn't attached to anything but what if he'd applied something to it? Something that would make her suffer with the contact. Would an Adveni venom kill her if it only touched her skin?

"Not going to tell me?"

Georgianna glared at him. Far from being angry about her refusal, Maarqyn looked practically giddy at her silence.

"Oh good," he said, leering. "I was so hoping I would be the one to mark you, little bird."

* * *

Soon, Maarqyn returned. He opened the door but stayed outside as a petite woman with short, spiked blonde hair entered. She wore the familiar pale grey uniform but it had been modified and was almost unrecognisable as Adveni. It was pulled in at the waist to show off her figure without being skin-tight like the Tsevstakre uniforms. The sleeves had been cropped short and designs of blue and teal, green and deep maroon were woven over her skin. No, not over her skin; *in* her skin. The spirals and spikes were as much a part of her as the olive tone of her face. Even her eyes looked different; a deep red line had been painted along her lashes and her bright blue irises seemed all the more vivid for it.

She pulled a device on wheels behind her. Setting it next to the chair, she peered back at Maarqyn.

"Where would you like it, Volsonne?"

Maarqyn locked the door behind him and studied Georgianna, tapping the tips of his fingers against his bottom lip.

"Shoulder, I think. Seems fitting."

The woman nodded and flicked a switch on the device. It hummed and shuddered for a moment and then fell silent. Georgianna shifted, her chair creaking, and looked between them. She squealed as a sharp sting shot through her arm. The woman lifted a copaq-like device. The side of it blinked red three times before going dark.

"She'll need to be turned over," the woman said, calm as the breeze.

Maarqyn strode across the room and made quick work of undoing the knot around Georgianna's left wrist. He moved around the chair and paused, his hand inches from the other knot.

"If you try to fight me, I will make this worse for you. Do you understand?"

She nodded, her gaze flickering to the woman, and he undid the knot.

Rubbing her wrists against the burn of the rough cord, she watched the two Adveni and chewed the inside of her cheek. A small blotch of blood had soaked through the arm of her shirt. She touched it and winced at the sting as the woman continued to flit around the machine, pressing buttons and reading a screen.

"Get up!"

Georgianna did as she was told. Maarqyn stepped around her and leaned down to adjust the long chair. The leg rest shot out and the back fell down until it was flat and square to the ground. Only the arm rests still protruded up on either side.

"Shirt off."

"What? No."

Maarqyn didn't wait for Georgianna to refuse him twice.

He grasped her elbow, tugging her forwards. She thwacked her arm against his chest but he barely seemed to feel it. He manoeuvred around her flailing and gripped her shirt, tugging sharply, ripping it down one seam. Georgianna kicked him in the shin.

The back of his hand rattled her teeth and made her brain bounce inside her skull. He had hold of her, pulling the other side of the shirt free and flinging it away. He forced her forwards until her cheek pressed against the sticky leather and coiled the cord back around one of her wrists.

"Down!" he snapped.

No matter how hard she pushed against him, away from him, Maarqyn forced her against the flat chair and held her body down. Leaning over her, he was so close she could feel him smirk against her skin.

"You should do as you're told, or I'll have to find a more entertaining use for you in this position."

Georgianna slumped and stopped resisting. She allowed the woman to help lay her in the correct position. Maarqyn brought the cord underneath her and wrapped it around the other wrist. Pulling tight, her hands came together until she hugged the flat of the chair as he tied down her ankles. By the time he was finished, Georgianna could barely move.

"This is Neyka. Do you know what she is?" Maarqyn asked, crouching by her side so that she could see him. She couldn't look away.

"No."

"She's a Nsiqo," he said. "She is the one who draws the Nsiloq marks when an Adveni believes they are ready to become an adult."

"What?" Her voice was barely more than a breath as fear spiked through her, sharper than the sting in her arm.

Maarqyn pulled a scrap of paper from his pocket. There was some sort of pattern on it but she couldn't get a good look at the detail. He passed it over his head to Neyka.

"What are the Cahlven planning?"

"I don't know. I'm not important enough to know that."

He barely looked away from Georgianna as he smiled.

"Begin."

17 A Scream and a Song

Georgianna clung to the bars in the cell door and held herself steady. The Nsiqo had ripped her apart from the inside. Muscle and bone were torn through her skin, set alight, and replaced, still smouldering. Each touch was a round of torture in itself. The questions Maarqyn asked didn't matter. Nothing mattered but the pain. He murmured that everything would be okay and wiped the sweat from her forehead, but he didn't offer to stop the pain. There was no bargain to be struck between them. He grinned with every fresh scream. He had claimed his prize already.

The soldier unlocked the cell but she couldn't yet move to go inside. Her legs shook and threatened to buckle beneath her. She wondered whether she should let herself fall. The stones would be a cool relief to the fire in her skin, and lying down would steady the churning in her stomach. She needed water to put out the flames and rid the taste of bile from her mouth.

She yelped as the soldier took hold of her elbow and yanked her forwards. He shoved her inside without ceremony and locked the door. She stood, wavering, as Keiran came to her.

His face was a mess. A long cut ran from temple to jaw and was oozing blood, dribbling over his bruises. A large red bump swelled from his cheek and a clump of hair was missing behind his ear. She wanted to touch him, to reassure him, but she realised, with her fingers already halfway to his face, that she didn't know how. She couldn't fix what had been done to him and she couldn't take the pain away. She couldn't even promise that it wouldn't happen again; that the Adveni would pay for what they had done.

"George," he said, frowning as she flinched away from him. "Are you... what did they do?"

"I told them," she whispered. "I told them the Colvohan is coming."

He reached out again, this time taking her hand. Georgianna hissed, as the shirt she'd been given rubbed against raw flesh. Pain throbbed through her, carried by her blood, beating through her body. Keiran was looking at her wrists.

She hadn't noticed until she looked down and saw for herself. Red welts glistened in the dim light. Her wrists were wet and sticky with blisters, and loose skin was peeling away where they had popped. She'd pulled against the ropes, tugging and struggling as the vapours of pain travelled through her body as easily as air. The cord had burned her and she'd not even noticed. Georgianna glanced down, wondering if she had the same at her ankles.

"It's okay," he assured her, careful to avoid the wounds as he brushed his thumb against the back of her hand. "It doesn't matter."

"I might have told them more. I don't know, I don't remember."

The shirt scraped against the mark again. She whimpered and hung her head, grinding her teeth. It was no good. The pain wouldn't go away, no matter what she did. Maarqyn had done this to her; he wouldn't want her torment to be over so soon.

When she had asked why Jacob's Nsiloq still hurt him, when the Adveni didn't seem to be bothered by the marks, Edtroka had told her that they hadn't 'set' the branding. Apparently there was a way for the Nsiqo to treat the Nsiloq and stop the pain. Of course they wouldn't do that for her. They wouldn't have given her the mark if she wasn't forced to remember it every second, like Maarqyn wanted.

"It doesn't matter," he said again, leading her down to the floor.

"Did you tell them anything?"

Keiran looked down at his knees, flexed his bruised hands and shook his head. Maybe before, she might have wondered whether he was lying. She might have believed that he was avoiding her eyes so that she wouldn't see the truth. Not this time. This time, she knew that he was telling the truth. His avoidance wasn't because he was lying, but because he knew that she would feel worse to see the truth. He had withstood Maarqyn when she could not. He had protected the others and honoured the cause. He had shielded her, and she hadn't been able to do the same.

He looked up, but instead of meeting her gaze, he stared at her wrists, taking the shirt sleeve between his thumb and forefinger and glaring at it hatefully, as if it were to blame for the state she was in.

"What did he do to you?" he asked in a breath.

Georgianna chewed her lip. Knowing how he'd reacted to Alec's marking him, she didn't want to tell him that Maarqyn had branded her. She didn't want to see the anger and hate in him, even though she knew he already felt it. He leaned closer, sliding his hand up her arm. She flinched as his touch rustled the shirt and pulled it against her shoulder.

"Why did he tie you down, George?"

The anger was already in his voice, a fury that burned as hot as the brand on her skin. He released her arm, moving away.

"He brings you back here in a different shirt, knowing I love you and that he—"

Keiran smacked the side of his fist against the stone with a slap that made Georgianna jump. She touched the front of her shoulder and let out a breath, waiting for his anger to subside. It didn't. His bloodshot eyes narrowed and he pushed himself upright.

"No…" Georgianna grasped his hand and pulled him back down. "No, Keiran, not that."

She hadn't considered what he might think of the change of clothes. She was so preoccupied with the pain and guilt, she hadn't thought about how it would look, wincing away from his every touch.

"What, then?" he asked.

She turned, a whimper escaping. Lifting the shirt up her back was torture. Keiran slid his hands beneath the material and helped, his fingers cold against her skin.

"Careful."

He held the material away until it could be lifted up off her shoulder.

He didn't make her take it off; he could see well enough what had been done. She glanced at him over her shoulder as he studied the mark. He traced his finger an inch above it and she wondered whether his cold hands would be soothing.

"He said he wanted to mark me, to make me remember it every day."

"Like Jacob," he said.

Georgianna nodded. He drew the shirt down her back with care. When she faced him, he took her hand and kissed her fingertips, wincing at the pressure against his split lips.

"Do you think the others are okay?"

He shrugged and closed her hand in both of his, resting his chin on top. She watched him for a moment.

"Keiran?" she murmured. "The mark. What does it look like?"

When he smiled, it was sad and bitter.

"It looks beautiful."

* * *

Georgianna didn't get much rest over the following days, her sleep constantly broken by flares of pain. Keiran didn't complain, even though she woke him frequently by whispering and hissing as she peeled the shirt from her flesh.

She couldn't be sure, but she thought she'd counted three days before the gate into the cell clanged open again. Maarqyn left it open, two soldiers standing on the other side of the bars, as he strode through to stand before them. Keiran pushed himself up and was rewarded with a kick to the stomach. He hunched over, bracing himself against the floor as he snorted and held back a groan.

"What are the others up to in the city?" Maarqyn demanded, without pleasantries.

Kneeling next to Keiran, Georgianna placed her hand against the back of his arm. Maarqyn would take one of them. He would take them and try to break them and she wanted Keiran to know she was still beside him. It had been the feverish space between dreams that brought his words back to her. It had been pain and tears that had finally made her hear them.

Knowing I love you.

It had taken horrors to bring them back together after their fight. They had both refused to budge out of pride or stubbornness, but that was gone now. There was no pride left to hold onto and no reason to try to grasp it again. She had one thing left to keep, to protect, and he was right there beside her.

Keiran straightened and his knuckles brushed against hers. He linked their little fingers as he lifted his head and looked Maarqyn in the eye.

"We don't know."

This was it, she knew. He would take one of them now, his grin said as much. Maarqyn reached into his pocket and drew out a collar. Georgianna flinched. He'd said he preferred personal methods over technology and yet he'd used a collar on her before to get information. Perhaps he didn't want to mark them so much that it made them unrecognisable, leaving him no other choice.

Maarqyn tapped the collar against the side of his thigh, looking between the two of them.

Georgianna dropped her head but her gaze flickered constantly to the collar. He would put it on one of them and take that person away. The only question was, which one?

Maarqyn stepped forwards. The collar flipped open in his fingers and Georgianna squeezed her eyes shut, waiting for the chill of cold metal. He'd spoken of putting a collar on her before, should he buy her as his drysta. He'd expressed his surprise that Edtroka had not applied one himself. Had he known then that Edtroka had not wanted her followed? Keiran's fingers jerked against her own and Georgianna's eyes flew open. The clunk of the collar echoed in the small cell. He yanked his hand away and let out a yelp of pain.

"You came into the city with them."

A convulsion ripped through Keiran, buckling him over. He clawed at the collar, trying to yank it from his neck but it did no good.

"Stop!" she pleaded. "Stop! Please!"

Maarqyn gave her an expectant look and pressed his thumb down on the tsentyl, his grin growing broader with every shudder, every cry.

"What are the others up to?" he asked loudly. He jabbed his thumb repeatedly onto the tsentyl. "You can make this stop."

"Please!"

Keiran's scream echoed between the walls and re-bounded, forming a chorus of screams all around her. She buried her face in her hands. She wanted to leap onto him, to release him from this somehow, but there was no way. Tears splashed from her eyes and onto the stone floor. Even if she tried to help, it wouldn't lessen his pain, it would only add to hers. There was only one way to stop Maarqyn. She shuddered and dragged her fingers through her hair.

"STOP!" she screamed. "Stop, I'll tell you!"

He lifted his thumb from the tsentyl. Keiran slumped onto the floor, panting, sweat glistening on his face and soaking his shirt. Maarqyn pursed his lips and raised an eyebrow, tapping his foot against the floor.

"I'll tell you, just don't hurt him any more."

"What are they doing?" he asked again.

Keiran groaned and shook his head, but Georgianna turned away from him. She looked at Maarqyn and straightened up, pushing her shoulders back. His thumb hovered over the tsentyl. For a brief moment, she considered lying to him, but what lie was there to tell? What would he believe?

She couldn't think. Her brother's face kept popping into her mind, her father's voice, Braedon's hands, so tiny when he was born. The space between the tsentyl and his thumb was getting smaller. He snorted and shifted the device to his other hand.

"Alright!" She took a deep breath as Keiran groaned and reached for her. He shook his head but she looked away. "They're after the Mykahnol."

Maarqyn moved his thumb away from the tsentyl and fixed her with an expectant glare. It wouldn't be enough. He would want more. He would always want more; that was what Edtroka had said.

"They were going to try to find some Adveni to help them. Those Edtroka used to know or who didn't like what happened in Nyvalau."

"Where are they?"

She swallowed the lump in her throat. Keiran flinched and murmured under his breath but she couldn't stop. The moment she stopped, his pain would return. She couldn't let that happen. Not when he was only here because of her.

"They were at the house when Ehnisque showed up," she said. "They ran. I don't know where. They planned to go through the camps and into the city but that might have changed."

"Who are these Adveni?"

"I don't know."

"You came all the way to Adlai not knowing what you were looking for?" he asked. "I find that hard to believe."

"We didn't come here for that," she said, shuffling forwards as he lifted the tsentyl again. "We were following Edtroka. He was going to hand himself in and we... I don't know if they found Adveni to help them."

"What else?"

She gazed up at him, wondering what in his life could have made him so cruel. Was it really just his training or did he get pleasure from this? She shook her head.

"What else?" he demanded again.

"There's nothing else. That's all I know. That's all we know, I swear."

Maarqyn leaned over her, grasping her chin. His thumb and finger dug into her flesh, pressing hard against her jaw. She winced but made no effort to free herself.

"Let's be sure," he murmured.

A fresh scream. Maarqyn turned her head, forcing her to look down at Keiran writhing on the floor.

"Please! Please stop! I told you everything," she begged, struggling in his grasp.

Maarqyn moved behind her and pressed his knee between her shoulder blades. He forced her onto all fours, only inches above Keiran, who spasmed and flailed, legs jerking, fresh gouges in his neck as he tried to claw off the collar. The screams cracked. His mouth was still open and he twitched against the ground, but no sound made it to his lips. His eyes, previously panicked and desperate, rolled back into his head. Drool crept from the corner of his lips.

Maarqyn released her and she slumped down beside Keiran. He placed his tsentyl back into his pocket, straightened up, brushed down his shirt, and left without another word. It was only as the echoes of the clanging bars died away that Georgianna could hear her own sobbing through the pumping of blood in her ears. She crawled to Keiran, lowering her ear to his mouth. Warm shallow breath tickled her cheek. Another sob broke free.

"I'm sorry, Keiran. I'm so sorry."

Peeling herself off the ground, Georgianna sat beside him and stretched her legs out before her. She slid her hands under Keiran's arms and pulled his head and shoulders into her lap. She brushed her fingers through his short hair and down his cheeks.

She waited out the night, clutching his hand as tightly as she dared.

Maarqyn had claimed that he enjoyed the process of branding, for the long-lasting connection. But as she cradled Keiran to her, Georgianna knew that a Nsiloq was far from the most painful mark that could be left on a person.

18 Traitors

"Keiran! Keiran, wake up."

She shook him gently. He'd been mostly asleep since Maarqyn's visit and even when awake he was sluggish and twitchy. His eyelids flickered and he looked up. The first weak rays of sun were shining through the small window and they lit Maarqyn's face as he appeared on the other side of the bars and opened the cell gate. Georgianna gripped Keiran's arm and kept her gaze on the ground before her.

"Your information proved most helpful, Medic," Maarqyn said as he stepped inside.

A new collar hung from the tips of his fingers, glinting in the morning light. A shiver ran through her.

"It did?"

"Yes. We captured two traitors helping E'Troke. They have already given up everything they know, which coincides with what you told me."

Keiran pushed himself up, his arm wobbling under

his weight. He made the motion of swallowing, though Georgianna knew there would be no saliva to coat his sore throat. It had been at least five days since Maarqyn's last visit, though she didn't trust herself to say how long exactly. The guards sometimes brought them water and a cold mush to eat, but if she was right, the last meal had been at least a day ago. Whether Maarqyn was testing as many different forms of torture as he could devise, she didn't dare ask, but his methods were proving effective.

Maarqyn turned the collar over in his fingers.

"They will be executed today."

If possible, Keiran looked even paler at those words. His eyes were dull and listless as he straightened and stared back at the Adveni.

"And what does that mean for us?" he asked.

Maarqyn pointed the collar at them as his gaze flickered from one to the other.

"That," he said, pausing and looking over their heads at the small window, "depends."

"On what?"

"On whether you have anything else to tell me, Belsa."

Keiran huffed and dropped his gaze. Georgianna shook her head. She had no more information but she knew it would make no difference. Maarqyn wouldn't stop. He didn't care whether they knew anything else, he would keep torturing them for anything he could get, even if it was only his own amusement. She didn't dare think about what might happen when the Adveni decided they'd heard enough.

"Shall I take that as a no?" he asked.

"I told you everything," Georgianna murmured.

Maarqyn stepped forwards and crouched before her. He pulled on a lock of her hair and twisted it around his finger.

"That is a pity," he said. "If you had more information, I could have lobbied to keep you. As it is, I have no further use for you. I would have enjoyed the opportunity to spend more time together, but I fear I have more pressing priorities."

He pulled his finger from her hair and patted her on the cheek. Georgianna flinched, but he didn't come any closer. He got to his feet, looked down at the two of them for a moment, and turned on his heel. He marched back to the door and passed the collar to a waiting soldier.

She jumped to her feet.

"Wait! What does that mean? Commander? What does that mean?"

Georgianna leapt to the bars as Keiran got to his feet after her. The soldiers stepped into the cell, one after the other, four in all. Prising her grip from the metal, they shoved her back into a ragged Keiran. Taking her hand, he turned her towards him. The blue-grey of his wide eyes seemed to be the only colour in his face.

"I love you," he murmured.

"Keiran?"

He took her face in his hands and kissed her, a simple kiss so desperate it took her breath away. A hand clamped down on her shoulder, making her squeal against Keiran's lips. It yanked her backwards. Keiran's chest heaved as two soldiers flanked him. Each took hold of an arm.

"Keiran?" she asked again. "What's happening?"

The soldier restraining her kept a tight hold, his thumb pressing hard against the mark on her shoulder. She squirmed but couldn't look away from Keiran's face, set in grim determination. The first soldier held up the opened collar. This one, unlike Keiran's, had a loop hooked into each side of it. She'd seen a collar like that before.

Landon Cartwright had begged before it was put on him. He had cried and asked what he'd done wrong. His protests hadn't stopped them from putting it on, and his cries hadn't given them pause before they attached the electrical cord, turning his pleas to screams.

Georgianna didn't plead. She didn't kick and scream as the soldier stepped forwards. She didn't need to ask what she had done wrong like Landon had done; she already knew. She wasn't useful enough to keep around. Maarqyn had other things to keep him busy.

A small jolt made the hairs on her arms stand on end. The collar was loose on her, resting on her clavicle. The soldier moved to her side and took hold of her arm. She just managed to look over her shoulder as she was dragged away from Keiran.

"I'm sorry," she mouthed. "I love you, too."

* * *

The rubble of the podium had been cleared from the far end of the square. A single post was speared into the ground, with a hoop on top and a blue cord already attached. The sun shone weakly through the clouds, the sky grey and swirling. There were no stalls set up, no rowdy crowd waiting for the performance. The Adveni in the square were quiet and impatient. They stood separate, shifting their weight and glaring as she and Keiran were led through the crowd.

Keiran's collar had been swapped for one with hoops attached. It was only as they were brought out of the building that Georgianna realised they had been kept near Javeknell Square since being taken from the camps.

Ehnisque stood next to the post dressed in her Tsevstakre uniform. Her long dark hair fell around her shoulders, rippling in the breeze. Their guards brought them to a halt in front of her.

"This one first," Ehnisque said without pause.

Georgianna tripped as she was pushed in front of the post. Another Adveni wearing heavy black gloves stepped forwards. He picked up the end of the cord, drawing a long length through the first hoop on her collar and then again, coiling it around the metal. He did the same on the other side. The soldiers brought Keiran over and he was attached in the same manner before the free end of the cord was brought back behind them, attached to the post.

"We thought, since the Belsa was so desperate to be captured alongside you, and you told us everything we needed in order to protect him, that it was only fitting that we didn't take you away from each other."

"Thanks for that…" Keiran returned her sneer but his fingers trembled as he slid them into Georgianna's. She grasped his hand tightly. She couldn't bring any comeback to her lips. She couldn't think of anything except the feeling of Keiran's hand shaking in hers.

"Well, since the podium was destroyed, this might take a little longer than usual. We wouldn't want you to have to wait."

She chuckled as she walked away, leaving Keiran and Georgianna standing alone, tied to the post.

"You never should have come out of the house," she whispered, squeezing his hand. "I'm sorry, Keiran."

He stared at the ground and shook his head slowly.

"I'm sorry we were caught but I'm not sorry I'm with you."

"Do you think the others will make it?"

Keiran looked at her then and, despite everything, there was a small smile on his lips.

"You can stop worrying about other people now, George."

She nodded and gave him a sad smile.

"So, you don't believe in joining, but you're willing to die for a girl," she said. "Would have been good to know."

He squeezed her hand.

"I would have changed my mind on the joining," he whispered.

Georgianna hadn't imagined joining with anyone since she was a young girl. She'd imagined the dress she would have worn and the woven grass ring her partner would slide onto her finger for their entire tribe to see, for all under the sky to note. In her fantasies, she'd always had her hair braided with flowers, the way her mother had done it when she was a child.

Now, she and Keiran were joined only by collars and everyone in the square would hear their screams. They faced them in tattered clothes and weak from torture. She'd not thought about a joining in a long time—certainly not seriously—but she'd never imagined it would happen like this.

A rumble went through the crowd, drawing their attention. The prisoners now being led through the square warranted a far bigger guard. Each man was surrounded by six soldiers, every guard dressed in the slick black uniforms of the Tsevstakre. A short way before the post, the soldiers turned their captives to face the onlookers and forced them to their knees. Shouts of fury went up from the crowd. An open collar was handed to each captive. One of the men had his back straight, his jaw tight. He held the collar before him in both hands and, without waiting, clasped it onto his own neck.

The second man bent double, his breath rattling through his teeth. The collar shook in his hands as he hesitated. One of the soldiers drove the butt of his rifle between the man's shoulders, forcing him to straighten up. He glanced around and shakily attached the collar.

"Lehksi Tzam, you have been charged with treason," Ehnisque announced loudly, stepping before him. "State your crimes."

Lehksi took a deep breath and stared back at her. He hardly flinched.

"I, Lehksi Tzam, cooperated with a traitor. I gave information that was to the detriment of my race. I betrayed my people. I accept my death."

Georgianna couldn't believe it. Accepting his punishment without argument was absurd. Stating his crimes so plainly, *asking* them to kill him? Unthinkable. He hadn't pleaded, he hadn't asked for mercy. He knelt still as stone, waiting as Ehnisque moved to the second man on his knees before the crowd.

"Goedt Lynec, you have been charged with treason. State your crimes."

It took longer for Goedt to reply. He took heavy, uneven breaths and stared desperately through the crowd. Nobody came forwards. Nobody spoke.

"I, Goedt Lynec..." He choked on each word, forcing them desperately past his lips. "I cooperated with a traitor. I gave information and supplies that would aid my race's enemies. I have..."

He gasped and rubbed his hand across the front of the collar. Tears crept into his eyes and rolled silently down onto his cheeks.

"I have betrayed my people and disgraced myself. I... I accept my... my death."

"There are no hoops," Keiran whispered. Georgianna glanced at each Adveni. The collars were as smooth as those the dreta wore when under the ownership of an Adveni. These were not killing collars.

The soldiers moved out of the way. Two men stepped forwards to stand on either side of Ehnisque.

"You have both been sentenced to death. May you find peace and forgiveness for your crimes."

The soldiers raised their weapons, peering through sights on the heavy rifles.

"Fire."

Two shots cracked through the square. The bullets speared into the collars with a bang. The metal clattered away across the concrete and smoke rose from the necks of the two dead Adveni.

Ehnisque gave a nod to the shooters, who melted back into formation. Four new soldiers moved forwards, pulling on heavy black gloves. They grasped the two men by their wrists and ankles and hauled them up, dragging them off to the side. Ehnisque smiled blandly and returned to the post.

"Why don't you shoot us?" Georgianna asked. "Why drag this out?"

"You, Medic?" she said, snorting with laughter. "You're not worth the bullets. And this crowd could use a little entertainment."

She moved to the post and crouched to tap something into a panel on the side. There was no ceremony, no words of regret or promises of forgiveness. She smirked as she hit the last key and moved away. A shock zapped Georgianna from head to heel. Keiran groaned and tried to tug his hand from hers.

Ehnisque had been right; the shock wasn't as strong as the last time a cinystalq had been clamped around her neck. Pain shot through her, tightening her chest and pushing a scream to her lips. She remembered what Edtroka had told her when Landon was executed. Their collars were the type which would cut off electricity from the brain, allowing them to stay conscious and aware. They would feel every shock. They would suffer every pain until their bodies gave out.

Georgianna's knee buckled. She fell sideways into Keiran and clung to him as the first scream sliced through her throat.

"STOP!"

She barely managed to lift her head as her other knee threatened to give way beneath her. She could see him across the square, his dark eyes piercing as he strode through the crowd towards the podium.

Edtroka stopped in the centre, his arms spread wide. He held no weapons and he was out of uniform.

"Stop, Ehnisque. It's me you want!" he shouted across the square. "Stop the execution."

Ehnisque whirled around to face her brother and he straightened, staring at her.

"I demand to see the Volsonnar."

19 Family Reunion

The sudden absence of electricity shocked Georgianna as much as the first buzz that had shot through her body. Her legs trembled as she tried to straighten up. Keiran wrapped an arm tight around her waist, holding her close and keeping himself upright. His arm shook where he gripped her and sweat glistened across his forehead.

The Adveni soldiers backed away from Edtroka, leaving him alone in the centre of the square. He stood straight and proud like Lehksi had done before he was forced to his knees. Georgianna wanted to scream for him. She wanted him to come to them and she wanted him to run. His hands were still spread to his sides and with a slow nod to his sister, he turned in a circle to show that he bore no weapons. When he faced them again, his gaze flickered to Georgianna and Keiran before settling back on his sister.

"Send the message, Ehnisque," he said. His voice was

calm, almost pleasant, yet his lips were pursed and his eyes wary.

"You do not tell me what to do, E'Troke!" Ehnisque snapped back. "You do not tell anyone what to do."

"Then by all means ignore me, if you think our father would not be angry at you for ending this before he has the chance to question me."

Ehnisque moved in front of them, partially blocking Georgianna's view. Silent as shadows, a group of soldiers emerged from the crowd and took position around Edtroka. They drew weapons, but not a single rifle or copaq was raised to aim at the Volsonnar's son. Ehnisque's mouth fell open at the sight of the soldiers and Georgianna realised she had given no signal for them to surround her brother. Ehnisque looked just as surprised as the others in the crowd, who muttered with confusion.

"Your father has given the command to me, E'Troke."

Maarqyn followed the soldiers from the crowd. He wore a heavy coat over his Tsevstakre uniform and a satisfied smile beneath his cruel eyes. Edtroka looked over his shoulder and watched as the commander circled around to face him. With a single nod from Maarqyn, one of the soldiers strode forwards, holstered his weapon, and patted his hands over Edtroka's body. Edtroka did not flinch away from the search and, when it was over, he gave the soldier a cordial smile and lowered his hands.

"I was given to believe that I would be granted safe passage to my father, Volsonne," Edtroka said as the soldier returned to his place and redrew his weapon.

"The time for that has gone."

"Are you suggesting that he would allow you to kill me without questioning me?"

Edtroka's voice was confident, almost arrogant. Georgianna remembered finding him in the drysta yard at the compound and hearing the self-assured way he had spoken to a man wishing to buy her. He didn't feign politeness, and only when she learned that he was the son of the most powerful Adveni on Os-Veruh did Georgianna realise why he had been able to speak that way to those who would have been considered his superiors. He knew people were afraid of his father and therefore afraid of him.

Georgianna looked at Keiran and gripped his arm. She wrapped one hand around her collar, pulling it down on her neck. Keiran's warm breath rose in a cloud in the cold, wet air. They could both see that Maarqyn did not fear Edtroka.

"Get my father here and I will come quietly."

"You have already come quietly, E'Troke," Maarqyn said. "You have no weapon and you are surrounded."

Edtroka smiled.

"If you believe that, Volsonne," he said.

Maarqyn's nostrils flared.

"Ehnisque, get the Volsonnar and then start the current again."

"No!" Edtroka's shout was fierce as he pointed at Ehnisque. "You will get Father, but if you touch that current, Sister, you will be the first to die."

The fire in his eyes was vicious as he glared at Maarqyn.

"I told you I would come quietly but if those two are harmed, this deal is off."

"Why would I care for your 'deal'?"

"Because, under the terms of my surrender, they are to be released immediately, and you would not go against my father's orders. I am a far greater prize than two Veniche, don't you think?"

Maarqyn's hand flinched at his side. He took a step forwards. Edtroka was taller but also slimmer. It would probably be an even match between the two if it came to combat.

"Get the Volsonnar, Ehnisque," Maarqyn growled.

Ehnisque pulled a tsentyl out of her uniform and swiped it open. In the centre of the square, as she began tapping in details, Maarqyn and Edtroka faced each other.

"There is no need for that."

The man's voice was cold and calm as he stepped out of the crowd.

"I am already here, Son."

The crowd parted with a gasp of surprise. They cleared an even larger space than they had for Edtroka. The soldiers surrounding Edtroka and Maarqyn jumped to attention and three moved to the side to let the man pass.

He was tall, only a hair shorter than Edtroka. He had the same lean physique but he was slower and more reserved as he moved forwards. His dark hair was peppered with grey, slicked back against his head where it curled at the nape of his neck. His eyes were lighter than his children's but he had the same penetrating gaze. There was no doubt that this was Edtroka's father, the famed Volsonnar.

Georgianna had never met the man before. She'd never even seen him. She had no idea whether she was supposed to kneel or stand to attention and so she remained still, leaning against Keiran, who tugged her closer and gripped her wrist with his free hand.

"Father," Edtroka said. "I had no idea an execution would be to your interest."

"Traitors are always my interest, E'Troke," he replied

coolly. "That it is my own son who would convince others to turn against their race makes no difference."

"I never wanted anyone to turn against the Adveni. I wanted fairness. I wanted justice."

"And my justice is not good enough for you?"

Edtroka took a step forwards. Every soldier raised his weapon and pointed it at him. He jerked to a stop and raised his chin defiantly. Maarqyn melted away, sliding past the soldiers to stand at the inner ring of the crowd. While Georgianna was sure he thought himself important enough to control most proceedings, it was clear he had no intention of being a part of this family affair.

"Ehnisque, deesa, come here."

His daughter moved with the tight grace of someone trying to look calm and collected. The Adveni endearment brought a smile to Ehnisque's lips. Standing next to her father, she touched her hand to his shoulder and offered a respectful smile.

"Volsonne, you know me," Edtroka blurted. "I would die for any of my brothers. But events have changed them. Your promise when we came here was one of peace, of progression, not oppression."

The Volsonnar didn't speak. He stared back at his son, emotionless. A freezing shudder ran through Georgianna at the sight of his cold reception.

"There can be peace here, father. The Cahlven will meet, you know that. The Veniche want justice. If you offer it, we can live peacefully," he continued. His voice wavered and Georgianna could hear the crack of fear that slipped through.

The Veniche did not want peace with the Adveni, everyone knew that. The Adveni had destroyed too much and killed too many. No Veniche would ever be able to fully trust the Adveni, no matter what truce was made.

"You offered safe conduct to the Cahlven. That can still happen."

Every word from Edtroka became more desperate in the face of his father's silence. He took another step forwards.

"Father…"

The Volsonnar clasped his hands behind his back and straightened. Georgianna pushed herself off Keiran. Her lips parted. As the Volsonnar looked at his daughter and nodded, Georgianna wanted to scream.

Ehnisque drew her weapon in a single fluid motion. Georgianna lurched forwards.

"EDTROKA!"

And Ehnisque pulled the trigger.

20 Grey Sky Bleeding

The shot rang straight through Georgianna and out into the square. Edtroka's eyes widened in surprise and horror. His lips parted in a silent cry. The bullet hit him in the forehead.

His knees buckled, dropping down to the stones, as he crumpled to the side in a graceless arc. His head hit the ground and his hand fell outstretched towards his father, towards his sister, towards Georgianna. Blood pooled across the paving in a spreading lake. Edtroka's eyes were still open, but his mouth was slack, his body limp.

Georgianna was screaming. It wasn't loud enough. She wasn't strong enough. It was only at the pull of the cord attaching her and Keiran to the execution post that she realised she had been trying to reach him. It held her firm at the neck, crushing her throat until she could hardly breathe. The screaming came in strangled and soundless retches. She had to reach him. He couldn't be gone.

A second shot, then another and another. But Ehnisque wasn't holding her gun out any more. She jerked and spun around. One of the Adveni soldiers slumped to the ground and his gun clattered out of his hand.

Each shot created five blasts, rebounding between the tall buildings. One cry became two, ten, a hundred, until the cacophony was all Georgianna could hear. Somewhere in there were her own screams.

Ehnisque dived into her father. They tumbled to the ground as a spray of blood gushed out behind them. The ring of soldiers raised their weapons and entered attack stance. They turned and aimed high and low, searching for the shooter. Maarqyn was down, on the ground, blood flowing from his hip. He shouted orders. Tugging against the cord, Georgianna screamed over all of them.

"Get off me!"

Keiran tightened his grip around her waist and pulled back, dragging her towards the ground. Shots came thicker, faster; a din that drowned out everything except the screaming. A storm of boots rumbled in from the opposite end of the square. Adveni scattered, the unarmed ones running. They dropped, arms over their heads, blood bursting around them. The square was flooded with liquid red, spreading and swirling like the grey sky above.

Keiran abandoned restraint and flung Georgianna to the ground, landing on top, pinning her down. Through the crush and the chaos, she could still see Edtroka's wide eyes and his hand reaching for her.

"Edtroka!" she screamed again. "Stop!"

Everything was blurring, light spotting before her eyes. A wall of indistinguishable bodies moved into the square, each holding a weapon, firing indiscriminately. A blanket of bullets soared through the air towards them.

Edtroka's body jerked and his blood splattered, splashing into the growing flood. Bullets struck his back and legs. The collar pulled tight on Georgianna's throat as she tugged against it. She wriggled out from underneath Keiran and scrambled at the cord. Grasping it with both hands, she yanked so hard that it slid through her palms with a searing burn. She didn't feel it. She had to reach him. She clawed at Keiran's arm. He had to understand, he had to let her go to him. Scrambling to her feet, Georgianna yanked at the cord again. It didn't budge.

The man who appeared before her was bulky and muscled. He had come from behind them, a knife in his hand. He was too short to be an Adveni but Georgianna didn't care. She swung a punch. It didn't matter whether she hit him or not, she just wanted to keep him away. The man swerved back and caught her by the shoulder. Georgianna let out a howl on reflex but didn't care about the pain of the mark.

"It's me," he hissed in her ear, wrapping his arm around her neck. He held her back against him, grappling for a grip. She recognised the voice, even though it sounded so taut that it would snap with the slightest touch.

Keiran pushed himself up to his knees, hunching his body and covering his head with his arms. Dhiren flicked the hunting knife, severing the cord between Georgianna and Keiran, and then once again, cutting them free of the post. He released his hold and tried to push them further from the fighting.

"Run!"

"Give me a weapon!" Keiran roared over the noise,

jumping to his feet. Whatever weakness he had from Maarqyn's torture was gone. There was a red fury in his face.

"You need to run," Dhiren repeated, shoving Georgianna. "Go!"

She stumbled away from him. The world pulsed and throbbed with noise: the thump of boots shuddered through her body; music of screams sang in her ears; a beat of gunfire drove her feet onwards.

"I'll kill her!" she screamed back. She snatched at Dhiren's knife.

Dhiren twisted away from Georgianna. His hand found her throat, and he pushed her aside with such force that she hit the post with a yelp.

"He's dead, George!"

His voice cracked and she didn't care.

Georgianna flung herself at him, knocking him backwards to the ground. She didn't care that he was supposed to be a friend. If he was stopping her getting to Edtroka, he was no ally of hers. She grabbed his wrist and grappled for the knife. She needed to do this, he would understand that. He *should* understand that. They needed to pay. For Edtroka, for her family. They couldn't live, not after this.

Screams echoed all around. The wall of men advancing into the square had spread, like rivers bursting their banks and flowing into the crowd. They came from all directions, running between the buildings and out into the open. Adveni wrestled guns from their fallen comrades. They hunched briefly, then ran.

Dhiren grabbed Georgianna and rolled her onto her back. He held her firm and she couldn't breathe for the weight of his body. She screamed and kicked. She raked at his face with her broken nails.

Then, the knife was pressing hard into her throat and she froze. His teeth were bared and there was such fury in his eyes that she didn't dare breathe.

"He just sacrificed himself for you, you stupid vtensu!" Dhiren roared. "I will knock you out and carry you if you do not move now!"

Tears poured down her cheeks and into her hair. The fight was leaving her as quickly as it had overcome the rest of the square. She nodded. Dhiren withdrew the knife and was up in an instant. Stretching out his hand, he yanked her to her feet and wrapped his arm over her head, pushing her down low. He drew a gun and tossed it to Keiran.

"Oprust!" he shouted. "Go!"

Gunfire rained down over their heads, bullets bouncing around their feet. A burning pain stabbed through Georgianna's side. She screamed and set off after Keiran, her feet pounding against the concrete. A splatter of blood now followed each step, the pain throbbing with every beat of her pulse. She kept her arms over her head, not daring to look where she was running. Dhiren kept pace at her side, tugging a device from his pocket.

"I got them! Get out!" he yelled into it.

The garbled reply was barely audible over the gunfire. Dhiren pushed Georgianna sideways and jumped over a body. Friend or foe it didn't matter; it was abandoned to the ground and the blood behind them.

Lifting the device again, Dhiren pointed it down the street ahead of them. Keiran turned and shot twice into the crowd, barely missing a step. Dhiren squeezed the device again.

"Cartwright, are they dead?"

Gunfire crackled from the device, almost as loud as the shots following them across the square.

"Two hits," a voice roared back. "Keep going! They're waiting."

Georgianna glanced over her shoulder as they reached one of the streets curving off between the buildings. Above the chaos, silhouetted against the grey sky, a man stood on the rooftop of the far building, a rifle hanging from his hand.

In the centre of the square, eyes open, hand still stretched towards them, Edtroka lay motionless as the fighting raged around him.

21 Slave to Pain

Scorch marks spiked from the entrance to the tunnel, where tongues of long-dead flames had licked along the ground and up the walls. Georgianna's entire body ached—from running, and the effort of holding back the urge to scream. Dhiren set a merciless pace as he disappeared down the steps and into the black of the tunnels. In front of Keiran, Georgianna steadied herself against the wall as she descended. At the bottom, Dhiren grabbed a lamp that had been left by the wall. He held it up and pushed on, his footsteps crunching in the centre of the pool of orange light.

The stench of smoke and flames made her eyes water. It had been weeks since the Adveni sent fires burning through the tunnels, but their memory remained in every gasp of air. She drew her shirt up over her nose and mouth, her breath hot and wet against the fabric. Dhiren led them down a wide tunnel, turning his head this way and that without stopping.

"Where are we going?" Keiran panted.

"Belsa," Dhiren said.

Keiran fell silent but for his heavy breaths as they struggled to keep up with Dhiren's pace. Georgianna's legs were close to buckling with almost every step, the stinging burn of the bullet shooting into her side matching the heat in her shoulder. This was coupled with the aftermath of the torture and lack of food, making her too weak to keep a steady running rhythm. Dhiren finally slowed and ran his hand along the wall. Keiran overtook him and reached for the lamp.

"I know where it is."

Georgianna saw Dhiren's jaw tighten, but he handed over the lamp. He drew his knife, turned it over in his hand and fell back. Keiran didn't need to slow to find the tunnel entrance. Normally, neither would Georgianna, but she was glad that navigation wasn't her role, today.

They slowed to a walking pace. Georgianna clutched her side and pulled her shirt down, gulping down mouthfuls of smoky air. Her throat burned with every breath. Tears ran down her cheeks and splashed onto her shirt. She was glad for the smoke, even though she knew the acrid air was not the reason the tears kept coming.

Lifting the lamp high above his head, Keiran ducked into the old Belsa entrance. In the slim tunnel, Georgianna ran her hand over the wall, letting it lead her along.

"Halt! Who is it?"

Georgianna walked into Keiran's back as he came to a stop. Steadying herself, she brushed her thumb under her eyes. A red light blinked on Keiran's chest and he looked down at it before lifting his head.

"Zanetti."

The red light blinked and vanished. A man strode

forwards, his legs and torso emerging into the light. He held his hands out and Keiran sobbed with laughter.

"Eli!" He embraced his closest friend and Wrench returned the hug with a tight grasp, gripping Keiran's shirt. When he pulled back, his gaze searched Keiran's, finding each mark that Maarqyn had given him.

He finally turned away from Keiran and looked at Georgianna, then Dhiren.

"Did it go according to plan?"

Dhiren pushed past them.

"E'Troke's dead. Let's get this done. Where is he?"

"I am here."

The man who stepped out of the darkness was tall and stocky. His mousy hair was plastered to his head with sweat and his smile faded the moment he saw Dhiren. He was Cahlven, Georgianna remembered; the technician who had set up the table with the map on it. He clapped Wrench on the shoulder.

"Come on."

The technician led them to a wider section of the tunnel. They had set up a stash of supplies on the floor and Georgianna noticed two distinct piles. Following them into the wash of light from two more lamps, she stood in the centre of the tunnel, looking around. Keiran was already wavering and Dhiren stepped forwards, helping him to sit. The technician gave Georgianna a tentative smile and indicated that she should sit, too. Georgianna slumped down and Dhiren returned to the mouth of the narrow tunnel, turning his knife over and over, his face hidden in shadow.

"You remember me?" the technician asked. "Tohma?"

"I remember."

"Alright. I need you to stay very still."

Georgianna nodded.

He picked up a sheet of sticky material and slid it beneath the collar, wrapping it around her neck. She stared at the wall as he drew out a knife and pried away a small section of the collar. Dropping it behind him, he moved the lamp closer, brushing her hair away and leaning close.

She stared at the lamp next to her, casting shadows in long strips across the ground. The pool of light burned orange and red, then dark red, and when Georgianna closed her eyes, she could see his face; the wide eyes that stared into nothing.

He had come for her. Sacrificed himself. She had tried to convince him of his own importance, but he had still put her safety first.

"You need to stay still," Tohma said again.

Georgianna didn't realise she'd moved. She lifted her hands to find them trembling. Everyone was staring at her as her breath came in sobs and tears burned across her skin. She'd not realised she was crying.

"She needs a minute," Keiran said.

"No, she doesn't," Dhiren said. "Get on with it!"

Covering her mouth, she took a few steadying breaths before lifting her chin, dropping her hand into her lap.

"Dhiren, come on, give her a—"

"We're vulnerable here," Dhiren said. "She can cry all she likes. It isn't going to help. Get on with it!"

Georgianna couldn't meet Dhiren's gaze as she hiccupped and covered her mouth again.

"I'm okay," she whispered through her fingers. "Do it."

Tohma cut the first wire. The first shock was little more than a tap against her skin. After that, a series of tiny zaps came in quick succession as he set about disconnecting one wire at a time. Opposite, Keiran's fingers twitched and he grasped his knees as Wrench worked on his collar.

Tohma made quick work of the wires within the collar. Georgianna counted the time along with her breathing, trying to keep it even. She needed to focus on something, anything other than the look of fear on Edtroka's face as his sister pulled the trigger. She'd only seen him that scared once before, when it was Dhiren who held the gun. She could hear the crack of his voice as he pleaded, told him he had *promised*. Exactly what had he promised? Would she ever know?

She remembered the cocky Adveni who had mocked her, claiming that she was always on time when working for him. He had been so charming and confident, and now he was gone.

"And yet you run every time I send you a message. Must be my irresistible charm. I should have that looked at. You don't happen to know a medic who can give me something, do you?"

Georgianna sniffed and dug her nails into her palms as tears welled into her eyes.

"I am sorry," Tohma said. "I know it hurts."

She wanted to tell him that he had no idea how much it hurt. Her chest tightened, her stomach clenched. She could see Edtroka there; the certainty with which he had strode into the square, the arrogance in his voice as he had spoken to Maarqyn. He must have believed his father would save him, that nobody could be that merciless. Maybe he believed that his sister might flinch and remember that he was her blood. They had betrayed him.

She had betrayed him.

"I am nearly there. This last one will hurt."

Dhiren fell to his knees and snatched Georgianna's hand from her knee, grasping it tight in both of his own. Tohma jumped back in surprise.

"Let go," he said. "You will not be helping her, only hurting yourself."

He looked at Georgianna but didn't let go of her hand. His eyes were red and raw, glowing in the lamplight. His teeth clenched so hard that his jaw shook.

"I'm counting on it," he growled. "Do it."

The pleading she had seen in Edtroka as the two of them had faced off in the cell was in Dhiren's face now. There was a desperation in his eyes that Georgianna recognised, and was now becoming a part of her. Physical pain was nothing compared to the hole opening up inside her. She gripped Dhiren's hands and nodded.

"Do it," she repeated.

Tohma nodded and slid the knife underneath the last wire. Opposite, Keiran gave a yell and panted through his pain. Dhiren's expression only hardened.

Lightning shot through Georgianna's body. It rebounded off her bones; sparks joining together, gathering strength. Sparks jumped from her skin into Dhiren's. He didn't mirror her cries or look away. His grip only tightened, his nails digging into her flesh. The collar clattered to the floor behind her.

The echoes of the shock immediately began to disappear, one by one, but the pain didn't fade from Dhiren's face. If anything, it intensified. Tears slipped over his lashes and down his cheeks.

He was shaky when he got to his feet. Georgianna's fingers slipped from his grasp, and as she panted and trembled, he walked away into the darkness without a word.

"You okay?" Tohma asked. He gave Georgianna a reassuring smile as he gathered his things.

She wasn't sure she was okay, but she nodded all the same.

"We should get going," Wrench said, packing his supplies carelessly into a bag.

Georgianna took a deep breath and climbed to her feet. Leaning on the wall for support, she shook each leg in turn, hoping the tingling would go before she had to move. Tohma finished packing his bag and it took a few seconds of his holding out his hand before she remembered the sticky material around her neck. She peeled it away and handed it over. It was slick with sweat and tears, but Tohma stuffed it into the bag without comment.

"We are done," he said to Wrench with a nod, slinging the bag over his shoulder.

Keiran came forwards and pried her from the wall.

"Are you okay?" he asked. Georgianna shook her head. His smile was apologetic as he nodded.

"Come on."

Tohma had already disappeared into the darkness before Georgianna thought to look around.

"What about Dhiren?"

"Leave him be," Keiran said. "He'll catch up."

"He knows where we're going," Wrench said. "Don't worry, George."

Keiran and Wrench grabbed the two lamps. Georgianna was about to follow when she turned back. Crouching, she picked up the collar and turned it over in her fingers. As she followed the others, she swept out her foot carefully with each step until she found Kieran's collar. She let both devices hang from her hands as she moved along the tunnel.

Keiran glanced at her over his shoulder a few times but didn't comment.

When they slipped out into the wider tunnel, Georgianna lay the broken collars at the entrance. It wouldn't matter now if anyone found them.

He had never put a collar on her. He had bought her, and under the Adveni rules he could do whatever he chose, and yet he had not hurt her. He had given her freedom. He had protected her, choosing his own death over hers.

Georgianna swiped her hand under her nose, brushing away fresh tears. She turned away from the collars and followed the others down the tunnel.

22 Patched Up and Pulled Apart

"Been here about four days," Wrench said as they trudged through the camps. "Been taking on troops where people are willing, letting them get behind us if they want to stay out of it. The Cahlven have their Densaii with the shield up, so people can stay safe."

The sun was setting in the west and a drizzle painted the world around in shades of murky grey. Georgianna wrapped her arms around her stomach as she walked, staring at the ground. Wherever she looked, she could see his face. She could see the blood seeping across the earth and the jerks as stray bullets hit his body.

"The Cahlven are allowing that?" Keiran asked.

"Beck's insistence, I think," Wrench said. "People with kids and stuff. After word got out about Nyvalau we had quite a few begging to join the fight. The Cahlven took a ship south to the border of the destruction. Managed to pick up some large groups who wanted to come back."

Keiran glanced at her. He opened his mouth, paused, and then closed it again. Georgianna followed the footprints in the damp earth, not really listening.

The houses around them buzzed with activity. Men in uniforms she didn't recognise swarmed in groups down the roads. Most of them had the look of Olless: eyes slightly too far apart, small nose, lips thin and pale. When she looked closely at Tohma, stomping along beside them, she realised he was from the same stock. He glanced at her and smiled in surprise to find her watching him.

A few of the men greeted him, and before long he split off to join a group of Cahlven soldiers huddled in a doorway. Wrench waved him off and indicated that they should continue on.

Georgianna rolled her shoulders back. Without the electricity to overwhelm it, the burning had returned. She peeled the shirt from her skin and held it out.

"We'll get something for it," Keiran said as he fell in to walk beside her.

Wrench looked over and raised an eyebrow.

"Nsiloq," said Keiran, answering the silent question. "Maarqyn's idea."

Georgianna didn't look up. She didn't want to see the pity in Wrench's eyes. She didn't think she'd be able to hear apologies from him or anyone without feeling like a liar. Edtroka had given his life. She didn't deserve any apologies.

Wrench guided them to a small house on the corner of two slim roads. The door was already open and the smell of cooking meat wafted down the corridor, but he didn't go in.

Instead, he dumped his bag next to the wall and stretched his arms over his head. Georgianna lowered herself to the ground and leaned over her knees.

"Welcome back, Mr. Zanetti, Miss Lennox."

Olless looked as though she thought it were a perfectly normal day. There was a small smile on her lips as she came closer. She patted Keiran on the shoulder but even as Georgianna stared at her, Olless didn't so much as glance in her direction. Silence stretched out.

"The troops are on the way back," she said, even though nobody had asked.

Dhiren hovered behind Olless. He tipped his head back, his face up to the rain. His cheeks were already pink and Georgianna wondered whether his eyes would be reddened, too. She stared back at the ground. She wasn't about to ask him if he was alright. He wasn't. None of them were.

The soldiers arrived, in dribs and drabs. Some strode in with the confidence of conquerors, while others hung their heads and trudged through in silence. When Alec appeared, flanked by Cahlven soldiers, he marched straight towards them, and Georgianna could see him checking each face. There was no joy in him. He had a rifle slung over his shoulder, longer and more formidable than any she had ever seen. He carefully propped it against the wall of the house, but as he turned and Olless stepped forwards to greet him, he moved straight past her, going instead to Dhiren, placing a hand on his arm.

"They took his body," Alec said, gently. "We tried, but it was too late."

Dhiren blinked and looked at him with bloodshot eyes.

"And her?" he asked. "Is she dead?"

"I don't know. We were pushed from the square pretty quickly. I had to follow to give cover."

Dhiren gazed at nothing, his eyes out of focus and his expression slack. He nodded and, without a word, turned and walked away.

"What are our numbers?" Olless asked, impatiently. Alec stared at the space Dhiren had left vacant and raked his short nails against his leg.

"You'd need to speak to Beck about that," he said. "They separated to pincer the Adveni troops in the square. I couldn't see the full assault."

Olless huffed and glared at each of them as if her ignorance was their fault. When she reached Georgianna, she sneered and turned away with barely a glance.

"I need to make the report. Send Casey to me the moment he returns."

"Will do, *boss*," Alec said with a disdain Georgianna thought he reserved for only Adveni and Keiran.

Once Olless had left them, Alec shuffled his feet. His gaze flickered and flitted, finding insignificant patches of wall.

"I'm glad you're alright, Zanetti," he said, finally, without looking at Keiran.

Keiran shifted his weight as he, like Alec, looked anywhere but at the person he was addressing.

"Thanks," he muttered. "For helping get us out."

Alec nodded. When he finally looked at Georgianna, his gaze softened and he moved closer, with slow, cautious steps. He crouched in front of her and rested his hand on her knee. Georgianna gave it a squeeze. Tears crept into her eyes and her throat tightened. With the smallest smile, he returned the squeeze and pushed back up to his feet.

"Wrench!" The flash of dark curly hair caught Georgianna by surprise. Jacob rushed forwards, his face red from exertion. "Are you alright?"

Wrench beamed and grabbed Jacob by the arm, tugging him forwards into a hug. Georgianna braced herself for Jacob to freeze at the sudden embrace, but Jacob returned the hug, grinning as Wrench ruffled dark fingers through his hair.

"I'm good, Jake," Wrench said. "Not a scratch. Told you."

Jacob pulled back and breathed in deeply. He nodded and wiped his palms on the backs of his trousers. Only then did he notice Georgianna and Keiran. The smile disappeared, replaced with a stern look of concentration.

"We should get something on those," he said.

Georgianna had never seen Jacob as anything other than shy and reserved. Even when he did speak, he usually blushed and quickly looked away. The young man before her seemed completely different, spurred into action. She didn't want to think about what could have happened while they were away that would put that sort of urgency in him.

"Can you see to George first?" Keiran asked.

"Of course."

Jacob studied Georgianna. She'd seen that look many times before, mostly on Jaid and Keinah when they were assessing a patient to see which injury needed the most urgent attention. Georgianna touched her hand to the top of her shoulder. Keiran nodded to her.

"Can we go somewhere private?" she asked.

Jacob pointed down the road.

"There's a house. It's not far."

Keiran grasped Georgianna's hand and helped her to her feet. She closed her eyes, head spinning at the sudden movement. Keiran kissed her on the cheek and she followed Jacob down the road.

He led her into a tiny shack. The old furniture had been pushed against the wall, replaced with boxes and bags of supplies. Jacob closed the door without needing to be asked. Georgianna drew her shirt up over her head. She clutched it to her chest and gave a small smile as a bright blush rose on Jacob's cheeks.

"Sorry," she murmured.

He shook his head as if the action hadn't bothered him, but with his cheeks, ears, and neck all now a rather impressive shade of red, she quickly turned away and swept her hair over her shoulder to reveal the mark on her skin.

"Oh."

Jacob's voice was barely a whisper. He stepped closer, sweeping the tip of his finger around the edge of the mark. He dragged one of the boxes further from the others and patted the top. Turning to one of the bags, he opened it and dug through it. Georgianna took her seat and watched.

"My side, too."

"There's another?"

He leaned around her and Georgianna shook her head.

"Bullet. We were running. It's just a graze."

"Alright, I'll get that next."

Jacob began searching through one of the boxes for supplies. He drew out a couple of linen bags and laid them on the floor next to her seat.

"Where's Lacie?" she asked.

"She stayed back. Beck wouldn't allow her to the front, said it was too dangerous. A family took her in under the shield."

The leaves he pulled out were bright mint-green. He grabbed a cantina of water and held it out for her. Clutching the shirt against her chest with one hand, Georgianna wedged the cantina between her knees and unscrewed the lid. The water inside was warm and stale but she gulped it down as fast as she could pour. It dribbled from the corner of her mouth and dripped onto her skin. Jacob took out a metal tin and moved behind her.

The first time he touched the mark, she yelped and almost dropped the water. He had smeared a cool balm onto his fingers, but the contact sent a searing pain down to her bones.

"Sorry," he murmured.

"No. No, it's fine."

He rubbed more balm onto the mark and each flare of pain was replaced with cold relief. She took another gulp of tepid water and dried her chin on the shirt.

"I would have thought you'd stay with Lacie," she said as he laid one of the large hyliha leaves over the wound.

He gathered a couple of strips of material and frowned. Twisting it around his fingers, he pulled so tight that the tips turned pink.

"I wanted to help."

He returned to his position behind and urged her to lift her arm to the side so that he could slide the material beneath. He wrapped it tightly over the wound, drawing another hiss from her. This time, he didn't apologise.

"I didn't want to be useless. I've been useless for too long."

Georgianna turned so fast that he jumped and dropped the second strip. The blush on his cheeks deepened as he picked it up.

"You were never useless, Jacob. After everything you went through, you... You are so strong. No one should make you feel useless."

His smile was timid and embarrassed. He gave a small shrug and urged her to turn back around so that he could place the second strip.

"I guess you have the same mark," he said quietly. "That means you're strong, too."

Georgianna didn't feel strong. She wrung her hands together and stared at the ground.

"Jacob," she whispered.

"Yeah?"

"What is it? The mark? Keiran didn't tell me."

He paused, examining the strip of material. She looked over her shoulder and saw he was frowning at it.

"Jacob?"

"It's a bird. It's abstract, but I'm pretty sure that's what it is."

"A bird?" she breathed.

"Yeah," he said, finally meeting her gaze. "In a cage."

Georgianna couldn't bring herself to say anything as he tied the strip in place, knotting it around the top of her shoulder. While the mark stung her skin, it was nothing compared to the scars the Adveni had left on her life. It wasn't what they had given that would haunt her, it was what they had taken away: the people. Her mother, lost to a senseless fight in the Oprust district.

RACK AND RUIN

Her father, brother, and nephew, devoured by the Mykahnol at Nyvalau. And Edtroka. Even the thought of his name made the hole in her stomach bigger.

She was being patched up and yet it felt more like being pulled apart from the inside out.

No matter what Jacob Stone said, she didn't feel strong. She didn't feel useful or worthy.

She felt nothing.

23 A New Plan

When Georgianna awoke, she found Keiran's arms wrapped around her waist, his hands pressed against the small of her back. His lips rested on her forehead and his breath fluttered through her hair. She wriggled in his grasp and he pulled back. His eyes were wide and alert.

"Hey," he said.

"Is it morning?"

He nodded. Georgianna pushed herself up to a sitting position, massaging her face. Keiran propped himself on his elbows and watched.

She had been alone when she finally fell asleep. Alec had brought her a bowl of stew and shown her a place to rest. He'd told her that Beck had arrived back safely but that they'd lost a lot of men in the assault. When Georgianna had asked if they'd come to the square because they'd known Maarqyn planned to execute them, Alec fell silent. Georgianna knew the answer was yes, and that only made her feel worse. She couldn't imagine Olless would have been happy about such a plan, since the Cahlven emissary had made it clear she held Georgianna in low regard. She wasn't happy about it herself. How many lives now hung over her head? A dozen? A hundred? She'd thanked Alec and retreated, leaving the stew steaming in the bowl.

Hunching over, Georgianna pressed her forehead to her knees, feeling the pull of the Nsiloq in her skin. It felt less uncomfortable than the day before, but she was still all too aware of its presence. The space behind her temples throbbed painfully and she pressed her fingertips against her head, rubbing in circles.

"How are you feeling?" Keiran asked.

"Like I wish people would stop asking."

Keiran stayed silent, and when she turned to him he was staring at the wall.

"I'm sorry. I don't mean, I just—"

"It's alright."

"No, it's not. Honestly, I don't know how I feel. Or... or I don't want to know."

He wouldn't understand if she told him the truth—that she wished they had never entered the square. He had been suffering, too, and she certainly didn't want that. But she couldn't weigh her individual life against all the others. Any relief she felt at having survived was soon eaten away by guilt and anger.

Alec appeared at the doorway. Georgianna welcomed the interruption and got to her feet, brushing off her sides.

"Olless wants to see you both," he said. "How are you feeling?"

Keiran touched her back as he passed her.

"Better, thanks," he answered for them both. "Alec, thank you for yesterday."

Alec's smile was small and uncertain. He clapped Keiran awkwardly on the shoulder.

"You got me away from Maarqyn," he said. "Figured I should help you do the same. Don't want to owe you anything."

Keiran laughed, though it didn't sound entirely honest. He strode from the room and out into the fresh air. Alec stopped Georgianna when she moved to follow.

"George?"

"I'm fine, Alec," she said without waiting for the question. If she allowed herself to directly face the question, she knew she wouldn't be able to lie.

The morning light had been washed away by a new onslaught of rain which slapped against her face in hard pellets, soaking through her clothes in seconds. But it was cold and it felt good.

They found Olless in one of the houses beneath the Cahlven shield on the outskirts of the camps. Like in the building where Jacob had patched her up, most of the furniture had been shoved against the walls to make way for supplies. A large table had been set up as the kitchen centrepiece and covered with papers, diagrams and maps. Notes spread over every inch of the papers.

"Good! You're here," Olless said without looking up. She turned some papers over and shuffled others into piles before she looked up. "I need to know what happened after you were taken."

Keiran dragged a chair from the corner and slumped down into it.

"We were kept in a cell, tortured, almost killed."

Georgianna remained in the doorway. The further she could stay from Olless, the better.

"What did they want with you?"

There was no delicacy to her words, no concern that the question might upset them, or that revisiting their capture might be painful. Olless looked between them, calculated and unsympathetic.

"They wanted to know what you were up to."

"What did you tell them?"

Keiran's gaze flickered briefly to Georgianna before he straightened in his seat.

"We told them that the Colvohan was coming, and about Edtroka's plans with the Mykahnol," he said, unabashed.

"*I* told them," Georgianna corrected him. "Keiran didn't say anything. I told them the plans."

As hard as she tried, she couldn't read the look Olless gave her. Maybe she was tired, or perhaps she had been expecting it, but her expression was blank as she returned Georgianna's gaze.

"It's of no matter," she said. "The first of the troops arrived after you left the encampment in the north. The Colvohan returned from Nyvalau in the night."

"And the Mykahnol? What's the plan there?"

"There isn't one. The inability to coordinate a full evacuation of Adlai now makes the point moot. We are certain that they will not try to detonate."

Keiran moved forwards in his chair and rested his elbows on his knees.

"So, what *is* the plan?"

"With the Colvohan now on Os-Veruh, we are waiting for confirmation that the Volsonnar will still meet to discuss terms."

"What?"

Georgianna stepped closer to the table. This was impossible. There had to have been a mistake. Perhaps it was organised before the assault. There could be no way the Cahlven would agree to a meeting after the Adveni's actions.

"You're still considering terms with these… monsters?"

Olless' lavender eyes were cool and impassive.

"Of course."

"They shot Edtroka in the head!" Georgianna cried. "His own father gave a nod and that was it."

Rounding the table, Olless lifted her chin and looked down her thin nose.

"This is bigger than one man, Miss Lennox," she said, emphasising each word. "We could save thousands of lives with these talks."

"Thousands of lives you wouldn't have known about if it weren't for Edtroka!"

She couldn't look at her. She wouldn't. Spinning on her heel, Georgianna marched back to the doorway.

"Miss Lennox, we are not finished!" Olless said. "Perhaps Grystch allowed you insolence under his ownership, but I will not allow it here."

The growl that grew from Georgianna was feral and filled with fury. She wanted something to throw at Olless. More than anything, she wanted to hurt the woman. She wanted to hurt her almost as much as she wanted to hurt Ehnisque.

"I don't take orders from the Cahlven. You elected leaders for the Veniche. I will talk to them."

She didn't turn back from the door. She didn't dare. If she looked at Olless, Georgianna feared she might try to punch her, or perhaps claw out those pretty eyes; anything to transfer a fraction of the pain crushing her from the inside.

"Keiran, talk to her!"

The chair scraped against the floor as he got to his feet.

"Which of the elected Veniche leaders will be at this meeting with the Volsonnar and the Colvohan?" he asked.

Georgianna glanced at Keiran over her shoulder. His expression remained calm, but she had known him long enough to sense when anger was bubbling under the surface. Olless spluttered, and retreated to the other side of the table. Keiran scoffed.

"Exactly!"

He didn't wait. He strode to Georgianna's side and took her hand, leading her from the kitchen and back out into the rain.

24   Bitter Medicine

Olless didn't bother them again. When Keiran went to find Beck, Georgianna set off in search of Jacob. Troops were now regularly scouting different areas of the city, and many were returning with injuries. After being shown where most of the medical supplies were kept, Georgianna joined the Veniche and Cahlven to help out. Keeping busy allowed her to focus on something other than the events of the last week; but every time she saw a head of dark hair she did a double-take, thinking that it might be Edtroka or her brother.

    Most of the Cahlven troops who returned didn't know Georgianna, and treated her with the standard respect they gave the other medics. A few looked at her in curiosity and a vague sense of recognition. Maybe she had been pointed out by a soldier who had been in the square, or they had seen her tethered to the execution post. She didn't know and didn't ask. Luckily, neither did they.

Alec returned from another scouting trip late in the afternoon. One of the Cahlven medics became free before Georgianna did, but Alec waved him off and waited until she had finished splinting a man's broken fingers before he took a seat on the box in front of her.

"How did you do this?" she asked as he lifted his shirt to reveal a large scrape down his side. He gave her an embarrassed smile.

"I slipped down a flight of stairs," he said.

Georgianna just about held back a snort of laughter. She rolled her eyes and gathered up a salve that Jacob had told her was good for superficial wounds. The stories the young man had told her about the Cahlven medicines were astounding. With each new patient, each new injury, he was gaining confidence. She wondered whether this bubbly young man was in fact the 'real' Jacob, the one he'd been before he was taken.

Scooping up three fingers of the salve, she smeared it liberally over the raw flesh. Alec watched her cautiously.

"Are you okay?" he asked.

She scooped more salve onto her fingers, focussing all her concentration into making sure she covered every inch of the wound.

"George, talk to me."

"There's nothing to say."

The grasp on her chin as he tilted her head back was gentle, but Georgianna wrenched away from him just the same. A flash before her eyes: the memory of Maarqyn's holding her and making her watch Keiran's pain. She turned away, rubbing her arm across her eyes.

"I heard you have a mark now," he said, dropping his hands back into his lap.

Georgianna gave a bitter laugh as she returned to applying the salve.

"Am I camp gossip?"

Alec sighed and took hold of her hand, pulling it away from the treatment.

"George, please. I know what Maarqyn is like. Talk to me."

She pushed herself up and tugged her hand from his grasp. Smearing the last of the salve across the burns on her wrist, she put the metal tin back into its box.

"I told you, there's nothing to say."

Alec made a great show of tugging his shirt down and straightening it against his body. He squeezed his hands in his lap.

"I'm not leaving until you talk to me."

There had been a time when that sort of statement wouldn't have surprised her. She would have rolled her eyes and told him that he didn't want to hear what she had to say, because he'd only get angry when she disagreed with him. She remembered that time so well and yet it felt like a different life, back when they would have been having this conversation down in the tunnels; when they would have been discussing whether or not she should be going into the Compound to help the prisoners. He always thought it was too dangerous, that she should be staying out of the rebellion efforts. She would have tried to distract him with a kiss, or would have changed the subject.

There was none of that now. That time was gone. Those people were gone. Georgianna rubbed her hands on her trousers and stared past him.

"Maarqyn told me they saw my family."

"What?"

"They passed a checkpoint," she said, fighting to keep her breathing steady.

"Are they okay?"

"I don't know. He wouldn't tell me."

"I'm sor—"

"Don't."

Turning away from him, Georgianna rearranged the contents of the box, lining up the tins and tidying the linen bags. Alec touched the side of her arm and she jerked away from him.

"You let him go into that square," she said. "You knew what would happen and you—"

"You would have been killed," he said.

"You paid for my life with his."

"What was I supposed to do, George? Let you die?"

"YES!" The word was out of her mouth before she had time to think about it. But even as she saw the flush of anger in Alec's face, she didn't take it back. He stared down at his feet.

"Do you really think I could have stopped him?" he said. "Edtroka was ready to hand himself over before your life was on the line."

"Like you even tried! You never cared about him. You just wanted your petty revenge on the Adveni for what Maarqyn did to you."

"Petty?"

He stepped back, his face red. Georgianna folded her arms. He had wanted her to talk and he was going to get his wish. He could have left her alone, but he'd had to push it. He'd had to demand answers she hadn't been ready to give.

"You think two years of torture is petty?"

"Edtroka didn't do that to you. If you wanted revenge, you should have gone after Maarqyn."

"What do you think I was doing?"

"You should have shot faster!" Her voice was on the verge of breaking. "You let him die! If you'd just…"

Alec's anger deflated as Georgianna gasped for air. Her hands couldn't brush away the tears of fury and frustration. They were flowing faster than she could control them, as the hollow in her stomach consumed her. Chest heaving, she gasped desperately for air.

"He would be here. He should be here. He saved me and I couldn't… I couldn't help him. I couldn't save them. I sent them away to save them from this and they still…"

Alec reached for her but she jumped away. She couldn't. Not now and not to him.

"They're gone!" she said with a sob.

Georgianna launched herself past him. She pulled her coat tight around her body, trying to hold the broken pieces together. Lunging into a run as soon as she was through the door, she splashed through the rain to the only place she could think of.

25 Army of Two

Georgianna didn't stop running until she was standing in the doorway of her family home. Breathing hard, exertion having fought off the tears for now, she leaned against the wall and gazed down the hallway. Every door but one was open. It looked like nobody had been here since Ehnisque sent the soldiers in to search. She moved slowly through the house, but everything familiar just made her want to scream. Why had she even come here?

Her bag still stood against the wall in the corridor, Braedon's stuffed toy sticking out of it. She tugged it free and clutched it to her chest. It wasn't surprising that the others hadn't returned to take her bag, even though there was medicine and food inside. It was just too dangerous to return to the house with Ehnisque's suspecting they were somewhere within the city.

The door to her brother's room was closed, though she couldn't imagine the soldiers would have left the room unsearched. She placed each step gently, creeping towards the door. Pushing it open, she let out a growl as a fresh anger flared up inside her. There was a man curled up on the ripped mattress.

She knew she shouldn't be angry. People had been displaced from their own homes by the Cahlven troops and it wasn't surprising that they'd taken shelter in the empty buildings. But to find someone on the bed her brother had once slept in, curled up with no mind to the fact its owner was now gone, made her blood boil.

She opened her mouth to yell, to scream and tell the man to get out. But before she could make a sound, he rolled over and looked up at her. It was Dhiren.

"What are you doing here?"

He pushed himself up and shifted along the mattress, leaning against the wall. His eyes were bloodshot and a crust of sleep clung to his eyelashes. He looked away from her and brushed a thumb across one eye.

"Nothing."

Georgianna chewed on the inside of her lip and brushed her fingers against the toy's back. Kicking off her boots, she padded across the room and sat down on the mattress next to Dhiren. He shifted along the wall to make room.

"Don't ask if I'm alright," he murmured.

"Only if you don't."

"Deal."

Pulling the toy to her chest, Georgianna picked at the rip in the mattress. She didn't know what to say without asking how he was doing. She wanted to say that she was sorry but it sounded hollow, even in her head. She had seen Dhiren cheerful, bawdy and cheeky. She had seen him so viciously angry that she feared him. She had even seen him restrain his anger into bitter obedience. But she had never seen him sad.

"Dhiren," she said.

"What?"

"You and Edtroka…"

It was an issue that had been burning in her head for a while, though she'd never considered pulling it from the flames. It was the little things, the big things, and everything in between. Was it Edtroka's fear or his desperate pleas to Dhiren in the cell, like he was the only one he could truly count on? Or had it been the anger with which Dhiren defended Edtroka's intentions in the forest? Had it been the way Edtroka mocked Dhiren about his skill, or the way Dhiren teased Edtroka about her? When Dhiren had asked how many people they were catering for, as they were organising supplies for a back-up plan, Georgianna wondered whether it had been out of logistics, or just plain jealousy.

"He wasn't just a friend, was he?"

Dhiren became intensely interested in the state of his hands. He turned them over and stared at the palms. There were scars there, old ones and new. Laying her hand over his, she leaned in closer. He didn't flinch or pull away. He simply stared, his eyes blank.

"You don't have to tell me," she said.

Enclosing her hand in his, he turned it over and traced the creases in her palm. His fingers were delicate as they peeled back her sleeve, revealing the blistering skin around her wrist. She wanted to ask if he was stalling to give him a chance to invent an explanation, or if the pause was his way of saying he didn't want to tell her. She held her tongue, letting Dhiren brush the unblistered edges of the raw skin.

His cheek twitched into an almost-smile and he dropped their hands back into his lap.

"I gave him so much shit about letting me rot in that compound," he said, his lip giving the slightest tremble. "I knew he saved me from a collar but I was so angry with him. He promised me and I'd trusted him."

Tears dripped off her chin and onto her shirt. Maybe it was as much of an answer as he was willing to give, this quiet regret. She licked a salty drop from where it hovered at the bow of her lips.

"There was a time I thought he liked me," she said. "He was always so flirty. He teased me even before I knew him properly. I'd been so scared of him and he—"

"And he was a charming bastard," Dhiren said, laughing. "Cocky as sin."

"He was. He mocked me once about running whenever he called."

Dhiren sniffed and took the rag doll from her hands. He examined it, smiling fondly. He'd told her once that he'd been a loner before he was put in the compound, that he'd never really been a tribe person. Had he ever had a toy like this? Something he treasured even though it was old and tattered? Had he ever been close to anyone before Edtroka befriended him?

"I almost denied him when he asked me to protect you in the block. It meant he cared about you. That he'd ask me—*me*—to be the one..." His voice cracked as he tried to force out a laugh. "It wasn't all a lie. He cared about you, George."

Was it resentment in his voice, or just sadness and pain? Georgianna moved to lean her head on his shoulder, but he stiffened and froze, and she sat forwards again.

• *208* •

"I don't know what to do now," she said.

"What do you mean?"

"My family is gone, Edtroka's gone. I wanted to help and I'm just making everything worse."

Dhiren pouted and held the doll out for her to take. She crushed it to her chest and drew up her knees. Dragging his finger across the mattress between them, he nodded absently.

"I'll leave," he said. "Once this is done."

"This?"

"Once I know Ehnisque is dead."

Georgianna looked at him over her shoulder. He had rested his head back against the wall and closed his eyes. She didn't know that revenge could make someone so content. She'd been hard on Alec about it, but there was a finality she couldn't place—about the idea of looking down at Ehnisque's body, at Maarqyn's. Maybe she didn't need to see out the war; she just needed to finish her own battles, *their* battles.

"You'll go back to living alone?"

"Well, it wasn't like I ever had a tribe."

She smiled weakly and shrugged, though he didn't see it.

"We could be a tribe," she said quietly. "However dysfunctional."

He cracked one eye open and peered at her. Behind his lowered lid, he rolled his eye and shook his head.

"You're a simpering idiot," he said. "But if a tribe is what you want, I suppose I can't stop you."

Georgianna shook her head and gave him the most self-assured smile she could muster.

"No. You can't. You saved my life."

"It wasn't intentional."

Turning to face him, Georgianna plucked his hand from his lap and pushed the doll into his grasp.

"Edtroka asked you to protect me," she said. "And I know he'd want me to protect you, whether you like it or not."

26 TAKING SIDES

Dhiren patted the small of her back as he scooted across the mattress. Georgianna wriggled her shirt back down her body and knelt once she was covered again. She'd not meant to stay overnight in the house, and Keiran was probably worried that she hadn't returned. But it had been nice to sit in the gathering dark with Dhiren. He didn't ask her to talk about how she felt, nor pester her for information. It was quiet and comforting, and when she fell asleep next to him, he covered her in a blanket and lay beside her through the night.

Gathering up the items from her medic bag, she made sure each lid was on securely and nothing had been spilled before putting everything away. There were still a few food packets down near the bottom. She took one for herself and tossed another over to Dhiren. They sat on the doorstep and ate in silence, scooping up the sandy mixture with their fingers.

Georgianna scraped the food off the roof of her mouth with her tongue, making a face. It wasn't particularly pleasant to eat, but Edtroka had said it was designed specifically to deliver nutrients to the body. Dhiren ate his without complaint and nudged her in the ribs, nodding down the road. Beck was walking towards them, flanked by Keiran and Alec.

"Can still make a run for it," Dhiren said under his breath. "I already know I can get over that back fence."

She chuckled into her food and met his gaze. The red rims had gone from his eyes and he looked a little better than he had the day before. She doubted it was the food that made him appear less hollow. He put on a mocking smile, continuing the transformation back to his former self.

"Dhiren, Gianna," Beck said warily as he came closer. "How are you both?"

There was the question again; the one she didn't want to answer. She didn't know how to. Her companion didn't seem inclined to say anything, either, although Dhiren didn't know Beck very well, after all. She knew that the best way to ensure the question wouldn't come up again was to answer and get it over with. She lifted her head.

"We're fine," she said, trying to sound reassuring, or at least not like she was being pulled in three directions at once. "How've you been?"

Alec and Keiran both looked out of place standing in front of her house, shuffling their feet and looking like they would rather be anywhere else. She wondered if Beck had asked them to come, or if they'd been looking for her.

"Needed a break," Beck said. "If you don't mind. My home is rather—"

"Burned beyond recognition?" Dhiren offered. "In enemy territory?"

Beck's eyes narrowed but he didn't comment on Dhiren's bluntness. Georgianna used the doorframe to pull herself to her feet and stepped out of the way.

"Well, the furniture is either broken or gone, but go ahead."

He nodded his thanks and almost touched her shoulder, before thinking better of it. He slid past into the kitchen, brushing his hand along the corridor wall. Alec passed Georgianna without a word, and Keiran only paused to place a soft kiss against her temple before following.

"Have we been kicked out of your house?" Dhiren asked. "Or are we supposed to go in there?"

She rolled her eyes, reached out for his hand, and pulled him to his feet. Dhiren took a fleeting look down the road towards the outskirts of the camps—and his potential escape—and trudged through the house after her.

Keiran had already made himself comfortable on the floor, leaning against the far wall. He had placed a bag on his lap and dug out a large canister. The moment he opened it, the smell of warm stew wafted out into the air. Georgianna's stomach grumbled and she quickly moved in to sit at his side.

"Did we miss something?" Dhiren asked. He leaned against the doorframe, tapping his foot.

"The Colvohan went to meet with the Volsonnar," Alec said.

The frown that pulled at Beck's face was enough to answer her question, but she asked it, anyway.

"And no Veniche were asked to go?"

"Of course not," he said. "Since Edtroka left, they have dropped all pretence of actually caring for our opinion."

Keiran filled the silence by drawing a collection of mismatching bowls from his bag and pouring stew into each one with a series of satisfying sploshes. Alec collected them and handed them round. Dhiren looked thrilled and put the packet of Adveni-made 'food' aside.

"Do we know what came of the meeting?" he asked, dunking his thumb into the stew. He sucked the juice noisily from his skin, grinning around the flesh.

Beck settled himself on the floor with the bowl in his lap, twirling a spoon absently in his fingers. Alec took a seat next to him.

"The Volsonnar claims the Adveni have been holding back," said Beck, bitterly. "They've given the Cahlven the opportunity to retreat, or they will mass for war."

"So much for good and friendly terms for peace," said Dhiren.

"Like we've not been at war, already," Alec said. "Nyvalau was just an accident, right?"

Georgianna didn't miss the dark look that Beck threw in her direction. At any moment he would ask another question she didn't want to answer, or he would offer condolences she couldn't accept. She was only just holding it together and she knew she wouldn't be able to continue if Beck forced the issue. But he stayed silent, turning his attention back to his stew.

"What about Maarqyn?" Keiran asked. "Do we know if he survived the attack in the square?"

"And Ehnisque?" Dhiren added. "Did the Volsonnar say what happened to his precious daughter, after murdering his son?"

Beck nodded.

"They both lived. Minor injuries. From Olless' report, he was quite smug about the lack of Adveni casualties so far."

"Yeah, because they have us to use as collateral damage," Alec said, stabbing his spoon viciously into his bowl. "The Cahlven send us in to fight for them, saying it's because we know the land. They don't lose any of their own, and the Adveni obviously don't care if they kill us all off."

Dhiren paced slowly around the room, staring out of the window. He stepped over Keiran's and Georgianna's legs and pushed the door open. He lingered, placing the empty bowl on the floor and rubbing his thumb over his bottom lip.

"Dhiren?" said Georgianna. "What are you thinking?"

He didn't turn away from the door or even acknowledge her question. He ran his fingers through his hair and tapped his foot against the wet ground just outside the door.

"Adveni casualties don't matter," he said. "And it doesn't matter whether they say they're going to go to war."

"How can you say that?" Alec asked. "If they think this hasn't been war so far, what are they going to do once it is?"

"I'm not sure I see your logic," Beck added.

There was a small smile on Dhiren's lips when he turned away from the doorway. He took his time in taking a seat, smearing his thumb through the remnants of stew in his bowl.

"*We* are what matters," he said, jabbing his dripping thumb at each of them. "The Veniche. Both sides assume that we're siding with the Cahlven. They assume that we can't cope alone, and so we need to hide behind one or the other. Obviously, we wouldn't ally with the Adveni."

"Well, they'd be right, wouldn't they?" Georgianna said. "We don't have the technology or the training to go it alone."

Beck frowned and placed his bowl aside.

"We have the land. It's been ours for generations. We know it better. We have numbers who will protect it."

Dhiren's thumb made a popping sound as his pulled it from between his lips and pointed it at Beck. There was a smirk of triumph on his face.

"That is exactly how we have to stop thinking!"

"You've lost me," Alec said.

"Me, too," Georgianna agreed.

Keiran slid his arm around Georgianna's waist and pulled her closer. He'd been unusually quiet since they arrived. But, as she was about to ask if he had any thoughts himself, she realised it actually wasn't strange for him to remain quiet in these discussions. She looked up to find him staring absently at the ceiling.

"Do you think the Adveni care if they damage this land?" Dhiren continued.

"They've already proven they'll do that," Beck said.

"Exactly. But what about the Cahlven?"

Alec raised an eyebrow but didn't answer. Beck seemed to be waiting for Dhiren to continue, and he did.

"The Cahlven care about this land about as much as the Adveni. They have back-ups if things get too bad. They have ships they can run away on. We are the only ones who don't have somewhere to retreat to."

Confused, Beck rubbed his hands over his face. He looked older.

"I'm still not following why this means we have to stop thinking of this as our land."

"Because, while we're thinking about defending our land, we're not thinking about doing absolutely everything we can to destroy the Adveni. And the Cahlven too, if necessary."

They let Dhiren's words settle in. Georgianna had to admit that she was still confused. How were they supposed to destroy the Adveni if they didn't have the weapons or the expertise? From the way they were talking, they didn't even have the Cahlven behind them. They would be alone.

"We need to fight dirty," Dhiren said, when none of them answered. "Show them we're willing to destroy as much as they are."

"If it's destruction you want," Keiran said slowly, finally looking around at them, "I think I might have an idea."

27 From the Start

The plan was questionable, at best. They all understood the merits of what Dhiren intended and what Keiran had proposed, but actually going through with it was more than any of them had ever imagined. They'd spent the last ten years trying to protect their lands from the Adveni.

They'd stayed in the kitchen late into the day, arguing and later compromising on the finer details, but in the end, even Beck was agreed that it was what had to be done.

It turned out that Edtroka had taught Dhiren and Keiran far better than any of them had ever realised. She could hear his skilful diplomacy in the way Dhiren turned them all round to his way of thinking. She could see his tactics in Keiran's insistence that they all keep their roles private; so, should one of them be questioned, he or she could only reveal a small part of the picture. And while they wanted to keep the numbers small to protect themselves, it was this sense of Edtroka's influence that helped her convince the others that they needed a few more people on board.

From Beck's conversation with Olless, they knew that the Volsonnar had given the Colvohan one week to comply with the retreat orders, before the Adveni intended to escalate the war. With a day and a half already gone, Georgianna set off through the camps to a house she had been directed to by Alec.

She had closed every door to her family house after the others had left. They would be back soon enough, and her home was out of the way. They could meet there without fear of being overheard. But that didn't make her any less dubious about returning. If she was going to be an active member of this plan, she knew that she would have to ignore the hollow space in her stomach. She had to focus, even though everything in that house brought her emotions painfully to the surface.

The building Alec had marked was quiet and seemingly empty. The front door stood open and the inside was dark. Cahlven soldiers passed back and forth in the street but they paid no attention to the blonde Veniche hovering awkwardly on the doorstep. She could ask one of them, she supposed. Wrench was cheerful and friendly and she didn't doubt that he'd gotten to know some of the other soldiers.

Georgianna hit the ground as the crack of a gun rang through the air. When she lifted her head to see where the shot had come from, she found nothing. A few of the soldiers were looking around in surprise and curiosity. They didn't seem to know where the sound had come from any better than she did. Realising that she wasn't at risk of being hit, and that training shooters was probably commonplace for them, Georgianna rose to her feet, a deep blush creeping up her cheeks as she noticed some of the soldiers smirking at her.

Desperate to get away from their mocking smiles, she slipped into the house and hurried along the entrance corridor. Even if she only came out the other side and continued from there, she would escape those looks.

As she emerged into the room at the back of the house, she heard laughing from outside the building. She held tight to the strap of her bag and opened the back door. The sound of the gunshot suddenly made sense, as she saw the rifle. But the reason behind it was still unclear, as the shooter turned around and brushed his dark curly hair from his eyes.

Jacob grinned down at someone she couldn't see and then looked up at her, his smile fading to polite surprise.

"George," he said. "Hi."

Georgianna pushed the door further and stepped out to find Wrench sitting against the wall, a weapon of his own across his lap. He looked up at her with a bright smile.

"Alright there, George?"

"I'm okay," she said, glancing between the two of them. "What are you doing?"

Jacob looked away and fiddled with the rifle in his hands. He rested the butt on the ground and grasped the barrel, rocking it back and forth.

"Kid here wanted to learn to shoot," Wrench said, as if it were the most natural thing in the world.

She looked away from them, at the holes Jacob had put in the fence. Wrench had drawn a wobbly target onto the wood and so far the young herber had only hit it once. She wanted to be angry with Wrench and tell him that it was inappropriate. Jacob had suffered enough, already.

He shouldn't be taught to shoot, so he could go off and kill people alongside the rest of the soldiers.

But the anger that bubbled up inside of her wasn't directed at either of the men in the garden. Jacob was still young, but he had seen more than most men of his age. He deserved to be able to protect himself, and knowing how he had considered himself useless, she wasn't about to take that away from him.

Her fury was reserved for the Adveni and what they had forced this young innocent to do in order to survive. Any questions she'd still held about the plan vanished in an instant. The Adveni deserved to pay for every ounce of pain they had given to the Veniche. They should have to pay for Jacob's torture and the loss of her own family. They needed to be held accountable for the destruction of a way of life, and the murder of thousands of innocent people. They deserved to pay for all of it.

Georgianna hovered in the doorway and dumped her bag down next to her, crossing her arms over her chest.

"Wrench, are you on good terms with that tech?" she asked. "The Cahlven?"

"You mean Tohma?"

"Yeah."

"Good enough," he said, nodding and scratching the back of his head. "He's been teaching me about some of their gear whilst I show him Adveni stuff. I mean, he knows most of it already but he likes seeing how I approach it."

Georgianna nodded absently. They were both watching her as she chewed on her thumbnail and gazed at the holes in the wood.

"You actually want something, George, or you just worried about my social life?"

She didn't feel particularly amused but chuckled just the same.

"I need some information on the Cahlven ship shields and I was wondering if you'd be able to introduce me. I don't think I made the best impression when we met before."

"He's a good guy. He knew you were upset."

"Why do you need to know about the shields?" Jacob asked. "It's not like we can fly the ships. From what Tohma has said, they're coded to react to certain individuals. Not to mention the language problem."

"He's right. There are biological controls on those things," Wrench said. "Something about voice and eye checks. It's a safeguard against tampering."

That would be a problem, especially since the whole point of the plan was to prove to the Adveni that they were willing to fight while also letting the Cahlven know they wouldn't just sit back and be walked over. If they needed a Cahlven soldier to work the ship, it didn't really speak to their independence. But she wasn't about to let the whole idea go up in smoke simply because they had to ask a favour.

"Well, maybe I can convince him into joining," she said. "It's only one person."

"George, what's going on?" Wrench asked.

"Just an idea. Dhiren and Keiran want to hurt the Adveni without getting the Cahlven involved. Well, certainly not the Colvohan."

"What do you plan on doing?"

Jacob came closer and rested his rifle against the wall. He brushed his hair back from his face and looked up at her with curious excitement. She couldn't send Jacob away so that she could tell Wrench and still keep Jacob in the dark. He'd been trying to prove his use. She had been the one to tell him he was important, and she couldn't go back on that.

"We're going to do what the Adveni have been threatening from the start," she said, crouching down next to Wrench and urging Jacob to do the same. She lowered her voice, grinning with satisfaction.

"We're blowing up the Mykahnol."

28 The Right Code

A space had been cleared in the middle of the front room. Broken furniture and discarded belongings had been pushed to the side and Dhiren and Keiran had spread out a number of maps. Some depicted the sprawling landscape from Nyvalau to Nyquonat, while others were more detailed, listing every street and landmark in Adlai. The larger of the maps had been discarded as the two men studied the Adlai map. They had placed a number of broken objects on top, even though, within the house, there was little chance of it blowing away.

Georgianna took the bowls over and handed one to each of them before she took a seat next to Keiran. Dhiren barely looked at his food. He put the bowl aside and reached for a marker stone that had been positioned on the map.

"Do they really need to be equidistant?" he asked, tossing the stone into the air and catching it.

Keiran swallowed a mouthful of food, tapped his spoon against the side of his bowl, and glanced between the other objects. As Georgianna leaned forwards, she noticed that they were placed in a circle, five points in all, not including the one Dhiren was tossing into the air. There was a sixth on the map, in the centre of the circle.

"If the information Edtroka got from Lehksi was correct, the pillars are spaced evenly," he said. He sucked the juice from his spoon and turned it around in his fingers. Using the handle, he measured the distance between the northern pillar and the eastern one, then repeated for the space between the eastern and southern. Last, he measured from the southern pillar to the broken splinter of wood in the centre of the circle. The distances were equal.

"But that's the pillars," Dhiren said. "The shield might be different."

"It's not," Georgianna said. "The ship needs to be at the centre of the field it covers, and apart from changing the general shape, we can't specify the barrier."

They both looked at her with wide eyes and slack jaws.

"Hey, I understood what Tohma told me," she said with a grin. "He said you can determine the size of the barrier to a certain extent but you can't fix it to specific points."

Dhiren scowled, placed the stone back in the circle, and picked up his bowl. He ate quickly and without fuss, keeping his gaze on the map. As he chewed, he tapped his spoon against his chin.

"So, either we don't destroy it all, or we destroy more land than needed."

"And we still don't know how long the affected area would be uninhabitable for," Georgianna said. "They didn't tell you that, right?"

"No," Dhiren replied. "But from the tales we've been told about how the destruction works, it would be a while."

Keiran looked at her.

"Did the tech say if the shield would withstand it?"

"Well, I was trying to keep the specifics to a minimum. Didn't want to risk him talking about it. In short, I don't know."

"Well, there's no point in moving forwards until we know," said Keiran. "And don't we need some information on how to actually detonate the thing first? At the moment, we're not even sure if it's possible."

"Oh, it's possible," Dhiren said, pointing his spoon at the centre of the map. "Our little Adveni friend told E'Troke how to do it. The main problem we're facing there is that we need Volsonnar approval."

Keiran dropped his spoon back into the bowl and stared at Dhiren with narrowed eyes. He rubbed his fingers into the bridge of his nose, shaking his head.

"Why did you even let me suggest this plan whilst knowing that?"

"Why wouldn't I?"

"Because getting the Volsonnar's approval to detonate the Mykahnol kind of defeats the point, doesn't it?" Georgianna said.

Keiran jabbed his thumb at her and nodded.

"You said the ship needs a Cahlven to pilot it, right?" Dhiren asked. "Something about biology?"

"That's right."

"Well, if this is the same, then maybe it's that tletonise stuff E'Troke was going on about."

Tletonise was the way Edtroka had explained how children had their parents' eye and hair colour, that it was the code they were made by. Apparently, the Adveni only bred from 'good' code. Those who were found to have undesirable code were branded Zsraykil and sterilised. Georgianna had no idea what they considered bad code, but in her opinion it was disgusting that a bunch of scientists decided whether someone could have a child or not.

"That doesn't help us," Georgianna said.

"Maybe, maybe not. If it is tletonise, then E'Troke might have been able to work it."

"Congratulations!" Keiran said as he leaned back onto his elbows. "How about we go collect his corpse and drag it to the Mykahnol, see what happens?"

Georgianna flinched and scratched her cheek. She didn't want to hear Keiran labelling Edtroka as dead so casually. The hole opened up in her stomach again and she stared down at the map as Dhiren leaned closer.

"Which means Ehnisque might be able to work it," he said.

"So what, we just go and ask her nicely?" said Georgianna.

Dhiren shrugged and collected up his bowl, scraping out the last of the food. He let his spoon hang out of his mouth, looking like a dog particularly pleased with a bone.

Keiran, on the other hand, was fixed on the map, his gaze roaming across the surface. He scratched his neck and the back of his shoulder, deep in thought.

"I might have a way," he said.

"What is it?"

He clambered to his feet and, as Georgianna moved to follow him, he waved her back down.

"Keep working. Figure out where we want this barrier to

fall and maybe bring the tech in to determine whether the shield will even do what we need. I'll be back soon."

He strode from the room without another word. The front door opened and closed and, when Georgianna got to her feet and ran to the window, Keiran was striding away through the rain, back towards the main body of the camp.

"Do you know what he's thinking?" she asked Dhiren.

"I'm hoping it's something to do with capturing Ehnisque and holding a gun to her head until she does what we want, but I doubt it," he said, sighing.

Georgianna doubted that, too. With nothing to do but wait for Keiran to share his idea, she returned to Dhiren to help decide how much of their city they would wipe off the map.

29 WHAT WAR IS

Georgianna closed the door against the rain, huffing and shaking off the water. She returned to the window. On the other side of the glass the sheets of rain reduced visibility to the length of her arm. The world was a wash of grey under dark clouds. It had rained all through the night, and the rising sun made little difference to the darkness spreading over her view.

"Will you sit down, please?" Dhiren said. "You're making me twitchy."

He was sitting against the wall, a shirt rolled up and propped behind his head. His eyes were closed and his arms and legs crossed. Georgianna rolled her eyes and returned to pacing.

"Why isn't he back yet?"

"Without knowing where he was going or what he planned on doing, I don't know."

Georgianna huffed again and balled her hand into a fist,

punching the side of her leg.

"Why didn't he tell us what he was doing?" she asked. "He's so secretive."

Cracking one eye open, Dhiren tracked her progress back and forth in front of the window.

"The plan was to have different people know different things so that—"

"Yeah, yeah, I know. So that I can't spill all our secrets again."

"Nobody blames you for that," he said.

When she snorted, he opened both eyes and abandoned his idea of sleep. Sitting forwards, he grabbed the shirt and shook it out, laying it across his lap.

"Anyone could have broken, George."

"But they didn't," she said, striking her leg harder. "I did."

"What's your point?"

She turned away from the window and leaned against the wall. Her palms were clammy as she rubbed her hands over her face.

"I don't know," she said. "I just feel like… oh, it doesn't matter."

"No, come on, tribe mate."

When she looked at him through her fingers, he was grinning. Behind the smile, his eyes were shrewd and calculating. Georgianna sighed.

"Even before Maarqyn, before Edtroka and the compound, they always treated me like someone to be protected and looked after."

Dhiren rubbed his jaw and rested his head in his hand, gazing up at her. He didn't say anything, he just stared, his lips pursed and an eyebrow arched, waiting.

Georgianna wiped her sweaty palms off on her trousers. She looked anywhere but at him. He just kept right on staring.

It was true. Alec had always been this way, even when she was young. She wasn't allowed to go on hunting trips because she was too young and might get hurt. Her brother didn't want her away from camp for too long and didn't like it when she went to help other tribes with medicine. All of them wanted to keep her in one place so she wouldn't hurt herself.

That was it. They didn't do it because they thought someone else would hurt her. They did it because they thought she would hurt herself.

"I'm not a child!" she said. "And I'm not Maarqyn's little bird, either. I don't need to be kept in a cage, protected from everything."

Dhiren still stared.

"Of course you're not."

Georgianna touched the top of her shoulder, brushing her fingers back and forth over her shirt. Maarqyn had branded her a caged bird and that was exactly how her own people were treating her. Edtroka had done it too, she realised. He'd given his life because he didn't think she could survive outside those bars.

She shifted her weight and dragged her fingers through her hair.

"I don't need looking after!"

"Clearly."

"Will you stop agreeing with me?"

Dhiren's thoughtful stare turned into a grin as she turned away from him. Leaning over his knees, he picked up one of the stones that secured the map and rolled it along his fingers.

"Alright, let's say they treat you like a child," he said. "How do you want them to treat you?"

Slumping down against the wall, Georgianna stared into her hands.

"I want to be their equal. I want—"

"That's your problem."

"What is?"

"Wanting."

She raised an eyebrow and stared back at his crooked grin.

"What?"

"You want them to treat you differently, but have you done anything to *make* them treat you differently?"

"How can I? They won't tell me anything! Keiran runs off any time he has an idea. Probably to talk to Beck or someone else he considers useful."

"And you let him."

His smug smile made her want to punch him, but apparently, wanting was wrong.

"So what? I stop him from leaving? Force him to tell me things?"

"No, that would just make you petulant."

Placing the stone back on the map, Dhiren got to his feet. He held up his hand and left the room, leaving Georgianna sitting against the wall. She listened to his footsteps and the rustling from the other room, wondering if she should have followed. That would probably make her petulant, too.

When he returned, he came to stand in front of her, keeping his hand behind his back.

"You really want to fight?" he asked. "You want them to treat you differently?"

RACK AND RUIN

She licked her bottom lip and drew the flesh back between her teeth. She wasn't sure she would like what Dhiren had in mind, but it had to be better than this.

"Yes."

He brought his hand out. He had a gun, loaded and ready. For a moment all she could wonder was where he'd been keeping it.

"Stop simply wanting things to change. Change them yourself."

Now, his smirk was a challenge. She was sure he thought she'd shrink away from it.

Getting to her feet, Georgianna looked down at the gun in his hand. Her gaze flickered up to that doubting smile.

She took the weapon, and Dhiren's smile grew broader.

"You and I are going hunting. If I'm going to be in a tribe with you, you're gonna be useful. You ready to break out of the cage, little bird?"

For the first time in days, the smile that came to her felt honest. She was truly excited.

"Ready."

* * *

The Oprust district bore some of the worst scars of the fighting. Windows had been blown out of most buildings and there wasn't a single shop that was open for trading. The streets were so quiet that Georgianna and Dhiren had to duck from alley to alley to avoid being seen, without the crowds to hide in. The rain had settled to a constant drizzle that clung to their bodies. The Heat was truly dying. Cold winds had set in and would stay for the weeks until they froze, along with everything else on Os-Veruh.

Dhiren hadn't told her what the goal was, and the longer they walked, the more she considered the possibility that he didn't have one. Instead, they just kept moving and he gave her helpful tips as they went.

"I swear, he stood in there for an hour before I finally told him he wouldn't find any fish in a Wash river," Dhiren said, sniggering.

"You let him stand there for an hour?"

Dhiren held his hand out in front of Georgianna, bringing her to a stop at the mouth of an alley. He peered around the corner and, after a moment, waved her onwards.

"He was so determined to do it himself and, let's face it, those Tsevstakre uniforms don't roll up in the legs."

Glancing sideways at him, she raised an eyebrow.

"Are you saying he'd stripped down and you were just enjoying the view?"

He rocked his head from side to side.

"That Nsiloq was pretty good to look at."

Georgianna snorted and decided she didn't want to know any more. She'd known that Dhiren and Edtroka had some sort of history since the moment she'd seen them fight the guards in the compound. They worked together too well, complemented each other in such a way that couldn't be a coincidence. Even so, it was hard to think about the fact she'd lived with Edtroka and realise she knew next to nothing about his life. Now, she had offered to stay with Dhiren, and she knew nothing about him, either.

Running her hand along the brickwork as they walked along a row of shops, Georgianna glanced frequently at Dhiren, wondering. From what she'd seen of him, he was incredibly private, only sharing things when he absolutely had to. Even when she had asked him what he'd done to get thrown into the compound, he'd only told her why the Adveni had caught him. She didn't know which tribe he'd come from, if he'd ever had one. She knew nothing about his family or even if he had any friends before Edtroka had come along. She didn't even know how Dhiren and Edtroka had met.

She opened her mouth to ask the question but changed her mind, looking down the road, instead. Dhiren paused and looked both ways.

"What is it?"

"We're never going to get anywhere from down here."

Georgianna followed his gaze.

"What do you suggest?"

Rubbing his hand over his mouth, Dhiren squinted through one of the windows into a shop.

"We need to get higher."

"I know where we can do that."

Ducking into an alley, Georgianna led Dhiren to one of the main roads through the district. She'd always avoided this path if possible, but, as Dhiren had said back at the house, if she wanted to stop being protected, she needed to act like someone who didn't need it. If that meant facing some uncomfortable memories, that was what she would have to do.

The gilding on the door was flaking away and the moss-green sign that was once a fixture in the window was missing. A large hole was left where the handle had once been, and the door swung open with the lightest touch. Their boots left prints in the dust across the floor and up the stairs.

Georgianna led Dhiren into the shop where she had been captured, up to the second level and to the back corner where another door led out onto the roof. He had to barge his shoulder against it a few times before it swung open with a creak, and they stepped out onto the row of flat roofs.

They walked carefully and Dhiren looked around so frequently that she thought his head might pop off. It was only as they came to the corner and turned left, clambering up onto a higher roof, that she realised they were heading towards Javeknell Square.

"How many Adveni have you killed?"

Dhiren glanced back at her.

"I'm sorry?"

"You said you were imprisoned in the compound for killing three Adveni, and Edtroka said there were a lot more bodies they could have pinned on you."

"Oh."

"So, how many?"

"Does it matter?"

Georgianna shifted the gun into her other hand and climbed over a ridge of wall separating two buildings.

"Don't you remember?"

"I remember," he said.

"Then why won't you tell me?"

He stopped and turned to her, using the barrel of his gun to scratch his jaw.

"Because when I tell people, they only see me as a killer."

"Is that a bad thing?"

"You saw how people reacted to me back at Nyquonat just for being in the compound. Cartwright thinks I'm some kind of monster."

"But I know you're not," she said. "You weren't doing it for fun, right?"

"No, I wasn't."

"So, how many?"

Frowning, he glanced along the row of roofs.

"Thirty-four."

Georgianna blinked and stared at him.

"Wow!"

He set off without another word and she was left to hurry after him, watching her feet.

Entrances to the buildings below spiked out of the rooftops the same way the entrances to the tunnels speared from the street. They passed five before reaching a corner doorway. When they stepped out from behind it, Georgianna realised she could see down into the square, where the stones, cracked and uneven, were stained with blood. They stood in silence, staring down at the same spot, right in the centre: the place Edtroka had died.

"They'll pay for what they did to him," she whispered.

"They can start now."

Georgianna looked at him in surprise and he pointed down the row. She edged around the doorway and saw a soldier standing on the roof, a large rifle hanging down his back. Dhiren adjusted his grip on the gun and drew his knife.

Scanning the rooftops, she spotted at least five more soldiers stationed around the square. Dhiren stalked past her, rounding the entrance. She grabbed him by the arm and yanked him back.

"What are you doing?" she hissed.

"What we came here to do."

She peered out from behind the entrance to the building below. The soldier paced along the edge of the roof, watching the square from above.

"There are five other guards on these roofs, Dhiren. Even if we get this one, they'll shoot the second they spot us."

"You wanted to fight, didn't you?"

Georgianna glared at his crooked smirk and yanked him back further.

"I wanted to fight, Dhiren. I didn't come here to die."

He pushed her away easily, his humour now gone. Georgianna stumbled back a step, bracing herself against the wall.

"There's always a risk of death, George, that's what war is," he said, sneering. "And if you're not going to take that risk, then maybe it's better that people keep treating you like a child, because it's certainly the way you're acting."

She didn't wait to hear any more. Yanking the door open, she ran down the steps, not caring what she would find at the bottom. She needed to get away from the roof, away from the square, and away from Dhiren's revenge-fuelled death wish.

30 Law and Lies

It didn't take long for Georgianna to realise that Dhiren was following her down the steps. She checked behind at every turning to make sure no Adveni were onto them, but instead she saw Dhiren, keeping his distance and not saying a word. Part of her wanted to tell him to go back and start his revenge, since he seemed so keen on it. But she felt comforted, knowing he was at her back.

For all he had said, claiming that she should be treated like a child who needed protecting, he didn't catch up and check the corners himself. He left it to her, and she was grateful. Perhaps this was only a small step in truly joining the fight against the Adveni, but she was glad she was able to take it on her own.

The longer she walked, heading back towards the camps, the more she realised that Dhiren may have been right. She had always known that there were risks to fighting and she'd paid the cost of that risk with her family's lives, but she'd never walked willingly into a fight before. She didn't even count the moment when she had faced Ehnisque outside her home. She'd been gradually giving up, and now was the time to change that. Five soldiers would not turn the tide of a war, and she didn't regret walking away this time. Soon, though, she knew she would have to push towards the fight instead of turning her back.

Of course, that didn't mean she was entirely ready to forgive Dhiren for calling her on it, or to overlook his reckless desire for revenge.

As they entered the camps, he fell into step at her side, slotting his weapons into his belt and pushing his hands into his pockets, as if he didn't have a care in the world. If he was feeling bad for the things he had said, he didn't show it. That only made Georgianna angry, and she held the silence, keeping the gun in her hand as they walked through the rain.

"Where the hell have you been?" Keiran shouted as he came running to meet them. The unbruised part of his face was pale, and a long scar sliced through the mottled purple and fading yellow down his cheek and jaw.

Tucking the gun into the back of her trousers, Georgianna glanced at Dhiren. He didn't return the look.

"Back from what you were doing, then?" he said.

"I came back and you were both gone," said Keiran. "No message, nothing. No one knew where you were."

He placed his hand on the small of Georgianna's back, urging her towards the house.

"Where the hell were you?" he asked. "I've been going out of my mind."

Through the doorway and into the front room, Dhiren rubbed his hand through his hair and shook off the water.

He glanced at Georgianna and quickly looked away through the window.

"Well?"

"We went to scout in the Oprust district," Georgianna said, turning away from Dhiren and back to Keiran. She gave him a placid smile. "We were trying to work out where the shield should fall. Dhiren and I aren't as good with these maps. We needed a proper look."

Keiran took a step away, wringing his hands together.

"I was worried about you. I thought maybe they'd sent troops in."

"Oh, suns, no. I'm sorry. We didn't know when you'd be back and we figured this couldn't wait. The sooner we have a plan and all that."

"That was really dangerous," he said, rounding on Dhiren. "You were heading into their territory. Was this your idea?"

Dhiren blinked with an innocent ignorance and spun his knife in his hand before tossing it down beside the maps. He brushed off Keiran's question as casually as he brushed the rain from his hair.

"The Oprust district is too close to the target," he said. "We'll never be able to destroy every Adveni building in the area unless we want a high number of Veniche casualties. It looks pretty deserted down there but you never know who's still around."

Returning to the maps, he shifted the stones they had placed in a circle and moved them further into the centre.

"If we try to evacuate, we'll give the Adveni the jump on what we plan to do. So, George and I were thinking that the best option is to use the Mykahnol to destroy a smaller area.

It would only take out a portion of the land we wanted, but it removes the threat of the Adveni using it later."

When he glanced up, he stared right at Keiran as if Georgianna wasn't even in the room. She had to admit, she was glad for it. If he drew attention to her she wasn't sure she would be able to hold up the lie as well as he did. It was so convincing she wanted to ask if that had been his plan all along. He'd known Edtroka for a long time and she was starting to think that maybe he had learned far more from the Adveni than she'd realised. Or perhaps Edtroka had learned his secrecy from Dhiren; she'd never know.

Keiran scratched the back of his shoulder where his shirt hid the mark Alec had carved into him. He glanced between them and pursed his lips, finally nodding.

"That is helpful," he said. "But you should have told someone you were going."

"Next time," Dhiren replied, thumping his fist against his chest in a crude show of the Adveni salute.

"You could have asked Alec or Wrench, you didn't need to take…"

Keiran fell silent and glanced at Georgianna. He looked away but not quick enough to hide his meaning: Dhiren didn't need to take her with him, because she, like always, was to be left out of it and protected.

Moving to Keiran's side, Georgianna shook off a trembling anger and settled her hand against his chest. Leaning close, she kissed a healing patch of bruising on his cheek. Her pulse throbbed painfully from her injured wrists, and her shoulder and side seared in pain as she stretched up to reach him. She kept on smiling.

"I'm fine, Keiran. See. You should stop worrying. I can help."

When he looked down at her, his expression softened. He gave a small nod and closed the gap, kissing her with tentative passion.

"I know you can," he murmured. "I'm sorry."

Even as he walked away, taking a seat next to Dhiren and the maps, Georgianna loved him, but she didn't believe him.

* * *

Georgianna hadn't seen the little house so full of people for a long time. Alec had brought Wrench and the Cahlven technician, Tohma, back with him. Though there were only six of them, the constant flow of discussion and interruption made for a lively room. The four walls were filled with life and yet Georgianna felt alone without her father in the corner. She could imagine him sitting quietly, listening to the conversation before interjecting some thoughtful comment.

Dhiren had remained silent, only speaking when addressed, and Georgianna knew his worry. They'd agreed that they would need to bring a Cahlven in to manage the technology, yet it was clear that Dhiren was as disillusioned with the Cahlven and their methods of war as she was. Keiran was more dynamic, which surprised Georgianna, with Alec in attendance. Instead of being sullen and resentful, he was mission-minded, responding to Alec's questions and asking some of his own.

They were forced to lie to Tohma, telling him that the discussion was hypothetical, to be used if they had to retreat. He nodded and didn't dispute their reasoning, but his eyes narrowed and he had watched Wrench and Alec for a long time after that with a small smile on his lips. He didn't ask why they would need a Cahlven technician if the attack was only for a last resort.

"The shields would withstand the blast," he said, picking up the central stone and lifting it high above the map. "The ship, on the other hand—"

"Any ship would need to be contained within the shield, right?" Wrench asked.

He nodded and rolled the stone around in his fingers.

"Exactly. It is what the shields were designed for. We can expand them to contain an extended area, but you cannot remove the ship from the field. Whichever ship was used, it would be lost in the—"

Tohma lifted his head, turning to look at the window. Keiran raised an eyebrow and leaned forwards, watching him intently.

"In the what?"

"Shh!"

Keiran blinked, his lips parting. Georgianna shuffled closer to the map, but the sound of shouting and heavy boots cut her short.

"I hear it, too," she murmured.

Clambering to her feet, she hurried to the window and peered out, shocked at the sight before her. She grabbed her jacket and slung it around her shoulders, shoving her arms into the sleeves as she half-ran to the door.

"What's going on?"

Georgianna didn't turn back to see who had spoken. A flurry of shuffling and breathy curses followed her outside.

A long red braid slashed through the air as Olless stopped and turned on her heel, propping her hands on her hips. Her pale skin was flushed a deep mottled pink. At full height, she was still shorter than Beck. He was red, too, his top lip curled into a sneer.

"I told you already, I have no power to make those decisions," Olless said.

"You were the one who named me Leader of the Veniche," he snarled. "So you have the power to elevate people to these positions, but not to make sure their roles are met with any semblance of decency?"

Olless looked around, suddenly realising how many people had stopped to listen. She stepped closer to Beck.

"Can we talk about this in private?"

Beck snorted, glaring down at her.

"So you can promise things you can later deny?" he asked. "Do you think I don't know how the Cahlven work?"

Olless shrank away. She took another look around, her gaze raking through the crowd. A small group of Cahlven soldiers had gathered just down the path, doing a bad job of pretending they weren't paying attention. She signalled to one of them and made a scratch-like gesture just in front of her ear, before drawing her thumb down the centre of her chest. The man nodded and pulled something from his pocket, turning away from his friends.

"Just like the Adveni," Beck added.

The slap of flesh on flesh cracked through the close air. Beck shook his head and lifted his hand to his cheek. Despite the red mark darkening his skin, he laughed.

"Don't get what you want with lies and promises, so you use force," he sneered. "If you were trying to prove yourself different, Olless, you failed."

"How dare you?" she screeched. "We have helped you, we came here to—"

"You came here to take control! You promised that we would be involved, that we would govern ourselves alongside you and look at what has happened."

"What is it you want?" Olless demanded. "I've already told you I do not have the right to—"

"Exactly!" Beck flung his arms out to his sides. "That's exactly what you don't have. You don't have the right to tell me, or anyone here, what to do. You have no rights here."

"What do you mean?"

"You left. You left us here on Os-Veruh and gave up your claim, just like the Adveni. If you want to stay here, if you want to work peacefully alongside us, you have to defer to the Veniche. It is our rights that matter here."

Georgianna jumped as an elbow drove into her side. She looked at Alec and followed his gaze as he nodded down the path.

The man approaching them didn't look like anyone special, and yet the group of Cahlven soldiers jumped to attention and backed away. Georgianna was reminded of the Adveni soldiers making space for the Volsonnar as he strode through the square.

He was a short man. His neck-to-ankle suit fit tight across the shoulders, accentuated by the blue lines that ran from neck to wrist. His black hair had been oiled down, gathered in a short, neat ponytail. Heavy lines were worn into his forehead but he carried them well.

"Mr. Casey," he said, looking up at Beck as he stopped to stand by Olless. "Please take a moment to gather yourself. We can discuss this privately once you have had time to reconsider."

Beck shifted his stance and folded his arms, glaring down at the man.

"I don't need time to reconsider, Aomel. I've made my position quite clear. Either the Cahlven defer to the Veniche, or they leave."

Aomel smiled, blinking as he looked Beck up and down. Georgianna stepped closer to Keiran. She recognised that smile. It was the same look her father had given her whenever she asked for something ridiculous or impossible. Keiran wrapped his arm around her waist and tangled his fingers in her jacket, drawing her to his side.

"That's the Second Colvohan," he murmured in her ear.

"Surely you must realise that your demands here are not sensible," Aomel said after a long pause. "The Cahlven are more technologically advanced, we have better numbers, and our men are trained. A war has begun, Mr. Casey. If we were to remove ourselves from Os-Veruh, do you believe you would stand any chance in winning against a superior force such as the Adveni?"

"That doesn't matter," Beck said with a snarl, stretching himself up to full height. He looked impressive, glaring down at the Colvohan, but even Georgianna couldn't follow his logic.

"It doesn't? Wasn't the whole point to drive the Adveni back from this planet?"

"It wouldn't matter because there is no point in winning a war against the Adveni if we were only to take up the same position beneath the Cahlven. If you're making decisions, we should be involved. We should be *equal*."

Aomel took a long moment to share a look with Olless. He turned full circle and peered at each person who stood to listen to the argument. Georgianna cringed away from his gaze. He gave her the same feeling Maarqyn did when he stared at her, waiting for the breaking point.

"I have another meeting scheduled with the Volsonnar," he said. "If it will placate you long enough to listen to our intentions, I will take you along."

Beck paused just a moment but, instead of looking at anyone else, he simply stared at the Colvohan, his expression steely.

"Fine."

"Good. Then I will send Olless with information of the time we leave," Aomel said briskly. "Come, Olless."

He swept past Beck without another word, heading back in the direction he had come from. Beck watched him over his shoulder. Turning away from the other Cahlven, Beck strode over, clapped Keiran on the shoulder, and marched away, further from the main camp.

"What - was - that?" Dhiren asked.

Keiran grinned, clapped Dhiren on the shoulder in the exact way Beck had just done to him, and went to the doorway.

"Nothing," he said. "We should continue working."

"Working on a hypothetical attack?" Tohma asked, smirking.

"Exactly."

Georgianna stared after Beck. He swung his arms as he walked and—wasn't that a faint whistle on the air, a bounce in his step?

Someone had just been played for a fool and, for the first time in a while, Georgianna didn't think it was the Veniche.

31 THE MEETING

No matter how Georgianna stretched, she couldn't reach the centre of the Nsiloq that Maarqyn had applied to her skin. She stretched her arm over her shoulder, smoothing the hyliha paste over the top of the mark. If she brought her arm up behind her back, she could just about brush the bottom of the design with the tips of her finger. But no matter how she twisted and turned, she couldn't get to the middle and soothe the constant burning ache.

Sitting on the edge of the ripped mattress in her brother's room, Georgianna smeared the last of the paste on her fingers over her arm, kneading it into her skin. Beck had left for the meeting with the Colvohan and the Volsonnar hours earlier, and all there had been to do was wait. Keiran and Dhiren had tried to stay busy, but even their efforts had ground to a halt, leaving them staring at the walls.

"Maybe you should ask one of the Cahlven if they have something for that."

Georgianna lifted her head just long enough to see Alec standing in the doorway. He rested his shoulder against the frame and stared at the wall behind her head. Picking up her shirt, she covered the front of her body and hunched down over her legs.

"It's not so bad," she said.

Alec snorted. He walked further into the room and took a seat next to her on the bed. Holding his hand out, he waited until Georgianna picked up the small clay bowl. He smeared paste onto three fingers, swept the hair away from her shoulder, and paused before smearing the paste over her skin. Georgianna hissed and jerked under the pressure.

"Everything's ready?" she asked.

Blades of pain followed his fingers as he covered the mark. He scooped up a little more from the bowl and held her shoulder to keep her steady.

"Just waiting on Beck," he said. "If he comes back with what we need, we're ready to go."

"And we'll go straight away?"

"Yes. Better to get the element of surprise."

Georgianna nodded and fell back into silence until Alec squeezed her shoulder and began scraping the remnants of hyliha paste off his fingers and back into the bowl. Keeping herself low over her knees, she pulled on her shirt, adjusting it when it stuck to her shoulder.

"Alec?" she breathed.

"What?"

"How did you deal with it? You know, when your family… How did you deal with losing them?"

He took the bowl from her and placed it on the floor between his feet.

"Distraction," he said, looking at her. She twisted the bottom of her shirt in her fingers.

"Oh," she said. "So that's what I was to you back then. Just a distraction? I mean, I guess I knew but—"

"No, Georgie. You weren't just a distraction."

She moved back onto the mattress, drawing her knees in tight to her chest. She didn't have the heart to admonish him for the use of a nickname he knew she hated. She stared at the floor, resting her chin on her knee.

"I grew up with you," he said. "You're Halden's little sister and I cared about you. But that only made it worse, I guess."

Gulping, Georgianna gritted her teeth and sniffed.

"Worse?"

"I felt guilty every time. Like perhaps I was betraying her, or even you. I shouldn't have used you the way I did, not when I couldn't move on from what happened."

"Is that why you told Beck to let people think you'd died? So you could move on?"

His nod was slow and steady.

"I did care about you, George," he said, his voice barely more than a whisper. "But I didn't... I never should have been with you like that, letting you think that—"

"That what?" Georgianna asked, her voice cracking.

"That I loved you, or that maybe I would someday. I didn't, not like that, and I wouldn't have, not the way..."

She sat up straight and turned towards him, crossing her legs.

"Not what way?"

After staring at the floor for a few seconds, Alec finally lifted his head and faced her. His eyes were wide and he brushed his dark hair back from his face.

"Not the way he does."

Her mouth dropped open and she wasn't quick to close it again. Alec had been so virulent in his dislike of Keiran that she couldn't hide her surprise that he'd comment on him in that way. It had been Alec who had said Keiran was using her. He told her she was naive and would go along with the lies Keiran told her. He'd been sure that Keiran wouldn't care, that he wouldn't love her, not the way she wanted or needed. Now it seemed he had changed his mind, but she couldn't work out why. Had it been the moment Keiran had walked out to join her in front of Ehnisque instead of saving himself?

"Have you forgiven him?"

Alec's grimace was thoughtful and he stared past her.

"I don't think forgiveness is the right word. I understand what he did but I don't think I will ever forgive him for it."

"That's..." Georgianna frowned as she paused, looking for the right words. Maybe there were none. "That's a little ridiculous, Alec."

He shrugged and met her gaze.

"Perhaps, but even if he didn't do the right thing for me, he did it for you," he said.

Leaning across the gap, Georgianna wrapped her arms around Alec's body, grasping his arm as she pulled him close. He patted her elbow and rested his temple against the top of her head.

"You'll move on, George," he murmured. "He'll help you move on."

She nodded, but even with these kind words about a man he'd wanted dead not a month before, she felt the guilt more than ever. She'd let Keiran distract her—from her family and from Edtroka. If she loved him the way Alec said

Keiran loved her, did that make it better, or worse?

A cough came from the doorway. Georgianna sat up and stared at Keiran. His gaze moved between the two of them, his body tight. He took a step back as Georgianna pulled away from Alec.

"Keiran, we were just talking about—"

"Beck's back," he said

"He is?"

Keiran didn't look at either of them. Staring at the floor, he shuffled his feet and took a deep breath.

"There's a problem."

He turned away and stalked back through the house and out onto the path. Georgianna followed him at a run, Alec on her heels. Keiran didn't look back, proceeding with his long strides, keeping Georgianna at a jog as they headed further into the camps. People had congregated along the path, muttering to each other. As Keiran came to a sudden stop, Georgianna gasped.

Three Cahlven soldiers surrounded Beck, each holding onto a thick metal chain. Shackles had been attached around Beck's ankles and wrists, connected by a thicker chain around his waist. He held his head high as he shuffled along between the soldiers, being led by the Colvohan, Aomel.

"What's going on?" Alec whispered.

Keiran didn't look back. He folded his arms and adjusted his stance, keeping a murderous glare on the Colvohan.

"Beck went with Aomel to the meeting with the Volsonnar," he said over his shoulder.

"Yeah, we know."

"Well, Olless told me he stabbed the Volsonnar."

Georgianna gasped. Alec let out a snort, somewhere between surprise and amusement. Keiran turned and glared at the both of them.

"The Colvohan only just got him out of there. The Adveni would have killed him," he snarled. "The moment the Colvohan got Beck free, they arrested him."

"That makes no sense," Alec whispered. "Why arrest him for killing their enemy?"

"Why would Beck take a risk like that?" Georgianna added.

The look on Keiran's face said everything he couldn't put into words. He turned away from them, looking back to Beck.

Olless hurried past to meet the Colvohan, who ignored her completely, leaving her staring after him. Her face twisted as Beck passed her with his guard. He smirked at her and she trembled with rage.

Keiran shuffled forwards and Beck used his limited movement in the shackles to twist the chain around his waist. He gave a small nod.

"Stay here," Keiran muttered over his shoulder.

"Keiran, what are you—" Georgianna tried to grab his arm but he was already gone, striding forwards to meet with the soldiers.

They closed ranks around Beck, but not fast enough. Keiran shoved between them, grasping Beck by the shoulders and enveloping him into a hug. Alec snorted, shaking his head. Georgianna stared.

One of the soldiers grabbed Keiran by the scruff of the neck, hauling him back and sending him tumbling into the dirt. He got to his feet, shouting curses and threats as they dragged Beck away. Sneering and muttering under his breath, Keiran stalked away into the crowd, carrying a small cloth bag dripping a thick, dark substance.

32 Colours and Cooperation

"I'm not saying that we should forget about it," Alec snapped. "But the Cahlven have shown their colours. They're more interested in cooperating with the Adveni."

"You don't know that," Keiran said quietly. He'd taken a seat in the corner of the room, the map of Adlai spread over his lap. Everything had now been planned, from the size of the shield to the route to the building that housed the Mykahnol. It was marked and outlined on the map draped across his legs. At Dhiren's insistence, they'd even planned three routes out of the city to move north; not that any of them believed they'd make it that far if the Cahlven didn't back them up.

"Dragging Beck off in chains didn't tell you as much?" Alec asked.

Despite admitting that he understood Keiran's logic in

helping Edtroka, and his insistence that the other Belsa had Georgianna's best interests at heart, Alec's snide tone didn't do much to convince Georgianna that he wasn't taking the rebuttal personally.

"It tells me they're angry that they were humiliated in what was supposed to be a peaceful negotiation," Keiran said. "You think Beck wouldn't have done the same if it had been one of us in his meeting?"

"But that's different. Beck was our leader. We followed his orders. We never agreed to follow Cahlven orders."

"Then what's your point?" Dhiren asked. "You're bitching about the Cahlven but, from where I'm stood, you're agreeing that we should back down."

A blotchy red blush rose until the scars on Alec's neck stood out bright white in contrast. A web of Adveni abuse stretched across his skin for all to see. Georgianna averted her gaze to the floor.

"If we don't have their support, we shouldn't be doing this," he mumbled at last.

Dhiren shook his head. Glaring at Alec, he stood square in front of him.

"I disagree," Dhiren said with no hint of the malice that had been in his voice when he had grabbed Alec in the forest. "Not having their support is all the more reason we should go ahead and prove what we're willing to do. Beck has already proven how far he'll go. He stabbed the Volsonnar. We should be celebrating."

Georgianna lay her hand on Dhiren's shoulder, tugging him away from Alec.

"How would it even work?" she asked. "We need a shield and for that we need a ship."

Keiran folded the map with slow, precise movements.

"Yes, the Cahlven arrested Beck. But they're still against the Adveni. They might still be on board if we tell them the plan."

"Without a ship, the entire plan is pointless," Dhiren agreed. "We could try getting the technician to steal one but I don't think it'll work."

Alec closed his eyes and let out a heavy sigh.

"So we're just accepting what they've done to Beck?"

Picking up the map from Keiran's lap, Georgianna ran her finger along the edge and turned it over, shaking her head. She held it up in front of Alec.

"Dhiren's right. We're proving what we're willing to do. They wanted their peaceful negotiations and it hasn't worked. They need a new plan and we have it. We can use this to negotiate Beck's freedom."

Georgianna wasn't sure which made her feel proudest: that Dhiren grinned and patted her on the shoulder; that Alec nodded in agreement; or that Keiran got to his feet and took the map from her, smiling. Dhiren had told her back at Nyquonat that she was a balance. He'd said that she evened out the people who would never act and those who would act too fast. She hadn't felt it; she thought he was ridiculous. But now, standing here with three men who she never thought would be able to stand working together, all agreeing with her—for the first time she felt that he might have been right. She wasn't a warrior like they were but that didn't mean she wasn't useful to the fight.

"So what, we talk to the Colvohan?" Alec asked.

"Yes," Dhiren said.

"Sounds like a—"

"No," Georgianna said. "No, we talk to Olless."

"Olless? Even she said she doesn't have the power for that sort of decision," Alec said, sneering.

She smirked.

"No, she doesn't, but there is no way the Colvohan will listen to us. If it came from her, though…"

"What makes you think she'll listen to us?" Keiran asked. "She listened to Beck and he ruined their little meeting with the Volsonnar."

"Exactly," she said. "She's been made to look stupid. I bet she'll do anything to improve her standing and our plan could be just the way to do it."

Dhiren laughed and slung his arm around Georgianna's shoulders.

"You know, Med, you're pretty devious when you put your mind to it." He chuckled, his lips next to her ear. "Reminds me of him."

* * *

"It's insane," said Olless. She shifted in her seat, pulling her long braid over her shoulder and fingering the ends. "Even if I could get the Colvohan to agree to it, it would take too long to organise. By the time we have the information we need and everything is in place, the Adveni will be in full attack mode and we'd never get a ship over the centre of the city."

Alec stepped forwards, bending over the table. He spun the map around to face Olless and placed his finger down in the centre, marking the building that they were now certain housed the Mykahnol.

"We have the information we need," he said. "We've done the planning. Wrench and I have worked on the pillars before. We know the technology we'll be dealing with."

"Everything is ready to go, Olless," Keiran agreed, stepping up to join Alec.

"Don't even need your troops," Dhiren interjected. "All we need is a ship."

Olless stared at Dhiren for a few moments before leaning back in her seat.

"And a pilot," she said. "But the number of lives is not the problem here, gentlemen. You are asking us to give one of our ships to a risky mission that, however it plays out, means we lose the ship."

Olless brushed her braid back over her shoulder. She hadn't stopped moving as they'd explained the plan, always twisting in her seat or pacing back and forth on the other side of the table. Unlike the Olless Georgianna had seen on the Cahlven ship, she was not poised or convincing. Georgianna wondered whether it was the unfamiliar ground that had put her so on edge, or the unfamiliar people. Back on the ship, Olless had been certain that she could mould the Veniche to her wishes. After the way Olless had treated her back at Nyquonat, Georgianna wasn't upset that the emissary had been brought rather sharply back down to the ground.

"Yes, you would lose a ship," Georgianna said, moving to stand at Keiran's side. "But your negotiations with the Adveni have not worked. After the attack on their Volsonnar they'll already be organising a response. We need to strike first."

Georgianna knew that Olless didn't like her. She was aware that the emissary had only kept her around because of her connection to Edtroka. But that didn't make the way Olless looked at her any easier to bear. Her nostrils flared as she sneered, her wide eyes narrowing.

"We've already told you we don't need troops," Keiran said, drawing Olless' attention. "Your losses, compared to the Adveni's, would be minimal. If we don't get out in time, you would have fewer than a dozen casualties, where the Adveni would lose hundreds of trained men and women."

"Puts you in a pretty good negotiating position," Dhiren scoffed. Olless seemed to like that even less.

"I can't make the decision," she said, getting to her feet and addressing Keiran. "I'll need you to come with me to explain."

Keiran licked his lips and took a deep breath. Glancing along the line, he reached out and slipped his hand into Georgianna's. He squeezed her fingers, nodded, and turned back to Olless.

"I need Cartwright to come with us."

"Me?" Alec blurted out.

Keiran nodded again and kept his gaze on Olless.

"Cartwright knows the technology better than I do. If your Colvohan has questions, he'll be the best person to answer them."

Olless looked between the two of them and threw her hands out to the side.

"Fine. You will both explain."

Alec looked pale. He gulped and straightened up.

"Okay then," he said. "Let's go."

33 Something of His

"I don't know how much will be useful," Dhiren said, tugging a bag towards him. "E'Troke kept these to survive, not to fight."

"It's worth looking," Georgianna said.

She grabbed the end of another bag and loosened the strap. There was no knowing what they would find inside. Edtroka had split most of the clothes and food between them when they'd travelled north from the forest to Nyquonat Lake. He'd given the weapons out for protection. He'd even handed over the medical kit to Georgianna. She couldn't think of anything else that would be useful for them, but once Jacob had told her that their belongings had been packed away and brought back to Adlai in the Cahlven Densaii ship, she knew that she had to check.

Alec and Keiran hadn't returned. It had been hours since they followed Olless from the house. Wrench had managed to get hold of a bag of tools and he sat against the wall, in front of an array of metal devices. Jacob sat next to Wrench, his plants forgotten as he watched and listened.

One of the small tents had been packed into a lumpy canvas bag. Georgianna set it aside and dug in again, pulling out a blanket, a few shirts, and a small leather pouch. Keeping the pouch in her lap, she also found a bag made of metal links so thin that it bent and hung like fabric. A fine chain held the bag closed, wrapped around many times. She unwound it carefully, glancing over at Dhiren.

"Do you know what this is?"

Dhiren looked up and moved to kneel beside her, shaking his head.

As the chain fell away, Dhiren took it and wrapped it around his hand, admiring the work. The metal links fell open across Georgianna's lap like a blanket, revealing a pile of items balanced between her thighs. She picked up a disk and turned it over, recognising it immediately.

"Absorbers," she whispered, digging them from the pile.

Dhiren looked at her, nonplussed.

"They make copaqs useless," she said. "The Belsa called them absorbers."

"Oh. You mean, Qol-tdro," he said, plucking one from her hand. He balanced it on the crook of his finger and flicked it up into the air, catching it easily.

Georgianna laughed and shook her head as she gathered the last of the tabs.

"How do you do that?" she asked.

"Do what?"

Dhiren grabbed a few other items from the small pile, inspecting each one. Although she only recognised the copaq gel chambers, Georgianna had the feeling that the metal bag was the most useful thing they would find in Edtroka's belongings.

"You pronounce things the way they do. Even the way you say Edtroka is Adtvenis."

Cocking his head, Dhiren stared at the absorber tab in his hand. He shrugged, his absent smile exploding into a bark of laughter, but he shook his head.

"What?"

"Nothing," he mumbled, still smiling. "E'Troke taught me the names and I guess they stuck."

She wanted to ask Dhiren what was so funny about Edtroka's teaching him Adtvenis, but as he turned back to dig through the bag for more hidden treasures, his smile faded, and she held her tongue. She dropped the tabs back in the metal bag and placed it at her side.

Georgianna studied the leather pouch, flicking the clasp. It opened across her thighs and she saw the small pockets fitted to the interior, just like the medical kit he'd given her in the forest. A thick leather cuff lay freely, the only thing not slotted into a compartment. She began to investigate each pocket, tucking her fingers inside. Most were empty but in the largest she found a collection of metal badges, each painted. Every one was different in shape and size, and there were a dozen in total. Laying each in her hand, she stroked a finger over the polished surfaces.

"They're from his training," Dhiren said, looking away from the badges. "That pouch, he… He kept important things in there. There's some from his…"

He trailed off and Georgianna placed each badge carefully back into a pocket. She recognised them now, though not in this configuration. Some of the other Adveni soldiers wore them, particularly when they had a special one. Edtroka had kept his hidden away instead of displaying them for all to see. There were enough to impress anyone and yet they had been left to gather dust and tarnish.

Opening the next pocket, she drew out a thin leather cord. It was knotted, with old and fraying ends. Unlike everything else in the pouch, it was not Adveni-made. A coil of wire was wrapped through a hole in a wood and stone pendant.

"Important stones," she said with a quiet snort of laughter.

Dhiren looked at her. His gaze jumped to the cord draped over her fingers and the stone in her palm. The polished gem was deep red, with flecks of black just under the surface and a coil of rich polished wood curled around it, holding it in place. It seemed as if the stone, just the sight of it, had siphoned all the blood from Dhiren's face. He gulped and returned to the bag in front of him.

"Do you know what this is?" she asked.

He didn't look up. His hands froze inside his bag.

"Dhiren?"

"It's mine," he said. "I thought I'd lost it."

"He was keeping it for you."

Georgianna held it out towards him, but Dhiren ignored her and rose to his feet, striding across the room to collect one of the other bags. She wound the cord around her fingers and tucked it back into the pocket she'd found it in. She kept the leather cuff, closed the pouch, and set it aside with the metal bag. The cuff was too big for her, but she kept it just the same.

It was right that she had something of Edtroka's with her while they did this.

* * *

"So why can't I go?"

Jacob's voice, usually so quiet and reserved, rang through the room. Georgianna stared down at the supplies in front of her and picked up Dhiren's knife, feeling for notches and dents.

"You're just a kid," Wrench said. "I don't want—"

"I'm an adult by every law."

Wrench sighed as he sat down. Georgianna glanced over at them before fixing her gaze on the weapon in her lap. Like Keiran, Wrench had a worn look, his eyes hollow and mouth slack. Jacob, though, stood tall, his curly hair pushed back from his bright eyes. He folded his arms and tapped his toe.

"I've been learning to shoot," he said. "You've been teaching me to shoot. Why do that if I can't fight?"

"I taught you to protect yourself, not to go running off into a fight."

"By fighting I am protecting myself. I can't sit around and—"

"How do I look?"

Georgianna jumped to her feet and swept past Wrench and Jacob. Dhiren stood in the doorway, scuffing his boot against the floor. He stared at the wall and scratched the back of his shoulder, tugging the material at his hip, then bent his knees and straightened up again. It was the first time she'd seen him unable to keep still.

It had been her idea and she was sure that if Dhiren had his way, she would pay dearly for it. Dragging her lips between her teeth, she tried to suppress the smile that wanted to burst free.

"It's great," she said, quickly pursing her lips again.

He glared at her, his expression murderous, and turned away. Georgianna jumped forwards and grabbed his arm, yanking him back.

"No, come on," she said. "That expression was perfect. Very Adveni."

"I feel like an idiot."

Drawing him further into the room, Georgianna looked him over again. He shuffled and adjusted his stance, rolling his eyes and staring over her head. His hair was too scruffy, his jaw unshaven, but it would do. They only needed to get past a first glance, just long enough to make an Adveni pause and doubt himself before shooting. They wouldn't get out of this without blood, they all knew it.

"You and Keiran are the tallest. It had to be you two."

They'd found two Tsevstakre uniforms buried in the bottom of a bag of Edtroka's things. Dhiren had wanted to burn them, but Georgianna had told him her idea before asking him to try one of them on.

She moved closer and clicked her tongue. Dhiren's black uniform was creased between the plates of armour that had been built into it. He'd not done up all the buttons. Having never seen Dhiren in any kind of tight clothing, she couldn't imagine the uniform was comfortable for him. She reached up to fasten the top button, stopping short when she saw the leather cord hanging around his neck. Georgianna smiled and quickly averted her gaze, patting him on the shoulder. Dhiren fidgeted again and growled under his breath.

"E'Troke is a head taller than I am. I don't feel right wearing it."

Georgianna frowned and tugged at his waist, straightening the creases.

"He *was* a head taller than you."

He didn't answer.

Glancing down and busying herself with making the costume seem authentic, at least for a moment, Georgianna snorted and covered her mouth with her hand. When she looked up, Dhiren was staring at her with a scowl so hostile that it only made her laugh all the harder.

"What?"

"You rolled up the trousers."

He propped his hands on his hips.

"What was I supposed to do? They're too big."

"It looks like your legs have swollen to double the size!" She grinned up at him. "And gone lumpy."

"Well if you have a better idea…"

She stepped back and pinched her bottom lip. For the most part, the uniform looked decent on him. Keiran, too, would be able to fool an Adveni for just long enough to give them a window. But the length of the uniform was sure to cause problems. It would be obvious that the uniforms had not been made for them; not to mention the discomfort in having the extra material bunched around their ankles.

"Well?" he asked.

"Shh, I'm thinking."

She pulled up the waist of the uniform. It ballooned around Dhiren's stomach and chest, the plating unyielding and unsightly. It also didn't remove the problem. The trousers were still too long.

"Take off your boots."

Georgianna grabbed one of the knives from the pile of weaponry they'd managed to find in Edtroka's stash. When she returned, Dhiren had taken off his boots, the uniform now extending past his toes. He flinched away as she knelt, knife in hand.

"You sure about this, Med?" he asked.

Looking up, she rolled her eyes and went to work, cutting away the excess material. She wasn't great at making clothes, but the extra was easy to cut away and she doubted anyone would look closely enough to see the fraying edges.

"Stay still, will you?" she said as Dhiren once again shuffled, watching her. He huffed and stared at the wall, crossing his armoured arms over his chest.

She was just cutting at the second ankle when the door banged open and Keiran and Alec, sodden from head to heel, bustled into the house. Dhiren turned away and the last of the material came away in a noisy rip. Slumping back on her heels, Georgianna stretched the fabric in her fingers.

Alec looked at Dhiren, his eyes widening as his gaze travelled the length of the black uniform. He blinked, and looked away.

"The Colvohan agreed," he said.

"He did?" Dhiren smirked and cocked his head to the side, scratching himself under the tight collar. "Surprise."

Keiran approached Wrench and laid his hand on his friend's shoulder. They shared a look, both grinning.

"We get one ship, one of the small ones. One pilot and Tohma."

"I'll let him know."

He grabbed his gun and was out of the door, Jacob on his heels, before any of them could say anything else.

"Will it be enough?" Georgianna asked. "Do those ships—"

"It's not ideal," Alec said.

"It'll be fine," Keiran corrected. "The shields are the same, we'll have the same area covered, and it'll be easier to position us over the buildings."

Alec was doubtful, but he didn't argue with Keiran's assessment. Dhiren smoothed his hands down the sides of the uniform and glanced to the other one, draped over the chair. Alec followed his gaze and stepped back.

"Not a chance."

Getting to her feet, Georgianna picked up the second uniform. She stepped forwards and Alec recoiled further.

"It's not for you," she said, holding the uniform out to Keiran. "It's for you."

Keiran looked down at it. His jaw clenched, but he took the uniform just the same.

"Any advantage we can get, right?" Dhiren said.

Keiran nodded and took a deep, steadying breath. He held it up against his chest and it was clear that this one would need to be altered, too. Georgianna held a hand against his waist, holding it in place, and measured down his leg. Marking the spot with her fingers, she lifted the legs away from him. He released the uniform immediately, letting the rest of it slump to the floor at her feet. He barely looked at it as he stepped back.

"I've been allowed to see Beck," he said.

"Really?" Georgianna asked. "Are they letting him go?"

"Depends on how this goes. If we come back successful, then maybe."

"A lot riding on this then," Dhiren said.

"You mean aside from our lives? Yeah."

Keiran gazed through the open window and drew a cloth bag from where it had been hooked into his belt. Something dripped from the bottom, dark and thick. Georgianna grimaced. He dropped it at their feet and turned away.

"We're leaving at sunset. I'll be back soon as I can."

He strode from the room and the others stared at the bag and the small dark puddle it had made on the floor.

Dhiren was the first to step forwards. He pinched the bag at a clean spot and lifted it. Something shifted inside and Georgianna wasn't the only one who took a step back, wrinkling her nose. The smell was atrocious.

The hand slipped from the bag and hit the floor with a slap. The skin was almost grey. Blood had congealed at the open wound where it had been disconnected at the wrist.

They had known they would need the Volsonnar's approval to engage the Mykahnol, and it seemed, thanks to Beck, they now had it.

34 THE DALSAIA

Georgianna held tight to the leather strap hanging from the ceiling as the ship swayed through the air. Bracing herself against the wall, she kept her gaze through the windscreen as their pilot, Jeshrom, had advised. The rocking of the ship swirled through her stomach and each lurch sent her heart into her mouth.

Jeshrom was a small woman. Sitting at the front of the Dalsaia ship, her head barely cleared the back of the seat, her thin hands only just wrapping around the controls. Her dark hair was pulled into a tight knot high on her head with the straps of her headset settled around it. A device was wired into her ear with a microphone in front of her mouth and a cord that fed down under her uniform to a pad placed over her heart. When she spoke, her voice echoed through speakers at the back of the ship even though they were all close enough to hear her clearly. Tohma sat by her side, his Cahlven uniform undone at the neck and the sleeves rolled up to his elbows. He read out instructions in the Cahlven language, frequently turning to translate over his shoulder.

The Dalsaia ship they had been allocated had no seats for passengers and was so small that they had to remain standing in order to fit inside. Keiran's arm pressed against Georgianna's on one side, Alec's on the other. Dhiren stood opposite with Wrench, and when Georgianna risked looking away from the landscape spreading out before them, it was to find Dhiren looking as sick as she felt. He hadn't taken Jeshrom's advice, instead closing his eyes and tipping his face up towards the ceiling. He gagged and grimaced with each lurch.

Tohma spoke again in the Cahlven tongue and turned to look back at them.

"We are heading south, leading into the airspace over Adlai," he said.

"What's to stop the Adveni from just shooting us out of the sky, again?" Georgianna asked.

Though they had been planning the assault non-stop, now that she was actually in the ship it felt like all of their foresight had been useless. Pessimism had taken root, and no matter how hard she tried to focus on the plan, there was an obsession over the ways it could go wrong.

"Bringing ship down on buildings cause much damage," Jeshrom replied in her broken Veuric, her voice echoing from both ends of the ship. "Almost much as explosion."

"But it's only a small ship," said Georgianna.

"It does not matter," Tohma said, his Veuric much clearer than Jeshrom's. "With the velocity of the fall, we would take out too much. We are following a scenic route with the hope that the Adveni will think we are on a scouting mission. By the time they realise the truth, it will be too late."

Georgianna nodded to nobody and turned her attention back to the windscreen. The moment she did, the buildings rushing beneath her made her stomach heave again. Like Dhiren, she tipped her head back and closed her eyes, waiting for the nausea to pass.

"The Mykahnol is in the basement of the building," Wrench said. "If we're correct, it's seven flights down from the roof."

They all nodded. Alec and Keiran began checking their weapons.

"Everyone's on lookout except me and Tohma."

Opening her eyes, Georgianna glanced at Wrench across the small space. He was leaning back against the wall, hunched over to check the devices in his pockets.

They'd known it would be impossible to get in at ground level. They had no idea how many Adveni would be inside the building until Jeshrom and Tohma could scan directly down from the ship. Georgianna was starting to think that she would have preferred to go in at ground level, even if it meant she might have to stand in the ship and wait. She'd never been involved in any Belsa missions before, not like this. In Lyndbury Compound she had only had to set a single device and run. She'd not had to fight anyone. Now, she was one part of a team and, if she cracked, they would all fail.

Georgianna gulped and pushed herself back against the wall. She squeezed her eyes shut and tried to push back the rising bile in her throat.

"Who set you up, Med?" Dhiren asked.

She opened her eyes and looked back at him. His face was so pale it was almost grey and yet he unwound his hand from the leather strap and stepped across the gap.

"I did," she said.

"Figures." He attempted a laugh that fell flat as he pressed his hand against the wall above her shoulder to steady himself.

Drawing the gun from the holster that had been set around her hips, he held it up in front of her.

"Which hand do you shoot with?" he asked.

She held up her right. Dhiren pushed himself off the wall and wavered for a moment as he calibrated to the rocking of the ship. He pulled the knife from her right hip and replaced it at the left, fitting the gun in the knife's original spot.

"You and Alec both draw across your bodies," she said.

He grinned back at her.

"You'll also notice Cartwright and I don't have breasts," he said.

Georgianna rolled her eyes.

"You have a copaq at your back, right?" he asked.

"Yeah."

"Is the handle facing your right hand?"

As her right hand was currently tangled in leather, holding her in place, Georgianna reached back with her left to check. She nodded.

"And you have your extra bullets?"

"Yes," she said. "Why are you only asking me this?"

"Because you're the only one who looks like you're about to throw up all over my shoes," Dhiren said.

Georgianna blushed and he lay his hand over her cheek.

"You ready to die?"

"Hey!" Keiran shoved Dhiren in the shoulder, sending him staggering back against the wall. "Don't say that."

Taking Keiran's hand, Georgianna squeezed his fingers and gave him a tentative smile before turning back to Dhiren. It was comforting, having him there. He didn't lie to her and tell her it would be alright, that she would be safe. Though he could be blunt and even cruel, it felt familiar and she liked it.

"I am," she said. Dhiren nodded and avoided Keiran's glare as he moved across the gap.

"Alright," he said. "Now make sure you don't."

Reaching up, he stroked his fingers over the leather cuff around her right wrist. When he returned to his position against the wall, she rested her head against Keiran's shoulder. He kissed the top of her head and squeezed her hand.

"You alright?" he asked. "Remember your position?"

"Yeah. I'm ready."

Only the rumble of the engine and the whoosh of air over the ship remained as they sped over the city towards the centre and the building they had marked.

"Two minutes," Tohma said. "Starting the scan."

Wrench was the first to move, straightening up and stretching his shoulders. Alec was next, unwinding his wrist from the leather strap and taking a shaky step towards the panel which would open up into a door.

"What about you, Jeshrom?" Georgianna asked.

"I set shields and follow you," she said. "When in place, connected to weapon, I control from distance."

Tohma had undone the buckle that strapped him into the seat and tapped Jeshrom on the shoulder as he climbed back to join them.

"Once the shields are set, we will have fifteen minutes before they are impassable."

"We're setting them to solid?" Georgianna asked.

"Have to," Tohma said. "If we want to make sure the blast is contained, we need the highest setting. Jesh can change it remotely, but the connection and the original order must be made from the ship."

Georgianna wasn't the only one who looked uncomfortable at the news, but they all knew that Jeshrom would need to get down seven flights alone if she was to get out.

The ship shuddered as it came to a halt. Tohma moved between them gracefully until he stood next to Alec by the panel door. The ship jerked and rocked harder than ever and, when Georgianna looked at Jeshrom, she had a control in each hand, manoeuvring the ship down towards the roof.

"Go," Jeshrom said as the ship gave another ominous lurch and stopped entirely.

Tohma smacked a device on the wall and the panel slid out of place. Cold wet air rushed into the small craft as the door opened. There was no turning back.

Following Dhiren, with Keiran behind her, Georgianna took a deep breath, looked out across the Adlai skyline, and jumped.

35 Fight on Flights

The impact shuddered up Georgianna's legs and along her spine. She crouched as she landed, pressing her hand against the stone and springing back up. Racing across the roof after the others, she glanced back as Keiran thudded down behind her and was at her side within three strides. He grasped her by the elbow and pushed her along, wheeling her in front of him as they came to the door. Pressing her back against the wall, she looked up and saw the grim determination in his eyes.

Tohma crouched in front of the door, wiggling a long, thin device into the lock. He glanced at a silver cuff around his wrist and turned the rod until a small screen in the metal flashed white. When he jammed the device further into the lock, it clicked. He waited a breath, his hand on the handle as he glanced to each of them in turn.

"Ready?"

Keiran just kept staring at her.

"Ready," the others chorused. Georgianna didn't join them.

"I love you," she said instead.

He smiled, squeezed her arm, and then was gone.

Drawing the gun from her holster, Georgianna waited until Tohma had extracted the device from the lock. He tucked it into a pocket on his chest and clapped Wrench on the arm. The two of them set off down the stairs after Keiran and Alec.

The others carried knives. They wanted quick and quiet kills if they could get them. Dhiren looked at the gun in Georgianna's hand, but didn't say a word. She was grateful.

She counted out in her head as they had planned. Ten seconds. While most had agreed that going down as a single group would be safer, Alec had insisted on scouting ahead, arguing that, should he and Keiran encounter a problem, it would give the others time to turn back. Also, if she and Dhiren were stopped, the others would be further ahead with a better chance to escape.

She wasn't sure how much she liked the plan either way, but she nodded to Dhiren once they reached ten, and they both slipped inside.

Dhiren closed the door behind them and the two descended side by side, creeping down the first set of stairs. They gradually increased pace, dropping faster and faster until they were leaping down two steps at a time, hurtling around corners. Georgianna's pulse thrummed, surging with every step. Whether Dhiren was hanging back for her sake, or he didn't dare go faster, he stayed in stride as they passed the first set of doors.

One floor. Two...

She raced past doorways without giving them a second glance. Alec and Halden had taken her out hunting once, even though her brother was almost as terrible at it as she was. She remembered Alec's advice: don't get distracted, always look at where you want to shoot. Georgianna kept her gaze fixed ahead. She would be able to hear a door opening off her to side, but nothing other than looking would stop her foot missing a step and sending her tumbling down the stairs.

Three floors down and Dhiren had to leap over an Adveni out cold on the floor. Who had taken him out? Alec? Keiran? Georgianna's chest clenched and ached, a scream fighting to break free. She grabbed the railing and hurled herself forwards, eager to get as far away as possible.

Four floors. Five…

They were almost there. She could hear the echoes of the others' footsteps leading them along. Her heart pounded harder.

A door opened to their right. Georgianna leapt down the last three steps and spun around. The gun was already in her hand. It felt natural as she raised it, finding her target. The Adveni launched himself sideways into the wall, stumbling up the steps. The bullet tore off a chunk of concrete and the sound ricocheted along the stairwell.

Dhiren shoved her sideways.

"GO!"

He ran back up the stairs at the Adveni. The man scrambled to get away but Dhiren was too quick, slashing with his knife. Blood sprayed the concrete. A strangled, echoing cry—cut short as the blade jammed through the back of his neck. The Adveni slid from the knife. His fingers brushed the door handle as he fell to the floor.

Georgianna was rooted to the spot.

"I said, go!" Dhiren shouted as he leapt back down the steps. He flicked the knife and blood splattered across Georgianna's boots.

He grabbed her by the arm and hauled her along, the way Keiran had done. Her legs felt heavy, too heavy to run at the speed Dhiren wanted from her. She tripped down the last two steps of the next flight and crashed into the wall, pain blooming through her shoulder.

Wiping the back of her hand across her mouth, Georgianna tried to focus on her breathing and the rhythm of her steps, shutting out the look of horror on the Adveni's face. The man Dhiren had killed had been a civilian. He was just a normal guy, with no weapon and no armour. He probably worked doing reports, and hadn't expected to be shot at in the stairwell.

Still, she had missed. She had once again proved that she didn't belong here. Even though she had a gun instead of a knife, she still couldn't get the kill.

"George, come on!"

Georgianna met Dhiren's eye and fell into step beside him. This was a mistake, she knew it, but she could at least try to keep up and not put them in even more danger. She just had to focus on keeping up.

Dhiren kept a tight hold on her elbow all the way down, even swinging her around the corners. She kept pace now, racing past the sixth floor and down into the basement.

They were met by knives that were only lowered for a fraction of a second as they raced past. Finally letting go of her arm, Dhiren turned off to the left, Georgianna to the right, guarding the corridors as Wrench and Tohma went to work on the door.

Glancing over her shoulder, Georgianna saw Wrench slapping the Volsonnar's detached hand down on the reader. It buzzed in a long low drone.

"Vtensu!" Wrench snapped. "It's no good."

"They made fast work of protecting it," Dhiren said over his shoulder. "You're up, Tech!"

Tohma shoved Wrench out of the way and dropped to his knees. The device he'd used on the roof was back in his hand. He laid a sheeting over the reader and connected it to the thin rod before inserting it into the lock.

"We've got to hope they haven't had time to reconfigure the Mykahnol, or this has been for nothing," Alec said over his shoulder.

Georgianna turned away, steadying the gun in her hand as she aimed down the corridor.

"Come on, come on, come on," she said under her breath.

Tohma muttered to himself rapidly in his own tongue. He jerked the rod this way and that, according to the commands on his cuff. He readjusted the sheeting over the reader twice and even fitted what looked like half a cloth ball over the handle. The door continued to buzz in that low, monotonous tone.

"Come on, Tohma!" Keiran said. He crept up three steps and looked up the next flight before jumping back down. "How long?"

"Just quiet, alright?" Tohma muttered.

Hopping from foot to foot, Georgianna kept her gaze down the corridor. She longed to look over her shoulder, but stayed facing forwards.

Tohma slapped his hand down on the sheeting that covered the reader, turned the rod, and the door beeped, high and shrill. It swung open and Wrench let out a hoot before covering his mouth with both hands.

Alec waved them in before him. Georgianna walked backwards through the open door before she dared turn around.

"Suns," Keiran whispered.

"Wow," Alec said.

Georgianna couldn't find the words.

The room spanned two storeys and the device in the centre stood all the way to the ceiling. Four metal pillars surrounded it, mirrors of the pillars that stood sentinel around the city. The core swirled and flickered, white flames of energy coiling around each other in a sea of blue and peach. From ceiling to floor, it burned so bright that it hurt to look at it.

She'd never known what it looked like; the weapon that killed thousands in one go, the weapon that had kept the Veniche under the control of the Adveni for so long, the weapon that might have killed her family. But there it was.

36 THE MYKAHNOL

"There are two other doors," Wrench said, pointing. "Dhiren, George, get them."

Bright white spots blossomed in front of Georgianna's eyes the moment she turned away from the Mykahnol. Blinking rapidly, she looked around. It was a large circular room with tall black boxes around every wall, each one whirring and beeping. The heat from the Mykahnol was so intense, it felt as if she were standing in the mid-Heat sun. She took the door on her left, between two tall black cabinets.

She pressed down on the handle; it was locked. A small display was fitted into the wall next to the door, but, unlike at the entrance, there was no palm-print reader. The door Alec and Keiran were guarding had a similar black panel beside it, gleaming amongst the bricks in the wall. It seemed that the Adveni didn't care about people getting out of the room; they only cared who could get into it.

Dhiren took up a position opposite her, testing the door. He watched Tohma with interest as the Cahlven technician came to stand in front of one of the pillars and began furiously typing into a screen not much bigger than a tsentyl.

"Jesh," Tohma said, and paused. A murmur replied through his headset and he began speaking rapidly in his own tongue.

He drew the screen towards him and checked something on the cuff around his wrist, relaying the information to Jeshrom up in the ship. Georgianna could hear the replies through the device in his ear, but it was too quiet to hear what was being said. Even if she could have heard, she assumed they were speaking the Cahlven language and she wouldn't have understood it, anyway.

Tohma glanced around, spotting Wrench and waving him over.

"We need the permission."

Wrench grimaced as he once again drew the Volsonnar's grey dead hand from the cloth bag. He lay it against the reader, leaving a smear of blood along the edge. The screen blazed blue and faded. On the far side, a second screen lit up and whirred in time with the boxes along the walls. It extended from the pillar, tipping up to face the ceiling. Tohma jumped to the side, peered around the core, and nodded.

"Did it work?" Alec asked.

"Yes," Tohma said.

Wrench dropped the hand back into the bag, which he hooked through his belt. Moving around the Mykahnol, he drew the screen further from the opposite pillar and tugged it out as far out as he could, before crouching to get a look underneath.

"Putting in the transmitter," Wrench said. Tohma relayed the information to Jeshrom.

Wrench pulled out a box the size of his palm and slid it underneath the screen. He turned and sat with his back against the pillar, his hands disappearing up and inside. Sweat was already creeping down his face and neck. Grunting, he looked over to Georgianna.

"George, come here."

Georgianna holstered her gun and went to join him.

"I just need your hands, alright?" he said. "Get down here."

He spread his legs as wide as he could and patted the ground between them. Georgianna knelt down. He took her hand in his and guided it up underneath the screen. Her fingers brushed hot metal.

"That's it, just hold that as still as you can."

He guided her other hand into position. The box was already warming with the heat of the Mykahnol. Her fingers twitched. This was no different from holding someone still while Jaid drew out an object from a wound. It was just another injury.

Wrench went to work. She couldn't see what he was doing. The screen shone in her face until, after a snap of a wire, it flickered and changed.

The metal burned against her skin. She tipped her head back and breathed hard through her nose.

"Just one more…"

His fingers brushed against hers as he worked, and a searing pain shot through her little finger.

"Shit!" Wrench hissed. "Sorry."

"It's okay. Keep going."

He fitted the last connection in place and tapped her

elbow. She pulled back to find blood dribbling down the side of her hand. A thin slice ran from nail to the pad of her finger. She wiped it on the side of her trousers and rose to her feet, helping Wrench up.

"Transmitter is in," he said as he pushed the screen back into place.

"I am almost past the countdown," Tohma said. "Jesh, start the connection."

Pressing her finger against her thigh, Georgianna returned to the door. Across from her, Dhiren was smiling.

Wrench and Tohma continued to work. The Cahlven typed with a speed Georgianna had never seen before. His gaze never wavered from the screen as Wrench moved around the pillars and the devices along the walls, prying things open here, tweaking them there.

"Sixteen-minute countdown," Tohma said. "Are you ready, Jesh?"

"Wait," Wrench cut in, wrestling with a sheet of panelling. "I still need to reroute the warnings."

Alec sprang away from the door and came to Wrench's side, pulling at the panel.

Dhiren stepped away from the door. Tohma said something in his own tongue into the headset and waited.

Keiran peered at the panel.

"Come on, guys."

"It's stiff," Alec said. "Just a little more…"

"I can get my hand in," Wrench said. "Hold the panel."

"We've got to get out of here."

Dhiren moved out of his spot by the door, already halfway across the room when they heard it.

They all froze as a gun was cocked. The machines continued to whir. The screens bleeped in perfect time, but it was like every living person was rooted to the spot. Georgianna peeked out from her space next to the door.

Ehnisque stood behind Keiran in the doorway. Her grin was broad as she took the knife from Keiran's hand and tossed it behind her. He didn't fight. He raised his hands to either side of his head as she drew the weapon from his hip, throwing that aside as well.

"Actually, since my brother isn't here to create another diversion," she said, nudging the barrel against the back of Keiran's head, "this time, you're not going anywhere."

37 Their War

"You really thought we would be so stupid that we wouldn't protect this, after you told the commander that you were targeting it?" Ehnisque said, pushing Keiran forwards with the muzzle of the gun.

"Well, you did miss your brother's treason for three years," Dhiren said. "It was possible you were that stupid."

Keiran glared at Dhiren, who simply shrugged, turning the knife in his hand.

Ehnisque lifted a tsentyl to her side. It was still closed into a cube and yet blue lines snaked across it as she spoke.

"Confirmed sighting. All available Tsevstakre to the basement of—"

"Wrench, keep working!" Keiran said quickly. Ehnisque pointed at them with the tsentyl.

"Stop right now or I blow his brains all over that core!"

Georgianna braced herself against the door, between the two cabinets. She covered her mouth with her hand, trying to keep her breathing quiet. She couldn't be sure whether Ehnisque had seen her or not, but it was fear that was keeping her in place. She already had her gun out. She could fire the shot.

But she couldn't move.

"Get to the Mykahnol," Ehnisque said into the tsentyl. "All available Tsevstakre. Breach in progress."

"They won't get here in time. Or they won't get out," Keiran said.

Ehnisque's cruel, mocking laugh reminded Georgianna of Maarqyn. It sounded nothing like Edtroka's laugh. Ehnisque Grystch was nothing like her brother.

"You'll never get that far," she said. "You know that the commander has taken over from the Volsonnar, don't you?" Ehnisque asked. "Your little leader did us a favour. The new Volsonnar won't hesitate in ridding us of the little rat problem we've suffered for so long."

"She can't stop you alone, Wrench. Keep going!" Keiran said.

"I told you to stop!" Ehnisque squealed. Her voice cracked and Dhiren stepped towards her.

"You won't be here to see him try, *deesa*," he said, sneering. "You cared about your father as little as you cared about E'Troke, didn't you?"

Ehnisque scoffed and shoved the gun against Keiran's head with a thump.

"E'Troke was weak and stupid," she said. "My father was a great man and his legacy will live on. The commander will reward me when I return his toys to him. Come to think of it, maybe I'll keep you for myself. My brother seemed to enjoy you well enough."

Dhiren's grip tightened on the knife. His eyes narrowed

to slits and he leaned back on his heel, ready to pounce. Steadying her grasp of the gun, Georgianna edged forwards. Dhiren shook his head and she froze.

"Oh, what? You think I didn't know my brother's tastes?" Ehnisque asked. "Men, women; it didn't matter to him as long as they amused him. I always knew."

Dhiren shook his head again. Georgianna couldn't be sure whether he was telling her to stay put, or simply denying Ehnisque's mockery. She didn't know if there was anything she could do, anyway. Even if she sprung out from the cabinets, she would never be able to aim faster than Ehnisque, who had trained since she was a child. She would get herself shot; or, worse, one of the others.

Pressing herself back against the door, Georgianna's elbow knocked against the handle.

"STOP!" Ehnisque screamed.

Georgianna pushed her hand against the panel and pulled down on the handle. The door swung outwards. Tohma glanced at her and quickly turned away.

"Start the countdown, Jesh," he ordered, repeating the command in his own tongue as Ehnisque growled. A shot ricocheted off the pillar above Tohma's head. Georgianna jumped back into the corridor. Tohma dropped to the ground but there was no blood. Ehnisque had missed.

Georgianna forced herself back against the corridor wall and took a deep breath. Her hands were shaking so hard that she could barely holster the gun. She drew the knife from her left hip and moved it to her right hand.

She took one last look at Tohma and crept along the inside of the curved corridor.

"Where are my Tsev?" Ehnisque demanded.

Georgianna turned, stomach against the wall. She leaned

back as far as she dared without risking Ehnisque's seeing her. She had to get close. Dhiren had always told her that she couldn't be scared to get close.

Around the bend in the corridor, she could see Ehnisque's back. Her long hair was tied in a ponytail that hung down her back. She was standing half in the doorway.

Each step took an age, each breath so loud in her head that she clamped her mouth shut and didn't dare draw another. The handle of the knife was slick with sweat. She stood, fixed against the wall.

She told herself again and again that she could do it.

This was their war: hers and Dhiren's. He had said that he would be out of the battle when he knew Ehnisque and her father were dead. The Volsonnar was gone; Beck had taken care of that for them. Now it was her turn. Only Maarqyn would remain. She could end it if she could just get close enough.

She could do this.

She had to do this.

Georgianna pushed away from the wall, sprinting the last few steps around the corner. She grabbed Ehnisque by the hair. The Adveni shrieked in surprise and anger.

Georgianna tugged back Ehnisque's head and lifted the blade. She sliced deep into her throat, tearing her surprise from her. The scream was replaced by the crack of her gun. She jerked and fell to the ground.

Ehnisque's blood poured across the stones, the way Edtroka's had done. She lay sprawled face-down, her eyes wide; the exact shade of brown as Edtroka's. Georgianna found her breath with a burst of nervous laughter.

She looked up. The laughter died with Ehnisque. Dhiren looked on in horror, Keiran's blood splattered over his face.

38 Blood and Lightning

"So, do you have a name, Sergeant?"

"Keiran," he said. "Most of the guys call me Zanetti."

Georgianna looked up from the wound across his palm—the wound she had caused—and was met by deep grey-blue eyes. Despite the slice across his hand, Keiran Zanetti was still smiling and joking even though it had been the knife in her back pocket that had opened up his palm.

"George."

"You're going to be a hard one to forget, George the medic," he said, flexing his fingers. "Not many of my dates actually stab me when I try to feel them up."

She grinned and wrapped the bandage around his hand.

"Oh, so this was a date?"

"It will be when I tell the story."

The knife slipped from her fingers and clattered to the floor. She stared at Dhiren, unmoving, not breathing.

Blood was dripping down his face and soaking into his clothes. She didn't dare look down.

"Zanetti?"

Alec tripped across the gap and fell down to his knees. Georgianna could see him out of the corner of her eye and yet she couldn't look. This couldn't be happening. Ehnisque's blood was still warm on her skin. She could still hear the scream. She couldn't have taken an Adveni life only for Keiran to lose his.

"Come on, Zanetti…"

Dhiren looked down first and it was only as his expression broke—a deep breath snorting out through his nose—that she risked doing the same.

In the black Tsevstakre uniform, it was difficult to see how much blood was seeping from the wound, but there was nothing to hide the hole the bullet had ripped through Keiran's shoulder. His face was screwed up tight, as pale and grey as the stones beneath him. Georgianna jumped over Ehnisque and fell to her knees beside Alec.

"Keiran?"

"Vtensu," he muttered through gritted teeth.

Georgianna gave another nervous laugh. She hunched over him, pressing her forehead against his cheek.

"Suns."

"What's going on?" Wrench demanded from his place by the panel. "He alright?"

Pushing herself up, Georgianna glanced around them. They were all staring.

"He'll be fine. Finish working," she said. "Alec, help Wrench and Tohma get those controls in place. Dhiren, help me."

Alec, Wrench, and Tohma sprang into action. Alec took over holding the panel in place and Wrench began fitting something in amongst the wires while Tohma went back to relaying information to Jeshrom up in the ship.

Dhiren didn't move. He stared at Ehnisque's body, his jaw set.

"Dhiren!" Georgianna snapped.

He shook himself off and crouched beside her.

"Hold him still. I can't get the bullet out here. I'll just have to dress it."

Snatching up her knife, slick with Ehnisque's blood, she cut through the arm of her shirt and tore it away. Keiran cried out when she pressed it down on the wound. She murmured apologies and wedged it in under the tight uniform.

"You'll be okay."

"George?"

Pressing down hard on the wound, she leaned over him.

"I'm here."

"Always good to have a medic around," he said.

He groaned and wriggled beneath her.

"Hey, Keiran," she whispered, leaning close. "You're not marked."

"What?"

"The bullet, it went through the mark."

He chuckled, his strained amusement slipping into a moan. Blood was soaking through the makeshift dressing and even as she pressed down on the linen, it slipped against his skin.

She glanced at Dhiren.

"It's no good, I need something to hold it down."

"No, it's fine," Keiran said. "Help me up."

"You'll never get that far."

Dhiren already had his arm around Keiran's lower back, helping him kneel.

"He'll have to," Alec said, releasing the panel. It slapped back into place. "We've got to go."

Georgianna opened her mouth to argue but was cut off as Tohma spun away from the panel.

"We are not ready. We do not have remote detonation."

"How long?" Wrench asked.

"I do not—"

The mumbling came through the headset and Tohma fell quiet. He turned back to the panel and pressed the mouthpiece closer to his lips.

"No, Jesh…"

He said more in his own tongue and when the mumbling came back through the earpiece, he rubbed his hand roughly over his face. "Jesh…"

Keiran staggered to his feet, his good arm draped heavily around Dhiren's shoulders. Sweat rolled in rivers from his forehead and down his cheeks and neck. He stared at Tohma.

"What is it?" he whispered.

Tohma smashed his fist against the screen. It smacked into the pillar. He turned away from the Mykahnol.

"Jesh has set the shields. We have fifteen minutes."

"Can she get down that fast?" Wrench asked.

"She is not coming."

"What?"

"She is staying to set the shields solid. She says we need to move."

Georgianna grabbed Tohma's arm as he moved to pass her out into the corridor.

"We can't leave her!"

"She is not coming," he said again. "We must go."

* * *

Wrench joined Alec at the front of the group as they ascended the stairs. Dhiren and Tohma wrapped their arms around Keiran's waist, half-carrying him. Georgianna brought up the rear, her gun in one hand, knife in the other.

They paused in the stairwell and Alec checked they were ready.

"Dhiren, take the front," Keiran said.

"What?" Dhiren raised an eyebrow and tightened his grip on Keiran's waist.

"The uniform," he said. "You're wearing the uniform."

Dhiren looked down at the altered Tsevstakre uniform. He nodded and waved for Wrench to take his place but Keiran shook his head.

"No, I can... I can do it."

Keiran brought his arm from around Tohma's shoulders and took a deep breath, straightening up.

"Head for the tunnels," he said.

Alec stepped out of the way, allowing Dhiren to take the lead. Georgianna had to admit that Dhiren, with his murderous determination, looked the most Adveni of all of them, even without the uniform. He grabbed the door and shoved it open as if he'd walked the halls a hundred times, striding out into the lobby of the building.

He had taken half a dozen steps, just as Georgianna slipped around the edge of the door, when the first Adveni noticed something wasn't right. He looked, turned away, and looked again. His hand drifted towards a copaq at his hip.

Georgianna didn't wait. She was the first to raise a weapon.

She missed and the bullet hit the wall a few inches to the right of the soldier. The crack was not missed by anyone. Before the echo of her shot had even faded away, three more blasts had been fired, this time at them.

All too fast, the open space in front of the main doors was closing up. Ehnisque's orders had called more soldiers to their location and they were running up the steps to confront them.

Georgianna didn't look at where or whom she was shooting. She just aimed away from their little group. They needed to hold the Adveni back. Even Dhiren had abandoned his knife and was firing indiscriminately at the oncoming troops.

As the soldiers advanced, other Adveni were running away, diving behind furniture or simply dropping to the floor. They were all trained, but most probably hadn't served in the military for some time. She spun and fired two shots behind her, holding them off.

Keiran fired using his uninjured arm. Alec was caught between two soldiers, gun in each hand. Dhiren bobbed and weaved in amongst all of them, always driving forwards. Georgianna reached for one of the extra clips of bullets she had brought along.

A lightning bolt, hotter and more painful than a cinystalq charge, seared into Georgianna's back. She hit the floor with a scream, head smacking the cold stone, blood seeping into her hair. She shook until she thought her bones might snap. The gel instantly burned in blemishes like the Nsiloq and began spreading over her body.

She shook and screamed, clawing at the gel splattered

across her lower back. Above her she could hear shouts. Waves of screaming rolled and crashed through her head, thunder to the lightning's pain.

Rolling over, limbs jerking aimlessly, she saw the Adveni standing above her. He didn't look like a soldier. The copaq hung from his hand, gel dripping from the barrel.

He pressed his foot down on her neck, the treads biting into her skin. She couldn't breathe. Even as she grabbed at his leg, the lightning just kept on shooting through her.

He aimed the copaq at her face, a sneer curling his lip and wrinkling his nose.

The bullet tore out half his neck as it hit. He was dead before he could react, landing on top of her. Georgianna did the screaming for him.

Dhiren was there in an instant, grabbing her around the chest and hauling her out from underneath the Adveni.

He howled as a knife slashed across his back and Georgianna hit the ground. Before he could turn, a bullet hit his Adveni assailant in the back and he tumbled, his face hitting the floor with a sickening crack. Dhiren wrapped his arm around her back.

"Cop... Copaq," she cried.

He lifted her, hooking one arm underneath her knees and hauling her up against his chest. She continued to fire at the soldiers, sending them leaping out of the way, but couldn't see if she was actually hitting anything. The copaq gel fired jolts through her nerves, sparking across her eyes. Her skin burned and sweat soaked through her clothes.

Dhiren broke into a run and Georgianna bounced in his arms as he made for a gap between the soldiers. No matter how much she screamed or begged him to stop, he didn't. He kept on running, jumping down the steps and sprinting along the road without a backwards glance.

Georgianna couldn't see if any of the others were following them.

39 Through Rock and Mud

"Dhiren, put me down."

He had slowed to a jog, his breath fast and uneven. He was soaked with sweat and had turned a pale shade of green. He didn't stop to even speak.

"Put – me – down!"

With a reluctant glare, Dhiren stopped and lowered her legs. He kept his arm around her back as her shaking feet found the ground. With a heavy breath, he touched his back and brought his fingers away dripping with blood.

"We have to go back," she said.

"No."

"Dhiren…"

"No, George. We're not going back!" he said, pulling away from her. She trembled under her own weight and staggered to the nearest building, steadying herself against the wall.

"The others—"

"Would do exactly the same. We don't have time. If they're not already out, they're gone. You have to accept that."

"But—"

"No!" He groaned as he leaned forwards, once again touching the slash across his back. "Now, come on."

He waved her back over to him. Staggering, Georgianna shook her head as he moved to lift her up.

"Just get this shit off me."

Dhiren's knife was sticky with blood. He used the blunt edge to scrape as much of the gel from her skin as he could. When he flicked the knife, blue gel and blood splattered the pavement.

He set off slow but within a dozen steps he was running again. She ran as best as could behind him, stumbling with every other step. The entrance to the tunnel came into sight around the corner. She could have cried at the sight of Wrench standing at the top of the steps. He waved them over.

"Suns, guys, you scared us," he said, turning to look down the tunnel. "They're here!"

Georgianna gripped Dhiren's arm as they descended the steps into the gloom of the tunnels. Wrench waved them on and there was no pause to gather her breath or steady herself. Tohma had fished a light from his multitude of devices, joining Alec at the front of the group and leading them along. Keiran fell in behind them. His breath came as a constant moan forced out of his body with every step. Wrench wrapped his arm tight around Keiran's waist and helped him along.

"We need to keep heading south," Dhiren said.

"The Belsa tunnels will lead us southwest," Alec shouted back. "And without Adveni."

Tohma's wrist cuff flashed almost as bright as the lamp he held. He shoved the lamp into Alec's side and handed it off, stumbling when he tried to enter something into the cuff as he ran.

They were approaching a split. One path would lead them south, the other towards the camps through the Belsa tunnels.

Blood dripped down Georgianna's temple and across her eye. Wiping it with the back of her hand, she grimaced at the tacky smear across her skin, a mixture of her own blood, Keiran's, and Ehnisque's.

"The Belsa tunnels are smaller," she said. "If anything happens when it goes off, we'll be trapped."

"Risk it!" Wrench shouted. "The other goes through the Rion district and too many Adveni. We can handle rocks. We can't go another round with Adveni like this."

She didn't argue as Alec glanced over his shoulder and nodded, veering off into the right hand tunnel.

Wrench was right about one thing. In their state, they wouldn't last five minutes in another fight with the Adveni. It was a miracle they were able to run at all. Keiran looked ready to drop at any second. Georgianna's vision was blurring and her entire left side shuddered with each step. Wrench's fingers were bent at a strange angle and blood was trickling down Alec's leg. Dhiren hadn't complained, but Georgianna could see the blood soaking through the back of the Tsevstakre uniform, and wasn't sure how he was still running. Tohma alone seemed to have avoided injury, though with the way he wobbled, she couldn't be sure.

They needed to run faster. What if they didn't reach the barrier in time? Jeshrom and Tohma had been clear. After fifteen minutes the barrier would be impassable. They would be trapped inside the shield when the Mykahnol went off, destroying everything it touched.

Georgianna had seen the devastation a Mykahnol could leave. Nyvalau had been reduced to a crater. There wasn't even any hint of the buildings that had once stood there. Everything had been destroyed, rock and ash left to the elements.

As they ran, she couldn't see a glimpse of the shield's shimmer. She couldn't remember if it only glowed ever so slightly blue in the sunlight. What if they were heading in the wrong direction? The tunnels twisted and turned underground and while Tohma was keeping an eye on the cuff on his wrist, he could only lead them in the general direction. They couldn't run through rock if the tunnels forced them away from the southwest.

Keiran was flagging at the back of the group. Wrench was helping as best he could to support Keiran's weight, but it was taking its toll. When Georgianna dared to glance away from her feet, Keiran looked like he was about to be sick. The tunnel down here was too narrow for two people to carry him. Wrench was already falling behind them, pressing his hands against Keiran's back and pushing him along where the tunnel became too thin to walk two abreast.

Alec skidded to a stop, bringing them all to a halt.

"It's there!" he said, spinning around. "I felt it."

Peering through the gloom, Georgianna couldn't see anything different about the patch of ground where Alec was pointing. Tohma stepped forwards and ran his hand through the air.

"He is correct," he said. He walked through without hesitation.

Dhiren paused before he stepped forwards. As he passed through, Georgianna realised that she could see it—his skin tinting blue, the light rippling across his body. He took another step and as she looked to the others, the blue began to glow brighter.

"Quick!" she cried. She reached for Keiran's hand and jumped forwards.

An uncomfortable ripple of static ran through her body. She lifted her foot and found the shield was harder to penetrate than it had been up at Nyquonat Lake. It pulled and stuck, but her body glowed as she passed through, bright as the summer sky.

Wrenching her foot free, Georgianna stumbled into Alec's waiting arms. She turned away, plunging her hand into the shield to grab Keiran's arm.

Keiran heaved himself through, his skin shockingly pale. He shoved and grunted his way towards them.

"It's like mud."

"Get through, come on!"

Air rippled through the tunnel, and it sounded as if he were pulling his body from glue. The shield was darkening. Neon deepened to dark water.

"Wrench?"

She could barely see Wrench on the other side now. Shadows smothered his features, his outline blurring behind the barrier. Before any of them could stop him, Keiran launched himself back at the shield. He hit it like running into a wall.

Keiran froze, his hand pressed against the solid blue.

"ELI!"

40 THE MARK LEFT BEHIND

"ELI! COME ON!"

Keiran pounded on the shield, now as black as the night sky. The sound of his fists hitting the solid barrier reverberated in the tunnel. Alec joined him, shoving against the shield with his shoulder.

"Come on!" Keiran cried again. "You can get through. Push!"

"It is too late," Tohma said, his voice quiet and nervous. "It is solid. There is no changing it."

A murmur broke through them. This time it did not come from Tohma's headset in some undecipherable tongue; it came from the shield.

"Run."

Keiran and Alec froze and leaned close to the shield.

"Run!"

Slamming his hand down on the black shield, Keiran's voice cracked and broke apart.

"No, I'm not going!"

"Wrench, we're not leaving you!" Alec shouted.

Georgianna looked back at Tohma to find him shaking his head. From what she had seen, Wrench had been closer to Tohma than any of them. He was the one who had introduced him to them, who discussed technology with him. Taking a step further away, Tohma glanced at Dhiren.

"We must go. We are not safe."

"I said we're not leaving!" Alec snapped.

"Run. Go!"

"The tunnels might not survive the explosion," Tohma said. "We must."

Looking back at Dhiren, Georgianna moved out of the way, letting him shuffle past her. They only had a few more minutes. He took a deep breath, steadied himself, and, while looking like it was the last thing in the world he wanted to do, wrapped his arms around Alec.

"Come on, Cartwright," he said.

Alec wrestled against Dhiren's grip, but it was half-hearted.

"I'm sorry, Wrench!" he cried into the dark. "I'm sorry."

She watched as Dhiren half-dragged, half-carried Alec down the tunnel, his protests fading into the gloom. Creeping forwards, Georgianna lay her hand over Keiran's against the shield.

"We have to go," she whispered. "Keiran, you can't save him."

"I can't leave him."

"He's already gone."

"He's not. He's just…"

Keiran leaned against the shield, pressing his forehead to it. A tear rolled down the solid barrier.

• 310 •

"Brother," he whispered. "My only…"

She drew him away from the shield with the same delicate urgency with which he had let her collapse into him back in the woods. He came willingly, just like she had done—the need for something to cling to overtaking the will to be strong. Wrapping her arm around his waist, he draped himself around her shoulder and they sidled away through the dark.

Each of his breaths came with a gasp, his wound forgotten for his pain.

The tunnel opened wider and she urged him into a run. The footsteps of the others pounded ahead of them, marking a rhythm.

There was no warning, no rumble or boom to announce its coming. The ground beneath them cracked and the shock of the explosion lifted them off their feet.

Georgianna stumbled into the wall of the tunnel, sending Keiran crashing into her. Before she knew what was happening, she was face first on the ground as rock tumbled down around them.

* * *

Georgianna prised herself off the ground, arms trembling under her weight. Keiran groaned beside her. Kneeling, she looked both ways down the tunnel. A dozen feet ahead, she could see the gloomy shapes of Dhiren, Alec, and Tohma as they moaned and peeled themselves off the floor. Behind them, a tumble of rocks had caved in, blocking the tunnel.

Keiran looked back, and flopped onto the ground, screaming into the dirt. Edging closer, she wrapped her arms around his shoulders and winced when he jerked and pulled away.

Climbing shakily to her feet, Georgianna pressed her hand against the crumbling wall and picked her way over the fallen rocks. Tohma's lamp shone down the tunnel, a foot from where Alec lay on his side.

"Everyone okay?" she asked.

Alec nodded.

"I am fine," Tohma said, rolling over and sitting up. "The shield worked."

"Too well," Alec grumbled.

Georgianna didn't answer him. She crouched down beside Dhiren and reached out. He hissed and cringed away from the touch.

"Hey, Yote," she said. He lifted his head and glared at her. She smiled in return. "I'm not dead, so you can't be either."

"Yeah," he muttered, spitting dusty phlegm onto the ground.

Georgianna clambered back down the tunnel to Keiran and, though he tried to pull away, helped him to his feet. He stared at the landslide of rocks, silent and shaky. His back was drenched in blood. She took his hand and led him across the rocks to the others.

"We should get out of here."

Tohma was already up and he helped Alec and Dhiren get to their feet. Georgianna took the lead this time, gripping Keiran's hand. He followed in a slow trudge, his head down. Alec, Dhiren, and Tohma held the silence, traipsing along behind them.

Rays of light shone down from the entrance into the tunnel, dappled across the ground. Raindrops splashed around them as they climbed the steps up above ground. The cold rain felt good against Georgianna's dusty, battered skin.

It wasn't the cold that had her hands trembling.

In the distance, she could hear screams and shouts. A ship rumbled and passed overhead, though none of them lifted their heads to see whether it was Adveni or Cahlven. Tohma checked his cuff and began walking towards the camps; he was almost halfway down the street before he realised they weren't following. He returned with a cautious curiosity. Without a word, they turned and headed north, back through the city.

The shield was visible even at a distance. Inky black, it towered into the sky in a mammoth dome. It was only as they came closer that they could see it was crumbling. It was disintegrating, piece by piece, flaking off and drifting through the air with the ash and smoke.

They crept closer in silence. Georgianna pulled her hand from Keiran's, wrapping her arms around her stomach. The street led them straight to it; the destruction they had caused. Ahead of them, buildings fell away to nothing leaving half-shells. The smell of burning filled the air, acrid and suffocating. Still they walked until they reached the edge of the ruin.

The ground fell away to a crater in the centre of the city. Ash and dust floated through the air, like snow on the wind. It whipped into them and stuck to their skin. Down and down, the hole drove straight into the ground, deeper than the canyon at Nyvalau. It fell in sharp jagged cliffs to a base of rubble. Rock and metal were piled on top of each other; spikes of beams and the dust of bricks. The sharp smooth lines of the Dalsaia was littered amongst them.

With every breath, Georgianna could taste the burn of what they had done. The Adveni had left their mark on

Os-Veruh at Nyvalau and now the Veniche had marked Adlai. This destruction belonged to them.

Georgianna unwound her arms from around her stomach and looked down at her hands. Ash and dust, rain and blood; it all clung to her. She was made of destruction and death.

Keiran's blood, Ehnisque's. Veniche buildings and Adveni. It was all the same against her skin.

She was no medic. She didn't feel like one, not any more.

As they looked on into the ruin, none daring to speak or perhaps even breathe, Georgianna could only think of Maarqyn. Ehnisque was in that rubble somewhere, her skin incinerated, her bones dust under the weight of the rock. Yet she felt no pleasure. Ehnisque, who had murdered her own brother, was dead, but Georgianna thought only of the man who had tortured and marked her, who was perhaps still out there.

He had said that a mark claimed a person, that they would remember who had given them the mark every day of their lives.

They had made this mark. They had made their claim.

And she didn't think anyone would forgive them for it.

MORE FROM THE
OUT OF ORBIT SERIES

I hope you have enjoyed reading *Rack and Ruin*. The fourth and final book of the *Out of Orbit* series will be released in 2016.

If you have enjoyed reading the *Out of Orbit* series, or are excited for what comes next, I hope you will get in contact. I love hearing from readers whether it is to talk about books, writing, or just to say 'hi'. You can reach me via Facebook or Twitter (*@CheleCooke*) or on my website:
http://chelecooke.com

Your support is very much appreciated.

Thank you for reading.

ACKNOWLEDGEMENTS

Thank you to everyone who helped bring the third *Out of Orbit* book to life and out of the black depths of writer's block.

Andrew Lowe, the only thing I enjoyed more than your fantastic editing was our rambling Skype chats. Thank you for all your hard work and great advice.

Thank you to Rachel Small for proofreading, and to Designs for Writers for the beautiful cover.

To the readers and reviewers. To the authors who helped me along the way. To everyone who kicked me to a computer and who told me they needed to know what happens next.
To Moa, who can make me smile no matter how bad I feel, and without whom this book wouldn't exist.

Thank you all. You keep me going.

ABOUT THE AUTHOR

Chele Cooke is a Sci-Fi/Fantasy independent author based in London, UK.

Chele is an English-born writer based in London. With a degree in Creative Writing from the University of Derby, Chele has been writing for over a decade, both original fiction and fan fiction. As well as the *Out of Orbit* series, she has a paranormal thriller series, *Teeth*, and a number of other projects.

For more information about Chele and the *Out of Orbit* series, and for promotions, giveaways, and future releases, sign up to Chele's mailing list and receive a free book.

http://chelecooke.com/freebook/
or visit
www.chelecooke.com

Printed in Great Britain
by Amazon.co.uk, Ltd.,
Marston Gate.